Two Finge

at

Agincourt

by

Walter Shields

Acknowledgments

Thank you to my daughter Barbara for here contribution and tireless efforts in editing this book.

INTRODUCTION

This is a book about the life and times of an English archer named Crispin Bowyer and his eventual friendship with his tournament rival Jack Smith.

The story is about his training, his detailed knowledge of making and using longbows and arrows and how from the tales told to him by his father and grandfather of past battles in England, Wales and Scotland, as well as the great victories in France at Crècy and Poitiers, he was eager to follow in their footsteps.

This came about in the year 1415 when he, at the age of twenty five, along with about 6000 ragamuffin poorly dressed English men who were mostly barefooted, tired, hungry, in poor health and extremely lacking in confidence, stood up to an army of over 20,000 Frenchmen.

The majority of English archers had little or no armour, were in fear of their lives and had no hope of winning the oncoming battle which was to be fought on ploughed fields between two small villages in France: AZINCOURT and TRAMECOURT.

Historians may argue and debate the number of men in each army but what is certain is that the French outnumbered the English by at least three to one. France like England had internal disputes and wars but after the fall of their walled town of Harfleur at the mouth of the river Seine they put aside their squabbling and united to face the English threat.

I have tried to keep to the main facts of the period and any historical errors in the story are entirely mine, therefore I leave it to the historians themselves to give you the finer points.

Weights, measurements, coinage, and how they were arrived at in the fifteenth century, will be shown in the appendix at the rear of this book, along with a glossary of terms and words used that are not in common use today.

THE SAINT CRISPIN DAY SPEECH

That he which hath no stomach to this fight, Let him depart; his passport shall be made and crowns for convoy put into his purse.

We would not die in that man's company that fears his fellowship to die with us.

This day is called the feast of Crispin. He that outlives this day and comes safe home, will stand a tip-toe when this day is named and rouse him in the name of Crispin.

We few, we happy few, we band of brothers, for he today that sheds his blood with me shall be my brother; be he ne'er so vile.

This day shall gentle his condition and gentlemen in England now abed shall think themselves accursed they were not here and hold their manhood cheap whiles any speaks.

That fought with us upon Saint Crispin's day.

Ascribed to Henry V on the eve of the battle of Agincourt

William Shakespeare 1564-1616

The Battle of Agincourt

25th October 1415

This is the most famous victory of the many conflicts that were fought during the One Hundred Year War, which lasted from 1337 to 1453 between England and France. The war has been dramatised in Shakespeare's play Henry V, where he coins the phrase 'his band of brothers'......Crispin was one of those brothers.

ROUTE TO AZINCOURT

CHAPTER ONE

Summer 1402

I was hurrying along the Oare creek towards the Swale looking forward to a cooling swim in the river and as I ran I heard this cry for help coming from the far side of the creek I guessed straight away what was happening ... someone had fallen in. On running to the edge I could see that this well dressed little boy had allowed his horse to come too close to the edge of the creek and that the horse's weight had broken the banking tossing them into the mud. The tide was coming in, but I still laughed at the boy who was facing down the slope struggling to swing around and climb out, but the more he struggled the more he slid down deeper into mud.

The horse was not moving so it had probably broken its neck or something and must already be dead, if the boy could grab hold of its saddle he would be able to clamour to the top of the slope and save himself. He cocked his head up when he saw me and desperately cried, 'help ... help me' but what could I do? He was on the far side of the creek in deep mud and the water would soon reach him.

I looked around for help but all I could see was a group of horsemen across the marsh. I waved and shouted but they didn't see nor hear me. The creek ended about a quarter of a mile from where I stood but to run around to the marsh side and shout again would take too long; and the boy would probably drown before I got to him.

He had managed to swing around and was now facing the top of the bank but he had slipped lower into the mud. The water was now well above his ankles and he was unable to move his legs. I knew that the water would be releasing the mud's suction and that if he had no boots on he might be able to pull his feet free, stretch out another yard, reach the horse and climb over it to safety. You could say I was a bit of an expert when it came to scrambling in the gooey mire as the creek was my playground.

"Take your boots off then you will be able to get your feet free" I shouted but he was too panicky to listen, forcing me to take a chance or he was going to die; so Crispin to the rescue.

I tossed my quiver onto the ground, slid down into the water and slithered the short distance to him, holding my bow above my head. He started clinging on to me so hard that I had to fight free of him before I could duck down into the rising water and slice through the lacing on his boots with my knife which allowed him to waggle his feet free. I hooked the horse's saddle with my bow and he scampered over me onto the horse which was stuck fast, then it was my turn.

From there it was just a short reach to the top of the bank where I stretched out to get my breath back but the boy had passed out. I hoped that he wasn't going to die as being well dressed he must belong to somebody important, making me a hero. More hero than I could ever imagine as the horsemen I had tried to attract were his men folk, who, having seen us climb out of the creek had come to see what was happening. A man jumped off his horse, washed the boy's face with wine from his canteen and hugged him to his body thinking that he had drowned but the boy spluttered back into consciousness.

I later learned that the boy was the ten year old son of Lord John Thornbury named William who had wandered away from the group and had gone into the creek without anybody noticing. His father, besides being a Lord was the Sheriff of Kent and he was also the man that had tried to find out who had injured Jack Smith the son of the local blacksmith and although it was a long time ago I was worried that he would recognise me as the main suspect but apparently not, as being covered in mud who would?

William was still in shock and by looking at his bare legs and seeing the dead horse it was obvious what had happened, if I had not come to the rescue William would now be dead. I was alright, perhaps a bit breathless but they whisked us back to the Manor where I was allowed to have a good clean up and given some dry clothing to put on. It seemed strange, having never been in the Manor before, to be walking on a highly polished smooth wooden floor, not like my families lumpy dirt one; but after having one of the best meals of my life, the hero Crispin was taken home in style riding on a borrowed horse.

Word had spread like wild fire about the rescue and there was a procession of cheering people following us to my home where my family were awaiting the hero, as requested by Lord John who had sent a rider to let them know what I had done and that I was safe. The borrowed horse turned out to be not borrowed at all but was my reward for saving William. Little did I know how my life would change from that moment on because I was given the chance to learn how to read and write; nor did I know what advantages it would give me as I grew up to be a man.

But first let's start from the beginning…….

I was born on Tuesday 25th October 1390, and lived on a farm of about two hundred acres at the end of the Oare creek, near Faversham in Kent. The old Roman road from Dover to London called Watling Street is the farms southern boundary and the river Swale the northern. The Oare creek is the eastern boundary and our land stretches west along the Roman road for about a half a mile ending at a forest.

My French mother had allowed my father to call my older brother John but as I was born on her favourite Saint's day she insisted that I was to be called Crispin, so my name is Crispin Bowyer; which is great for me as everybody in Faversham and Oare celebrated my birthday.

All summer, like all the other boys, I had been running about bare footed and the soles of my feet were as hard as clay. One Sunday I was playing in the creek when I stood on this hard thing which turned out to be a pointed copper nail near where the remnants an old boat had been rotting away. All of us budding archers knew that it was wrong to add points to our arrows because of the danger of hurting each other; we were only allowed to have blunt ends but I bound this nail to my favourite arrow to see if it would stick into anything and went into the woods to try it out. Whoosh, the arrow flew past the tree I was aiming at and a terrific scream came from the undergrowth, in a flash I was off home hoping that nobody had seen me. I raced into our dwelling, dashed past my mother and hid under my straw bed.

"Alwight" my mother shouted, turfing me out.

"What ave you did dis time?"

"Nowt, just playing" I said.

"Don't give me dat, what ave you did?"

"Playing bows and arrows but don't tell"

"Why what ave you bin up to?"

"Nowt" I whimpered.

My mother, who had her own way of talking never told on me but she later found out that Jack the blacksmiths son from Faversham, was lucky not to have lost an eye as the arrow had sliced his cheek and taken away part of his left ear. Jack was two years older than me and as he was part of the other gang it didn't bother me much. Our gang, the Oare gang, always used to do battle with the Faversham gang; across the Ham marshes and we hated each other. I never told my gang mates that it was me who had shot the arrow; as Tom, the Millers son, had relatives in Faversham. Anyway I had been hit on the knee with a stone last month, so it was fair justice weren't it? There was a big stink about it because Jack's father was well in with the Manor where Lord Thornbury lived.

John the Smith did all the Lords horseshoeing, so there was a hue and cry out to find the culprit. I was the main suspect as I was always using my bow and arrows but they didn't get me because my grandfather had said I had been working in the Flax field with him at the time of the dastardly deed. I never did get my favourite arrow back, but I knew that Jack blamed me and would get me one day.

Both Faversham and Oare were growing in population with about thirty boys between the ages of eight and sixteen and to save any more accidents bow and arrow fighting was banned and any arrow firing from now on was to be done along the Ham marshes towards the river Swale. We didn't really hate each other as it was only pretend battle, we even got dragged to the same church; St Mary's. Our battles were great contests and the pathway down the centre of the marsh was the border line between the two armies.

We had an agreement not to cross this path when doing battle, so the *Oare* gang lined up on our side of the path which was eighteen inches wide and the Faversham gang lined up on their side where we fought it out to the death or until it got dark; if you got killed you had to die in anguish taking your time to fall squirming and twisting to the ground then after a few seconds you could jump up and start all over. Sometimes a big boy would storm our side of the path which wasn't fair, so when this happened we wouldn't play with them anymore and fought ourselves; which wasn't as much fun but as time went by big boys fought big boys and little boys fought little boys.

It was in 1384 that my father brought my mother and my one year old brother back from France where he had been with one of many raiding armies sent to burn and plunder villages, towns and farms in the name of King Richard II. His family were amazed to see that he was still alive, as his soldier friends had seen him cut down and killed. His father, also called John celebrated his return by making him the owner of Bowyer's Farm which he would have inherited anyway. At first nobody liked my mother because she was French but when they learned that she and her mother had protected my father and saved his life they welcomed her with open arms. My parents had come to England on a Faversham fishing boat that had been forced to take shelter from the weather at a small French fishing port called EU, on the English Channel; and whilst waiting for the weather and wind to turn favourable, the crew learned of a wounded soldier living about a mile inland from the town, who the locals said came from England. Their curiosity was aroused and some of the crew went to investigate and lo and behold it was John Bowyer. My father knew most of the fishermen, so when they offered to take him and his family back to England at no cost, it took my parents no time at all to collect their belongings. So that on the following morning after a few tears between mother and daughter, they said their goodbye's climbed aboard the boat and parted with the promise of seeing each other again.

Whilst I was growing up my father had told me the story of what had happened when he was wounded.

"We were marching through the friendly province of Normandie" he said, "and as this area was in favour of their Norman connections with England, the population showed no hostility towards us. Our army consisted of about three hundred men; eighty men at arms and two hundred or so archers. We were passing the town of Eu, which was expected to have a French garrison, so we intended to give it a wide berth. Our army was normally on its guard" he said "but as it was such a beautiful day, with the sun shining and the birds whistling away we had relaxed our attention, however the French also had troops of soldiers roaming the country trying to intercept our armies one of which we met up with."

"The encounter," he continued, "was in a wooded area where the longbow could not take a decisive role so we knew it would be an unequal battle which we could very well lose and in the short mêlée that followed, I was hacked down by a French man at arms receiving a slicing sword blow from my right hip to halfway down my thigh and was left bleeding on the ground as the rest of our army ran back out of the woods; followed by the French who were too busy chasing after my comrades to bother about me, so I was able to crawl away and hide in the undergrowth knowing what would happen on their return. The next thing I knew was waking up lying on a rough mattress with my britches removed and my leg wrapped in a linen bandage, I felt lucky to have been rescued but was in so much pain that I passed out again.

I awoke to the sound of French voices and thinking that I had been captured, pretended to be unconscious but the voices were smooth and gentle, so I took a peek only to be caught by a peasant woman who said to me in part English and part French, allo, so yu is not deed then? vous are safe here, has we do not like der pigs fram Orleanais, woo just want to took all our nourriture, Betail et Mouton, and do udder not neece tings, I hid mon fille, but dey av gone now, so wrest and try to sleep and I shall got vous sum fromage, pain et d'eau for when you wake up."

"I figured" my father said, "that the pigs she was talk about must have been the same men who had wounded me."

The woman, he thought, looked about thirty five years old and with her was a pretty young girl around sixteen year of age who giggled at his bare body and that the woman had shooed her away for the bread, water and cheese. My father who was twenty one years old at the time, later found out that the young girl named Fayette was the daughter of his rescuer and that her father had drowned when his brother's boat, on which he had been a crew member, sank in a storm with the loss of all the men excepting her uncle.

My father was concerned that when he eventually turned up he would be posted as a deserter from the army so the woman told him that she would send word to the English army, who were camped about a mile north of her farm, to tell them that they were looking after a badly wounded soldier. The following day, mounted soldiers came to her dwelling and my father struggled to tell them that he was in great pain and that he would try to join the army when he could. The captain told him that the battle he had been in had resulted in a standoff and that the French, not surprisingly, had disappeared. He was told that due to his injury he would be a hindrance to their progress and would have to be left behind.

The captain took his name, so that his departure from the campaign would be noted; and gave him a written permit of dismissal saying that when he got better he should try to make his own way back to England. The wound to his leg had removed some of his muscle and he was lucky that the cut had not gone down to the bone. It took six months for his leg to heal and a further eighteen months before the chance came to return home; during which time he worked on the farm with Fayette's uncle who was now married to her mother.

My father told me that Fayette was eighteen years of age when they had first met and they had spent a lot of time together whilst he was recovering. Eventually falling in love, they had married at the beginning of 1383.

My first recollection of meeting my French grandparents must have been when I was about three years old. I had been very sick with the rocking of the boat as we crossed to France and you don't forget a thing like that do you. I don't remember coming home but I do remember the squawking baby my mother brought back to England with us who turned out to be my new sister *Yvette*.

On my sixth birthday I asked my mother why she called me after her favourite Saint and what happened to Saint Crispin. Crispin she told me, had a brother named Crispinian and that they had lived in Rome over a thousand years ago; they had become Christians and that during the persecution of Christianity they were forced to escape from Italy and went to France where they lived in a town called Soissons.

The brothers, still practicing Christianity became shoemakers and made footwear for the poor; "but France" she said, "like England, had to suffer the yoke of the Roman Empire and they were arrested and given the choice; disavow their faith or die. They refused to give up their beliefs and were killed by the Romans." My mother went on to say, "legend has it that the Roman authorities tied millstones around the brothers' necks and threw them both into the river Aisne; but the stones floated and they couldn't be drowned. The brothers were then boiled in oil, which had no effect, then in pitch but they still lived, finally the Romans beheaded them."

She then told me that when she came to England she was surprised to learn that Faversham claimed that Crispin and his brother were the sons of the Queen of Logia (Kent) and had to escape the persecution of Christians by the Romans and fled from the town of Canterbury to Faversham where they became apprentice shoemakers to a master shoemaker named Roberts.

"One day" she said, "Crispin was sent to Canterbury with shoes for Ursula the daughter of Maximinus who was a junior Caesar to Emperor Augustus Caesar and whilst there, Crispin fell in love with her and they married in secret. Maximinus was very angry about this union but when he found out that Crispin was of high birth, he confirmed their marriage on October the 25th which was celebrated with feasting and drinking which Faversham has celebrated ever since".

"But how did they become French Saints" I asked. "If they lived in England?"

My mother was unable to answer this question, so I suppose they must have gone off to France at some time.

**

CHAPTER TWO

We always seemed to go to France for my Brother John's birthday, or maybe it's because now that it's September and the crops are harvested, my father has more time to spare. Living near Watling Street is quite handy as it allows us to catch the London to Dover coach which stops overnight at the Anchor Inn. I don't know how much the journey to France costs but I think my mother's biscuit sales pay for it.

It took us six hours to travel the twenty five miles to Dover where the port situated just below the white cliffs was bustling with ships of all sizes. The smell of the sea was hanging in the air and luckily a fresh wind was blowing off shore towards France. There are always boats willing to take you across the twenty two miles of English Channel; so we were in Calais before nightfall and it seems strange that after only a few hours on a boat nobody knows what you are saying, so it was a good job my mother could sort out where to stay for the night. But catching a boat that is going down the coast of France was not as easy as catching a boat to France; because most boats going south from Calais were on their way to Paris and only a few were willing to put us ashore at Eu, but my mother's charm along with two Sou coins usually did the trick.

The sixty odd miles can be sailed easily in ten hours if the wind is right, and if it isn't, then sleeping on the boat gets us into Eu the next morning, after which it's a one mile walk to the farm. After the usual hugs and kisses and lashings of hot lamb and bread, I am allowed to play in the woods pretending to fight the French army; just like my father had done, he even showed me the spot where my French grandmother had found him wounded. On one trip when I was eight years old my sister's friend, a little tot of a girl named Catherine, started following me everywhere I went; she was two years younger than me, had jet black hair, a spotty face and couldn't say one word in English. She is the daughter of Philip Devereux (the son of my grandmother's second husband) Yuck, why do we have to put up with girls? The only thing good I could say about her, was that she didn't stink.

The stay usually lasted for about three weeks, where my father helped around the farm, my mother spent time with her mother or looking up her old friends whilst I tried to avoid Catherine. There was never any trouble getting home as my grandfather had bought another fishing boat, allowing us a leisurely sail back to Faversham. It was always good to get home to England because I could once again play with my small bow and arrows. I always use my left hand when placing the arrow nock into the string whilst holding the bow in my right hand but my father tries to make me use my right hand on the string; as he had a feeling that I may be left handed. If so, he was determined to make me right handed because it was generally believed that left handedness was evil and sinister; therefore when I was eating using my left hand to hold my spoon, I ended up with a slap on the wrist, which was always a problem but when alone I used my left hand. I didn't think it was evil neither did my mother, thus as I grew up I could shoot an arrow from both hands.

My mother and father were having a bit of a problem with people in Faversham regarding my father's friend, Uncle James who he had been in France with. He was not my real uncle we just called him that to be polite. They had met up again at an Archery contest in Maidstone, where my father had gone to sell his longbows and they swapped tales of what they had been doing since they had last seen each other. When my father found out that James had no family, he invited him to come and work on our farm. I was never told what the problem was but it was said that James had got some girl from Faversham into trouble; don't ask me what sort of trouble, but he wouldn't marry her and my father wouldn't kick him out as he had said that James has always been good at making arrows; so with him making arrows and me making longbows, we are a good team.

But it's not all about bows and arrows as my father has a farm to run where he grows hops which makes ale, and flax from which we obtain linseed oil and linen. My father could make his own ale but it's easier for him to sell the hops to a brewer then buy back the ale. He grows other crops such as corn and wheat but the best is flax, which we plant in the spring using some of the seeds we have saved from last year's harvest. Oil is squeezed from the plant's seeds and linen is made from the stems; each plant holds about ten tiny seeds in a pod and we squeeze the oil out of some of them which is used to waterproof our cloth or for cooking but we try to keep as many seeds as possible which we sell to a person we call the Whittington man who works for a wealthy London merchant of that name.

This man will buy anything for cash money and will take all of the seeds and plant stems we want to sell. From a fine harvest my father can make six pounds but what I can't understand is, why, after making his mark of eighteen nobles he has to pay back three pence for every noble to the Whittington man who claims that this money is to pay for his protection from robbers and for having to make a lot of the payment in small value coins. I thought that this was cheating and although my father knew what was happening, there was little he could do about it; perhaps one day I shall find out the truth as to why my father has to pay back four shillings and six pence after signing for twelve whole nobles and six nobles worth of groats, pennies, halfpennies and farthings, but as it happened I was able to get our own back sooner than I thought because as I was plodding my weary way home along the London road (Watling street) one day after playing in the woods, the Whittington man came galloping along in the opposite direction going towards Faversham nearly knocking me down.

He never noticed a large pot hole in the road and when his horse swerved to miss it, it stumbled causing him to side over its neck and fall off; he wasn't hurt but his saddlebag was thrown clear. I couldn't let him see me giggling as he collected the bag and its scattered contents, glowering at me as he re mounted his horse and rode away. My eyes have always been sharp and I saw that his whip was still lying in the road, so I went back to pick it up but decided to leave it where it was as I had noticed a gold coin in the roadside grass which he must have missed along with his whip when collecting up the rest of the bags contents.

I put the coin in my pocket, ran a short way along the road and crouched in the undergrowth to see if he would come looking for his money, my heart was pounding but he wasn't getting his coin back. He returned about half an hour later, picked up his whip, looked up and down the road and started to search the area. He stooped, picked something up off the ground and continued his search, cursing all the time at the grass and bushes; there were other men with him and they all started to tear away at the undergrowth.

Serves you right I thought, as I slowly backed into the bushes and trees in case they spotted me; but I was mad at myself as he must have picked up another coin that I had missed. It was only on making my way home that it hit me, he had seen me as he passed but I was not sure if he knew who I was; if he did know me he might accuse me of finding the coin, so I was glad that I left the whip where it was and decided to say nothing to anybody. I put the coin in my hiding spot under a stone in the pig sty and waited to see what might happen.

The Whittington man had recognised me and came to our dwelling just as I was eating my bread and soup and he asked my father to find out if I had picked up a noble on the road.

"Well Cris" my father asked, "Did you find the man's coin?"

I looked at my father with innocent eyes telling him that I had seen him climb back on his horse and that I had just carried on home. The Whittington man still suspected me but there was nothing he could do about it. I had put on such a great act that even my father believed me. All the next morning my friends and I searched and searched the spot where he had fallen off his horse as there was a reward of sixpence offered to the finder but nothing was found and we all went home disappointed.

I had considered giving the coin up but it was too late now; I was to suffer with worry and loss of sleep in case I was found out and for weeks and weeks I was in fear of discovery but now and then went to look at the coin wondering what to do with it. Should I just throw it away and forget about it? No, should I tell my father? No, should I try and spend it? No, because such a large amount could not be spent or changed in Faversham, only in London or Canterbury and a small boy with so much money was sure to give the game away. In the end I left it in the pig sty, where it stayed until I was eventually able to spend it.

It wasn't an easy life for us peasants having to work hard on the land for six days a week, nor did it leave much time for pleasure but there were many Saint's day holidays, like Saint George's day and my birthday Saint Crispin's day; then there were market days every Wednesday and Saturday which was a good place to sell your wares, where my mother always did well with her baking. The markets were important to everybody from near and far and farmers, who grew much more food than they could possibly eat themselves, were able sell their crops which enabled them to buy other comforts and needs. Therefore the market place was the only real place that town's people could get food but unfortunately a limit was set on how much a person could buy to prevent hoarding. For instance; you could only buy two corn loaves at one time as there was only one baker in Faversham, who was wilting in age and finding it hard to meet demand.

Two creaks flow into north Kent from the river Swale: the Faversham creek, which swings to the east then south west, and the Oare creek which carries on to the south west; resulting in parallel waterways with about a mile of the Ham marsh separating them. This marsh often floods creating a lake between both creeks, which looks strange when one is used to seeing land but once the tide goes out we are able to catch little flat fish that have been trapped in small muddy pools, which is great fun. The slow flow and ebb of the river Swale is unable to flush any sediment away from these creeks, so mud builds along their sides which can be anything up to ten inches deep at the lowest point and about an inch deep at the top edge and the depth of water at the centre of the creeks (when the tide is fully in) is about ten feet.

Children have lost their lives after been stuck in this mud, so we were warned to stay away from the waterways when the tide was entering but that didn't bother our gang as we loved sliding down the creek edges when the tide was out and getting completely mucked up. However trying to climb back up the side was a different thing, as you kept slipping back down but we could form a daisy chain and clamber over each other to the top, and being stuck in the deep mud was no problem either, as having no boots on you could waggle your legs back and forward to make the mud watery then pull your foot out with a sucking sound but you had to know what you were doing, little did I know how useful this would be in years to come. We knew it was dangerous if you were on your own; but even then, if you had a couple of strong sticks, one in each hand, you could dig them in and out of the mud and crawl your way to the top. To remove the mud from our bodies we went to one of the streams flowing into the creek or we walked to the Swale where all of the brown, hard caked soldiers swam in the river but it was not all play, I had my jobs to do around the farm and sometimes there was no play whatsoever especially at harvest time.

It was my responsibility to see that there was always clean fresh water to drink and cook with and I used to have to carry at least two bucketful's a day from a stream one hundred yards away where the banks narrow, causing the water to flow faster and where my grandfather had built a run of stones that formed a small waterfall so that the overflow would go straight into the bucket. I was taught never collect water from a slow moving stream or where there is no movement on the surface, such as a wide stretch or pool because it may support dirt, or floating bugs.

Before my brother started to go to war he was always in the woods learning about the forest, from a woodsman named Isaac who had taken a liking to him because of his interest in trees. Isaac was employed by the Manor to cut down and supply oak to the navy for shipbuilding and some of the things John learned from him he passed on to me. I could already recognise Oak, Rowan and Hazel not to mention the Yew tree growing in the church yard, and Silver Birch was easy because of its silvery bark but John must know at least twenty different types of tree. John told me that the inner side of Silver Birch bark can be used as a bandage and that it could also be used to make good strong binding string once it had been cut into strips then boiled in water, he also showed me how this tree could provide you with a sweet tasting drink by boring a hole into its side, then by pushing a hollow pipe made from the bark of a stick into this hole which allowed the sap to drip into a bottle to collect about a pint overnight.

I also learned that sap can also be collected from the Maple tree and the Pine tree in the same way. This Maple sap, when boiled makes Maple syrup, whilst the sap from a pine tree goes very hard but when heated will soften up as a black tar which is useful for sticking things together such as an arrow shaft into an arrow head.

"But what's important" said John, "Is that once you have finished tapping a tree, you must plug the bore hole to prevent it from draining its life away."

He also told me about a stone called flint, I knew that flint could be found in the chalky cliffs at the seaside but Isaac had told him that flint could sometimes be found under the roots of a fallen tree, so we went into the forest, found a tree that had been blown over in a strong wind and lucky enough we discovered a piece about the size of a small chicken. John picked up an ordinary stone and smacked it into the flint, knocking a lump off it.

"Watch your hands and fingers now" he said, "as the edges are sharper than a knife."

The colour of the flint ranged from grey to black and John picked up a black piece and struck it a glancing blow with his knife, creating a spark.
Great, I thought, *I can now make my own fire, providing I don't slice my fingers off.*

"What you need now" said John, "is something to catch the spark" and he had with him some fine soft moss.

He struck his knife against the flint causing a spark to jump onto the moss which immediately started to smoulder, he then wrapped an old piece of linen around the smouldering moss and started to gently blow on and off it, until it burst into flame causing the linen to set alight; then he added fine wood shavings to the burning linen and that was it, the fire was lit. John explained that if you didn't stop and restart blowing you may blow out the fire, and have to start all over again. I had lots of tries before I got it right, catching the spark was easy but the blowing was difficult, you had to blow softly at first then harder towards the end but the hard part is making the smoulder bigger; then make something catch alight. I also found out, to my surprise, that the spark did not come from the flint but from the tiniest bit of iron removed from the knife and you must have heard about the sparks flying when two swordsmen were in combat?

**

CHAPTER THREE

I didn't sleep much the night I saved William as my hero's head was spinning with joy. And now that I am the proud owner of a young mare valued at over five pounds as well as a saddle and tackle costing at least two Nobles, I was wondering what other treats were in store for me because the day after the rescue my family had been invited to the manor to celebrate.

Lord John has sent a coach to collect my mother, father and sister but I am going to ride in style on my six year old Chestnut mare which I have named Floss; waving to the admiring crowd lining the route….. Well what I really mean is, lined by my admiring grandfather and Uncle James. I was hailed for my brave and courageous act by Lord Thornbury who presented me with a purse full of coins which I couldn't wait to open to find out how much it had in it. Then William, who looked very tiny now that he was standing, thanked me for saving his life and gave me a new knife replacing the one I had lost in the creek. I had no idea how much was in the purse but I eventually learned that it contained: ten groats, twenty pennies, twenty four halfpennies and thirty two farthings, which added up to one noble.

Having given the bag of money to my father for safe keeping I had no trouble sleeping that night as I am now a rich person with six shillings and eight pence in coins, with the same amount hidden under the pig sty, and the knife William has given to me is ten times sharper than the one I had lost.

I went to the Oare creek two days after the rescue where lots of people had gathered to see the Lord's men trying to drag out the small horse from the lowest point of the creek with ropes attached to all of its legs, the saddle had been removed, but with ten of the Lord's men and dozens of willing helpers, all they could do was get the carcase to the top of the creek but not over the banking; eventually they were forced to cut the animal into small pieces, leaving no reminder of the accident.

Whilst celebrating the rescue my mother had found out that the Lord's wife was also French and came from a place called *Boulogne*; and an instant friendship was formed between them. My mother told her that she had always wanted me to learn how to read and write and asked her if she could help in getting me lessons from the monks at the Monastery. The Lord's wife said that she would to talk to her husband about it but thought it would be alright providing I was willing to learn; and I sure was willing because I could then find out if the Whittington man was honest or not. Lord John said that I would be offered the chance to work at the monastery three days a week where I was to assist one of the monks who tutored young William, saying that if I showed any ability the monk would educate me.

I was instructed to go to the monastery, on my birthday Wednesday 25th October 1402 at 7.30am to start my work. I didn't know how to tell the time so I walked there as soon as daylight came where I was met by a monk in brown robes who took me into the monastery adjoining Faversham Abbey.

This monk was not much taller than my five feet and I was told to call him Brother Benedict and that I was to help him with any jobs he asked me to do.
He must have been at least forty years old and of course had a bald head shining through a ring of hair.

I thought I was an early riser but Brother Benedict had been out of bed since four am, had done his morning prayers in the Abbey and would start giving me work from eight am until eleven am; then I was to go home and to come back every morning at the same time except Sundays, so it was to be six mornings not three days. I had to collect water from the well in the monastery grounds and sweep the stone floors of his two rooms, each one bigger than the dwelling where all our family had to live. After about a month I became a firm friend of Brother Benedict and as I was a willing helper and keen to learn as much as possible, he started to teach me.

At my age it came easy and I was soon able to say the alphabet and write small sentences, I also became quite good at telling the time. I could already count up to ten on my fingers but now, looking at Brother Benedict's timepiece and his sun dial, I had a better idea of time itself other than sun up, noon and night. I still had my jobs to do at home but less water carrying after the first morning carry. I could speak French but was amazed that a lot of the words I said didn't sound the same as the words spoken by Brother Benedict and it dawned on me that it was no different from speaking in English; with people in Kent using different accents than that used by people from other areas of the country.

William was pleased with my learning and because he was well ahead of me with his lessons he was able to help me understand more and more and as time went by, Brother Benedict could see that William was more attentive when he was learning with me, so he started teaching us together. He changed my lesson time to an eleven am start and finishing at three pm; as for some reason William didn't get up early in the morning. So now after seven months I have become quite good at reading and writing but I still have trouble with what is called arithmetic; adding up and taking away are alright but times and sharing are not so easy, still this is important if I want to sort the Whittington man out.

Winter is well out of the way, spring is turning the land green, putting new leaves on the trees and the flowers were filling the air with lovely smells. May is approaching and the people of Faversham and Oare are getting ready for the May Day Festival which will be this coming Sunday. May Day is the time when in folklore, farmers pass their livestock through hoops made from the Rowan tree to protect them from harm and to ensure fertility, so everybody wants branches from our trees.

It was said that good fairies live in the Rowan trees and that they are benevolent with their favours. If, for instance, a piece of this wood is sewn into a child's clothing it will protect them from evil spirits; the buttons on my doublet are made of rowan, so this will probably counteract my left handedness. There are lots of other customs and uses for this wood. Witches were supposed to use rowan sticks as magical wands, so that's what we children do, we wave our wands and cast spells on the Faversham gang with them doing the same to us; and if the sticks magically happen to turn into a sword, then its war to the death all over again.

Everybody will have a good time watching drunken men trying to manoeuvre their un-helpful animals through the hoops; but I will have to drive our pig home at the end of the day and my drunken father and grandfather will be guided home by my mother and Yvette. People only took one or two animals to the festival ground but pigs were a great favourite as they would not co-operate whatsoever and this was highly amusing.

At last it's May Day and everyone is off to the festivities on the common. All yesterday my mother had made eight lots of baker's dozen biscuits that she will sell at two for a farthing. They are about four thumb inches in diameter and half a thumb thick. She uses a secret French recipe, mixing wheat flour with honey or maple syrup and crushed hazel nuts; she gives the thirteenth ones to me and my friends about noon time when all the main sporting events are due to begin. My father hopes to sell some competition longbows at two shillings each and Uncle James has taken about sixty of his finest three farthing arrows along with the same number of cheap halfpenny arrows.

The first events in the afternoon will be the archery contests, starting with the junior twelve to fourteen year olds and then the fifteen to seventeen years followed by the adults. The small children's activities have been going on all morning, such as the three legged race and the sack race. My sister has been showing off her skills at maypole dancing but I have been waiting for the junior archery competition as this is the first year I am old enough to enter. There are twelve boys competing and we have six targets to shoot at, making two groups who will shoot five arrows each from a distance of twenty five yards. We are not allowed to have metal points on our arrows in the opening rounds of the competition, just shaved points, but we can use metal points in the final shoot off.

The targets were made of parchment stuck onto a tightly bound straw circle five feet in diameter and each target had a nine inch diameter red bull in the middle that scores five points if your arrow hits it.

A white ring is surrounds the bull and this is called the inner. It has an outside diameter of twenty seven inches which when hit, scores three points.

Then there is a blue outer ring that surrounds both the bull and inner rings, with an outside diameter of forty five inches which scores just one point.
In the dead centre of the red bull is a one inch circular disk of white parchment called the bull's eye which scores the highest and is worth ten points; the rest of the straw circle doesn't count in the scoring.

After the first round, the four lowest scorers have to drop out of the competition leaving eight to shoot again in two groups of four, this time at thirty yards with two targets removed, where again the lowest four scorers have to drop out.

I was one of the last four, as was Jack Smith, and I hoped that at forty yards I would be one of the final two contestants who will shoot at a distance of fifty yards. I was getting nervous as we all lined up on our targets, Jack was on target three and I was on target four, a boy named John was on target one and my friend Tom Miller was on target two.

As usual I had to use my right hand to fire my arrows and my father had told me to watch where the other boy's first arrow had hit the target before I shot, as this would give an indication of what the wind was doing but there was no wind blowing, so I loosened off my first arrow scoring a white inner below and to the left of the bull.

Jack scored a bull, Tom on target number two hit the straw circle but not in the scoring area and the fourth boy John, on target one, scored a blue one point outer.

After shooting the next arrow we all scored white inners for three points and on the third arrow Jack and I scored a bull. Tom scored a three point inner and John scored a blue outer for one point. John scored a bull on arrow four with the rest of us scoring inners.

For my final arrow I was going to wait and shoot last, but so were the others, so I fired scoring a bull which just missing the bull's eye.

Jack shot a bull and I knew that he was certain to be in the final shoot off with 21 points, I had 19 points.

Tom could equal my score if he hit the bull's eye for 10 points and John could beat me by one point if he hit a bull's eye. Tom shot an ordinary bull, so he was out of it.

John knew that he had to score a bull's eye for ten points, so he took his time and really concentrated, all of the watching crowd were quiet but I felt confident that he was not a good enough archer to hit the small bull's eye. He pulled the arrow right back to his cheek and SNAP! His bow broke.

John was using a bow made out of witch elm whereas Jack, Tom and I were using yew bows, all made by my father.

What do the rules say?

I hoped that John would be out but the judges said that as the arrow had not been released from the string he could use another bow and fire again. He wasn't having my bow! But Jack who was already in the final said gloatingly that John could use his.

I knew that Jack was going to get me sometime, for the pink scar on his face and the nick in his ear, so this was a start to getting his own back. I hoped that because John was using a strange bow it would put him off but no, a great cheer went out from the crowd, bull's eye they shouted.

How could it be possible? I couldn't look.

To score ten points the arrow only had to nick the white disk and that's what the judges were trying to decide. If there was the slightest scratch on the small circle, it was a bull's eye.

As it affected me, I was allowed to look at the target and I could see a slight nick on the white disk but said nothing; my father was one of the judges but he wouldn't give his opinion as he said it would not be fair to John. So it was decided that a three way shoot off would take place, which suited me, only this time Jack would not let John use his bow and he had to borrow one from one of his friends. The targets were set at fifty yards and we could now use an iron point which was needed to carry the distance; but I felt a cheat and decided to come third but my pride in shooting forced me to make some sort of effort and aim at something, so I chose to land my five arrows as close to each other as possible below the bull and in the inner circle scoring fifteen points. If I then won, it would still show what a good archer I was and I would feel less guilty.

I scored three inners and two outers for eleven points in exactly the place I wanted, below the bull, with all my arrows no more than six inches apart and I could have argued that one of the arrows in the blue ring was touching the white inner ring making my score thirteen.

Jack of course won with seventeen points and John scored thirteen points.

I felt quite pleased with myself as what is two pennies for coming second against knowing my aim was good.

Jack won a groat (four pennies) which he wasn't happy about because they are hard to spend and not many people trusted them for some reason.

I won a penny and was glad that I hadn't claimed the extra two points because I wanted to win not come joint second.

The men then held their competition; only this time they started the contest at fifty yards finishing up at one hundred yards which was won by my friend's father, Tom the Miller from Oare with my uncle James coming second. My father did not shoot as he could not keep a good stance due to his leg injury.

The ale had been flowing nicely all day so now it was time for my grandfather to do his act, the tug of war, but he must have a winning secret as his team has never lost a contest, There must be a reason why his side win's all the time and I shall have to find out how it's done. The rules of tug of war are: two teams of ten men are spread out facing each other along a strong rope about forty feet long with a marking ribbon tied to the centre of the rope between them. The idea is that each team has to pull on the rope in opposite directions with the winning team being the one that pulls the ribbon across their side of a line set at two yards from a central start line; they have three pulls and the champion is the team that wins two of them. Each team pick up the rope and a Judge tells the teams to shuffle back and forward, moving the rope so that the ribbon is directly over the start line and when he is satisfied that this is done he shouts 'take the strain' and then he shouts pull!

Each team then tugs with all of their strength whilst all along each side of them their supporters are shouting pull! pull!...... with their team leader giving instructions; and just like always, my grandfather's team won.

"How's it done Grandfather?" I asked.

"Team work boy, team work, you must all pull together" he said.

"Come on grandfather, there must be more to it than that?"

"Ask your father" he said. "If he thinks you are old enough to keep it to yourself, then I shall tell you."

However my father told me the secret himself.

"Your grandfather's team" he said. "Take no notice of any of its supporters or him, they just keep taking the strain by digging their heel of their right foot into the ground and not pulling. They lean back on the rope but keep their left leg backward for balance and just watch his helper."

"What helper?" I asked.

"Me!" he replied. "But the other team doesn't know that as they think your grandfather is giving the instructions. I walk along the side of the other team and watch for any weakness such as, not pulling on the rope at the same time. They also dig their heels in the ground at different times, so it's my job to watch for these differences and give your grandfather's team hand signals. When I raise my right hand the team all slacken the strain slightly which makes their opponents lose their balance; then when I lower my hand they put their weigh on the left foot and dig the right foot a little bit further back all at the same time and once again take up the strain, this is usually enough to make the other team completely lose their balance and the pull is won; but if the other team are able to recover we start again until the line is crossed. That's team work."

My father concluded, "And like your grandfather said, all pulling together and taking instructions from one man!"

This information stuck in my mind and was proved decisively in years to come.

I was still happy with my archery skill and was running through the woods when Jack blocked my way, I knew what was going to happen and tried to escape but being older and bigger than me he grabbed hold of my doublet and punched me to the ground where I lay still, hoping that it would all end.

Jack thought that he had killed me and was about to dash off when some grown-up people came along; this made me feel safe so I pretended to come alive. I could see the worried look on Jack's face and I told them that we had been racing and that I had tripped and fell. Jack was so relieved that I was still alive and that I hadn't got him into trouble that now, we have become good friends. We now practiced archery together as it was obvious that we would be a match for each other.

Jack was able to develop his arm and back muscles by working with his father at the blacksmiths forge; where it was his job to work the bellows that blew into a charcoal fire, then when the iron gets red hot, he sometimes did the shaping. I asked Jack how iron could be made into things but all he did was tap his nose a couple of times with his finger, this was a way of saying 'mind your own business, it's a secret.'

"Alright then, never ask about longbows and arrows" I said.

But as the years went by, we both learned all there was to know about archery.

Then when I was eventually allowed to enter his father's smithy I learn about forging metals and all sorts of arrow heads. I even learned how to make the iron arrow heads harder when Jack asked me to piss into a bucket which contained horse hoof clippings. He told me that his father had discovered this hardening when instead of cooling hot arrow heads in water, he dipped them in the pee mixture which for some reason formed a hard coating to the point; but as I grew up I learned that carbon was added to molten iron which made it harder still and this was known as steel.

It was now getting towards late evening, the sun was starting to set in the west and the best part was going start ……..

Herding the panicking livestock through the rowan hoops, with pigs, goats, sheep and drunken men going all over the place; it was a good job that the mothers and children were there to sort it all out.

When we eventually arrived home my grandfather, a great storyteller and having had more of his share of the tug of war prize, a firkin of ale, started to tell me of a past battle he had fought in. My brother had heard his stories before and warned me not to believe everything he said. Telling stories was the only way anybody got to learn about the past as there were no books for the ordinary peasants, not that anybody could read them if there were. The only books were in Faversham Abbey's library, so I heard his story about the Battle of Poitier's fought in the year 1356.

My grandfather said "When I was seventeen years of age (he was now sixty three) I was allowed to go to France with an army, led by the twenty six year old Edward Prince of Wales who was the eldest son of King Edward the third. We were trying to avoid a battle with the French and after much marching backwards and forward we were passing through the Loire Valley, retreating to Bordeaux.

I was in the advance guard and when we came upon their army we were forced to give battle at a place near the town of Poitiers, which is in central France. Our army consisted of about two thousand longbow men and roughly four thousand men at arms. We were lined up facing North West in a defensive 'V' formation on a high flat ridge with a deep valley protecting our left flank and to get to us the French army, who numbered at the very least twice as many as us, would have to cross a ditch then pass through a thorn hedge."

"The Prince had given no order to attack he continued, so we just stood there waiting for the French to make the first move which they eventually did when we pretended to retreat. I was on the left side of our army, close to the valley and could see three large armies of Frenchmen moving towards us. The first army was led by a knight holding a long banner showing a gold coloured image on a red background and once they were within our firing range of two hundred yards, we started to shoot our arrows at their horses. The French had to close ranks so that they could pass through the thorn hedge; making their army impossible to miss, we didn't even have to aim our arrows, just shoot at the mass of men. There were so many dead and injured that their formation broke up, causing their second army to get tangled with the first group. On seeing this, the third army panicked and fled. My comrades and I were nearly out of arrows, so we joined up with the men at arms and advanced against them; winning the battle and capturing the French King along with a lot of his knight's."

"I could see very few wounded Englishmen" he went on "and as far as I was aware, none of our men had been killed but the French were lying dead and wounded all over the battle field."

I didn't know if I believed my grandfather or not but I later found out that everything he had told me was true. There were hundreds of books at the monastery and on reading one of them about the Battle of

Poitiers, history has revealed even more details with certain facts coming to light which were not known to the ordinary soldier at the time.

Each army has a number of men called Heralds who have to conduct negotiations between the opposing armies and who, after any battle, have to decide the winner; not that it took much deciding in this case. They then wrote down their view of the battle, as did other people such as, learned soldiers that were in the battle which resulted in quite a difference in opinion. Naturally the French writer's opinions were on how they lost the battle, whilst the English opinions were on how the battle was won; this is what I read.

On Monday the 19th of September 1356, Prince Edward, with six thousand men, was marching back to Bordeaux with a great deal of plunder which slowed his progress. He had to decide whether to abandon the plunder and escape to Bordeaux, or to stand and fight; he chose to fight. The French had about twenty thousand men divided into four armies, the first of which was a strong force of three hundred knights and Pike men in heavy armour who were to break up the English archers.

They believed that an English arrow would not be able to penetrate their armour and that they could just march through the onslaught without getting hurt but they found out to their cost that an arrow may well glance off a curved surface but would break through with a direct hit; or where there was a link from arm to chest or around the groin area, allowing the arrow to go straight into the body.

Their soldiers were falling like flies.

Their second army, commanded by King John's son Charles, got tangled up with the retreating force and suffered the same deadly problem, so that when the third army led by the Duke of Orleanais saw what was happening, he and his men turned back in panic; leaving the fourth group, led by the French King, to the mercy of Prince Edward, who, with his detachment of horsemen had circled the French left flank and attacked their rear. The English dead and wounded was less than fifty but the French casualties numbered over two thousand five hundred killed or wounded with two thousand captured, including King John.

**

CHAPTER FOUR

My friends thought it was unhealthy to wash the skin and used to laugh at me for being clean but at least I didn't stink like them with their smelly bodies. The only time they washed themselves was in the river Swale. I did stink however, of lye soap, until such times this smell was washed away in the stream.

To make this soap you need three ingredients: lye, pigs lard and rain water, but there is one other ingredient, elbow grease otherwise known as hard work. Lye is obtained by using the ashes of burnt hardwood mixed with rainwater in a barrel or bowl which is then left to soak for several days making sure that the mixture is well out of the way of children or animals as it would cause burning to the skin.

I shall not tell you how the lye mush is finally formed, not that it's a 'nose tapping' secret because everybody makes it; it's just that it is dangerous when raw. The lye is then added to the pigs lard in an iron pot and heated over a fire until they are both fully melted together, then after removing the pot from the fire the contents have to be stirred and mixed until the stirring paddle becomes really hard to move which can take several hours. The contents are then scooped into a flat wooden box about eighteen inches by eighteen inches and one inch deep then left to set. Once the soap starts to harden, lines can be scored down into the mixture forming hand size blocks and the longer you leave the mixture the harder the blocks will set. Two weeks to a month is normally long enough for it to go hard but when washing yourself you must make sure that no soap gets into your eyes as it will really make them smart.

I had heard whispers that a lot of people had died about fifty years ago from the *Black Death* but nobody wanted to talk about it; so the next time I went to the Monastery I searched in the library to find what I was looking for.

The reason nobody would say anything about it was because The Plague as it is now called, was not over and people thought that if they were to talk about it, then it would bring the pestilence back. Monastery records show that in the spring of 1349 the Black Death came to Faversham and that thirty-nine people had died by the winter of 1350; two of whom, were my great grandparents. A diary left by a Faversham monk named Brother Gregory recorded the local disaster and its effect on the Faversham population.

Having been to London in the summer of 1349, he wrote:

The whole of London was in a state of panic as more and more people were dying and their bodies were being left unburied because nobody wanted to go into a dwelling that had a large red cross painted on its door; as they were afraid of getting the black spots on their bodies and the swelling lumps on their neck's, groins and armpits which signalled death. When I came back to the Monastery my report was hard for anyone to believe but other travellers told the same sad story. To catch the Black Death, it was thought that you only had to be in contact with a victim, so people were staying well away from one another.

Word soon spread around Faversham and it was decided that no strangers were to be allowed into the town including merchants, visitors or indeed any relations of the villagers.

Autumn was almost upon us, he wrote, and the townspeople were getting to hear more and more stories about this epidemic and how it was spreading further and further across England. If a person would not keep his distance he stood a good chance of being killed and left to rot where he lay.

One story the monk wrote, was about a Rochester man who had come to his family in Sittingbourne pleading for their help but he was beaten with a club by his brother and driven away.

The monk went on to write:

Guards were now placed on the London road to the east of Faversham as well as the west of Oare and that any person trying to enter the area was to be warned – stay away or be killed. Nobody had shown signs of black spots or swelling and once winter had come the panic started to die down but the guard was still maintained at the road entrances to the area; then as spring approached we had our first death, a ten years old boy. He had been playing in the fields chasing rats and within four days he was dead and his mother died two days later followed by his sister and father, so the Black Death had arrived.

People in Oare now stay away from the people in Faversham and killings were quite common on the outskirts of our community.

When I read what Brother Gregory recorded about my great grandparents I broke down and cried, they had been alone on their farm and nobody had seen them for a week; they were found dead in bed huddled together.

But, he wrote:

The Black Death was not only caught from people, it was also spread by rats and fleas. The whole of England was in panic and town's people who were not able to grow their own food were starting to die from hunger and in their attempts to get something to eat were coming out of the towns, only to be killed by country folks.

Eventually, I got the story out of my grandfather when I told him that I had read everything about what happened in Faversham and that I knew that it was only my great grandparents who had died in Oare. He had kept it to himself for over fifty years and I wanted everybody to hear his story, so I sat down with my parents and Yvette to listen to what he had to say.

My brother John was still away somewhere, fighting the Scots so wasn't there to hear my grandfather say, "I was scared to death, as it was my friend Paul who was the first to die. We had been playing together chasing rats, so like everybody else my family stayed inside and kept to ourselves; but after weeks of being cooped up and seeing no one, I was itching to go out and play. My mother told me that I could go out with my father and build a hideaway shelter in the woods to see what it would be like to be a soldier."

My grandfather then started to cry, saying "I didn't know what the black spots on their bodies were but my mother did and she was sending me away in the hope I would be saved. I was to pretend that we were being invaded and not to come out of hiding."

Then my father, in-between tears said "you needn't go on if you don't want to."

But Grandfather replied "It's about time you all knew the story", so he continued with all of us crying now.

He said "I was so frightened that I crouched in my shelter for three days without moving a muscle but hunger eventually made me eat some of the food I had with me and the stream was just a few yards away to have a drink. I had now got some black spots but I was feeling well and after a couple of more days the spots left me. I went out through the woods where the birds were singing away as usual, the sun was shining and everything smelt fresh. I was no longer afraid for myself but I was worried about my parents and as I walked towards my home I was shouted at to stop and come no further but when the shouter recognised me, I was told what I had already guessed; my mother and father were dead. I fearfully went back to my den for another two days but when people were shouting out my name to see if I was still alive, I came out of hiding."

I knew from my reading in the library at the monastery that the Plague had started to lessen its deadly grip during the winter of 1350 and that for reasons unknown there were people who had caught it and survived but I didn't know that my grandfather was one of them. Why he didn't die is a mystery.

My grandfather told us that he was sorry that he had never told the story before and was surprised when my father said "I have always known that our dwelling had caught fire and that my grandparent's bodies were never recovered for a Christian burial and that everybody suspected that you had started the blaze."

My grandfather admitted to us that he had burned his home down and felt guilty about the cremation of his parents.

However, I had read that the burning of the dead was the best way of disposing of a body even though no Christian ceremony had taken place and that Pope Clements the sixth and the Catholic Church were forced to grant remission of sins for those who had died without the benefit of the clergy.

I then asked my grandfather about the rats and he told me that when it was known that the Black Death came from rats everybody was killing and burning them on bonfires but it was impossible to kill them all.

I then asked "And what about the fleas grandfather?"

"What fleas?" he replied.

I told him that I had read about how it was the fleas just as much as the rats that spread the Plague.

"That must have been why everybody was burning their bedding and clothes" grandfather murmured as he went on to finish his story.
"After the winter of 1350 and spring of 1351 nobody was dying and people were beginning to have contact with one other and I tried to make my burnt out dwelling habitable again" he said.

"But I could only make a den out of the ruins and I survived by scrounging around and living off what food people left at the boundary of my hovel. As the summer of 1351 came we all thought that the Black Death was over, so the local men helped to clear away the ruins of my home and rebuild a decent shelter for me, as they felt that as it was only my parents who had died in Oare they should help me all that they could."

He ended his story there.

My reading ability was now as good as William's which he didn't mind, as once you can read that's as far as you could go; well as far as reading English was concerned but William knew that he would eventually have to learn Latin and more French. I wasn't interested in Latin and even though my French accent was different from Brother Benedict's the letters were near enough the same, so except from some spelling changes, I could work out the written word from the spoken word.

I now wanted to learn about another battle, the battle of *Crécy* which my great grandfather had fought in.

I already knew about my grandfather at Poitiers and my father at Eu, and wondered who will be next me or John?

Probably John I thought, so once again it's back to the monastery library to read about the battle of Crécy which was another triumph for the longbow; when will the French learn? But no, hang on, my Grandfather had already told me about Poitiers which was ten years after Crécy, so that's when they should have learned about the deadly effect of long range archery.

The battle of Crécy took place on the 26th of August 1346.....

I read:

The English had landed in Normandie during the summer and had won a battle at Caen in July and then another on the north side of the river Somme, two days before the battle of Crécy; at a place with heck of a name, Blanchetaque.

The French had planned to trap the English army led by King Edward the third, along with his eldest son also named Edward, between the river Seine and the river Somme; but they had escaped by wading across the Somme when the tide was low, with the water coming up to their waists.

The English army numbered: four thousand men at arms, seven thousand longbow men and five thousand spearmen. Opposing them was a French force of seventy four thousand cavalry and six thousand crossbowmen.

Edward's men were in a defensive position facing south east with wooded areas on both sides awaiting the French to make the first move. The King had ordered his men to dig ditches and pits in front of his lines to bring down the French cavalry horses. During the morning his men were formed into a forward pointing 'V', with the archers on each flank. The ground sloped downward towards where the French would have to start their attack, so all they had to do was sit down and wait.

There was a roadway from one wooded area to the other which was one hundred and fifty yards in front of the English lines therefore any Frenchman reaching the road was certain to be in killing range of an arrow. At about four pm the first wave of Genoese men started to advance carrying heavy crossbows and as they approached the well-rested English army stood up and fell into rank. Then due to a sudden rainstorm both armies were trying keep their strings dry to avoid stretching. The Genoese had to hide as much of their crossbows as they could under their jackets but their strings were still getting wet making them less effective, if not useless.

I knew that changing a string on a crossbow is not as simple as changing one on a longbow because you have to use both hands and feet or a special winding frame to do the job due to the greater tension required. Whereas an English archer can easily remove a bowstring with little effort by placing the longbow on his foot and bending it backward, then keeping the string protected in his clothing or under his cap it could then be refit once the rain has stopped. It is well known that the Italian crossbow men were no match for the English bowmen as they could only shoot two arrows per minute, whilst the English archers could shoot ten or more in the same time.

So reading on, I learnt:

Having had to use wet strings the Genoese bolts were falling short of the English lines but the English arrows were striking hard into them, therefore after sustaining heavy losses they panicked and started to flee; which was greeted with scorn by the French who attacked and killed a large number of these Italians who were considered to be cowards.

The English archers were now ranging their arrows into the French infantry who had started to advance but in so doing, they were colliding with the retreating

Genoese resulting in a jumble of men and bodies. Then as the French reached the roadway the English archers had no problem in creating a mass of fallen dead and wounded across the battlefield. The French cavalry then galloped up the slope in an attempt to break up the English formations but the ditch obstacles, along with their dead and wounded disrupted their charge. Each English bowman had started the battle with two quivers holding a total of forty eight arrows but these were soon used up, forcing the bowmen to fight alongside the men at arms using whatever weapon they already had or could pick up from the fallen enemy. Their cavalry made charge after charge but the English held fast resulting in more and more French men being killed; thus as night fell, the wounded French King Charles VI ordered a disastrous and humiliating retreat.

There were some English casualties, said to be no more than three hundred dead or wounded but the French casualties were vast and was estimated to be between eighteen thousand and thirty thousand dead or wounded. After the battle most of the French Knights were taken prisoner for ransom but those seriously wounded were dispatched with long daggers inserted between their armour into their heart; or through their visors into their eyes.

On further reading I discovered something that nobody in my family seemed to be able to tell me about…….

I knew that the English had a strong foothold in the French town of Calais but how this came about was now revealed to me.

After the battle of Crècy, Edward had marched his army another forty five miles on to Calais which was defended by high walls and two moats, as well as being partially surrounded by marshland. Edward had felt that as Calais lay on the English Channel it could easily be supplied from England and would therefore be an ideal launching site for future invasions of France, so he started to besiege the town. For several months the English were unable to stop food and water reaching the town from the sea but as the siege progressed Edward's navy was able to blockade any further supplies reaching them; so that after nine months of being under siege their food and water started to run out.

As I read on I was ashamed to be half English because the town sent about five hundred old people and children out of its gates to the mercy of the English. This was an attempt to preserve what little supplies of food and water remained for the defenders and I found it hard to believe that the English stopped these exiles, preventing them from passing through the surrounding cordon and forcing them to starve outside the town walls. The final fate of these poor souls was not written about but I hoped that the defenders would have taken them back into the town.

On the first of August 1347 after eleven months of siege, the town was prepared to surrender to the English but Edward was so enraged with the defenders that he wanted to kill all who survived. However, he was advised that if this was to happen the defenders would fight on, so he relented and the remaining inhabitants were allowed to leave Calais peacefully.

∗∗

CHAPTER FIVE

William and I had been learning sums but other than counting money I couldn't see what arithmetic could be used for, until Brother Benedict applied it to my favourite pastime ...... Archery.

"When an arrow is shot from a longbow" he said, "the speed and distance of its flight is determined by the amount of effort put into stretching the longbow, so the more it is stretched the further an arrow will fly and a strong man will be able to shoot an arrow a greater distance and more speed than a weaker man. However, with some alterations to the longbow a weaker man may improve his ability; therefore a longbow can be made to suit the archer."

"There are two things to consider" he said. "One is a man's stretch because the longer his arms the greater his stretch, the other is the amount of arm and back strength a man can achieve by training and strengthening his muscles."
"Yes" I said. "But where does arithmetic come into it?"

"Well" he said "it is important that a man can demonstrate his strength with a longbow, therefore I want you to borrow one of your father's finest longbows with a good string and we shall try to work out some pull strengths."

Brother Benedict told me to take a measuring stick home and ask my father to pull the string on his longbow as hard as he could, as if he was to shoot an arrow; then I was to measure the distance from the bow to his fingers on the stretched string.

"Get him to do this three times" he said "then get somebody else to do the same."

My father was not too pleased at lending me a longbow but after some begging and pleading he agreed to lend me one on condition, that if it was lost or damaged I would have to pay him two shillings. This was no problem for me as I had not spent a penny out of my reward money.

My father pulled 36 inches three times, uncle James pulled 33 inches three times. I pulled 18 inches three times and my mother pulled 23 inches, 22 inches and then 21 inches; my sister pulled 11 inches and 10 inches, then her face!

When I arrived at the monastery the following morning Brother Benedict was already there along with two men at arms. William had a parchment covered in lines going up and down making little squares; this we were told was called a grid which was to be used to make a plan of my numbers and that it was called a graph.
Brother Benedict then spread the tips of the longbow, with the string upwards, across two benches spaced as wide as the bow was long and we measured the distance from the longbow to the string which was 9 inches.

We then had to hang weights on to the centre of the bow bending it more, until the string was just slack enough to remove which took six pounds to achieve; then we had to hang the longbow from its centre, across a low roof beam about five feet from the ground with the re-joined string downward then bind the bow to the beam to stop it moving or slipping. The two men at arms then lifted two half hundredweight sacks of corn joined together with a rope and hung them onto the string using a butchers 'S' hook, this stretched the longbow as if a man was pulling it. This worried me as I thought the bow would break but it took the weight easily without having any effect on the string either.

William and I were then told to measure from the bow to the string and tell him the distance which was near enough 36 inches. He reminded us that the corn sacks hooked on to the string weighed exactly 112 pounds (one hundredweight). He then had the men remove the two sacks and replace them with one sack (56 pounds); the stretch now came to 27 inches.

"One more measurement to take" said Brother Benedict, and the half hundredweight sack was replaced with 28 pounds and the measurement was 18 inches.

Brother Benedict thanked the men and we untied the longbow. We now had to plot all this information on to the graph but before the men left he asked each of them to use the longbow as if they were shooting an arrow. The taller man pulled 31 inches and the other pulled 29 inches. Brother Benedict had already numbered the grid from the bottom left corner of the graph up the left side, equally spacing the numbers starting at nought then at 20 pound and so on, spacing them all the way up to 120 pounds but leaving five squares in-between each 20 pound marking with each square representing 4 pounds.

Then he numbered along the bottom starting again at nothing, followed by equally marked inches from 0 then 5 all the way along to 40 inches but this time each of the 5 squares in-between the markings represented one inch.

It was a good job Brother Benedict was doing the plotting as I was completely lost and I think William was as well. Putting a ruler on the graph across the line at 112 pounds and another ruler going up the line at 36 inch Brother Benedict marked a large dot where the rulers crossed then we had to check what he had done.

Poor William had to do the next plot.

"Put the ruler along the 56 pound line" Brother Benedict said.

William managed this, then he had to find out where the 27 inch line going up, crossed the ruler at 56 pounds, where he put another large dot on the graph.

I was watching fearfully as I knew I would be next but as it turned out mine was simple. Across at 28 pounds, up the line at 18 inches and where they crossed, I gratefully put my dot on the graph.
Then Brother Benedict said "Just one more dot to add, which is the start mark."

Asking me what the distance the string was set from the bow, I said "nine inches."

He then asked William what the weight was on the longbow when we started the experiment.

William said "six pounds."

So we marked a dot on the bottom of the graph for 6 pounds and 9 inches for the pull setting; this was a bit too much for me to take in and my head was reeling but Brother Benedict announced "you will shortly be able read what people's pull strengths are from the graph."

Brother Benedict then bent a ruler across the four dots and I had to draw a curved line along it which he called the trend line. It was still not clear to me or William what the graph told us until Brother Benedict asked me for my families pull distances which are:

My father 36 inches, uncle James 33 inches, my mother 22 inches, me 18 inches and my sister 10 inches.

"Now the next thing we have to do" said Brother Benedict "is to work out what amount of pull everybody can achieve. This is done by back plotting each measurement Crispin has just given me but this time, where the individual pull length going up the graph crosses the trend line we put another dot and from this new dot we go along the line to the left side of the graph and read the pull strength."

This just threw me completely but Brother Benedict told us "It will all become clear if we stick at it." So stick at it we did.

Where my father's 36inch line crossed the trend line (which in fact was already dotted from the testing) and plotted across to the 100 pound mark plus three squares of 4 pounds, it showed that my father had a pull strength of 112 pounds.

Wow! Information at last......

He can pull the weight of one hundredweight.

Uncle James next; up the line at 33inches, dot the trend line and read across for the result……… 92 pounds, easy peasy!

Then my mother; up the line at 22 inches, dot, read across……… 38 pounds.

I knew that my pull for 18 inches was 28 pounds which was also dotted from the testing.

I was not happy that my mother was stronger than me! And my sister had very little pull strength.

Brother Benedict let us finish early for the day and I took everything home with me including the measuring stick.

On arriving home Uncle James and my father were eagerly waiting for me and wanted to know what their pull strengths were. My father was happy with 112 pounds but Uncle James was disappointed to hear that his pull was only 92 pounds. I was to learn that although my father and Uncle James did not know what pulling strengths were all about, they knew the term and that it was expected to be 90 pounds or over for a good archer. My mother asked me what her pull was but never asked what I had pulled, Thank Goodness! And as for my sister, she couldn't care less.

Brother Benedict never told me what to expect when I got home but he had told me to take the measuring stick with me as well as the longbow and graph. I soon found out, as not long after I got home, six of my father's friends wanted their pull strength testing on this longbow; all of which were over 90 pounds.

Uncle James was determined to pull over 92 pounds, so he had another pull which came to 34 inches. I pretended to have trouble reading the graph, but a little tap around my head did the trick ... 100 pounds.

The next day I took everything back to the monastery where the men at arms couldn't wait to get their pull strengths. The tall man who had pulled 31 inches, had an 80 pound pull strength and the other man whose pull was 29 inches was about 68 pounds; which I thought was poor for such big men, when you consider what an archer can pull.

William pulled 20 pounds and Brother Benedict, not surprisingly, declined.

From the information we had plotted an archer will have to pull a bowstring about 32 to 33 inches, using my father's longbow, to reach the required 90 pounds pull.

Brother Benedict then invited another monk named Brother Arnold to come and have a go.

WOW! This monk must have been six feet six inches tall with arms like tree trunks. He pulled 38 inches which went over the top of our graph but by continuing the trend line up the parchment, he had pulled an unbelievable 120 pounds. It was no trick as Brother Arnold had been an archer who had turned to the church after all the death and destruction he had seen in English riots as well as the wars he had fought in against the Welsh and the Scots.

As the months went by, I pestered Brother Arnold to teach me all that he knew about archery which would be added to the skills and tricks of the trade that I had learned from my father and Uncle James.

Everybody knows that Yew is the best material for making longbow because this wood has a straight close grain which allows strength combined with springiness. The tree has a bushy round headed look and the branches spread out in an irregular way, the bark is fluted, similar to the shape left in the sand at the seaside when the tide has gone out fast. My father, following on from his father uses young tree saplings because the core of the wood is hard whilst the outside sapwood is springy. The saplings are cut at the end of the growing season, in late autumn, when less sap is needed to feed the foliage.

Unfortunately the trees that grow in England are not suitable for making longbows due to the seasonal weather changes which cause the trees to grow twisted and tangled; what is needed is a wood grown in a temperate steady climate and in limestone or chalky soil. My father gets his wood from Spain or Italy in the form of reasonably straight saplings, in lengths of about seven feet but different diameters ranging from one and a quarter inches up to about two and a half inches.

My grandfather had made a deal with a timber trader in Dover who buys the Yew wood from abroad, who allows him the first choice of the saplings as he passes our farm on his way to London. This suited the trader as he was treated to a night's lodging in Faversham with a good free ale session thrown in; whilst my grandfather was saved the trip to London. This tradition which occurs once a year in January or February is now undertaken by my father.

The thicker saplings are split down the centre enabling two longbow staves to be made from one piece of wood, whilst with the smaller diameter saplings a finer and stronger longbow can be made. Once purchased the saplings are left out in the open for six months to dry out the sap. This is called weathering and seasoning. The bark is then removed and some preliminary shaving can begin, creating a rough longbow stave.

These staves are again stored outside, only this time with a roof covering them and in separated layers leaving gaps between each stave. This further weathering and seasoning can take another six months or even longer, so a large amount of staves have to be bought on a regular basis to keep up a steady supply. Once the stave is ready to be shaped into a longbow, great care is taken to cut it to the length required and this is where all of the skill of a bowyer comes into play, as each longbow is individually crafted to suite the person who is going to use it.

The most popular length is about six feet and the middle distance of the stave is carefully marked off so that tapering from this point outward can begin. Each end of a stave needs to be tapered at the same rate otherwise there will be an uneven stretch when the longbow is in use which will have a vast impact on the longbows accuracy.

This is the guarded secret of a bowyer and my father does this tapering away from prying eyes.

The thickness at the centre of the bow, from front to a flattened rear will be just over one inch tapering to about a half an inch at the ends; with whatever shape of notch a buyer wants for fitting his bowstring, such as: a bone knob, a notch on the front side, or any means he wanted for holding the longbow in tension when the string is attached.

All methods of attaching the bowstring were fine but my father always recommended a curved groove with a piece of bone inserted to stop the wood splitting. He may leave the wood surface rough or he may smooth it down by adding sand and linseed oil on to a piece of linen and drawing it along the length of the longbow, steadily reducing the amount of sand to just linseed oil and then just linen until it becomes a joy to stroke your hand slowly down the length of the longbow. It is not uncommon to see archers caressing their longbows as if it was a woman's hair, using only the oil in their hands. An unsmoothed longbow takes two days to make and costs one shilling, whilst a crafted longbow using the finest single stave smoothed saplings takes him three days which he sells for two shillings.

Now we come to the making of arrows, anybody can make an arrow, you just get a straight stick put a point on one end some feathers on the other and that's it; but of course there is a lot more to it than that and an arrow is another crafted piece of wood.

An ideal arrow will be straight, does not waggle too much in flight and be heavy at the front and balanced with flights at the rear. My father and Uncle James consider that the wood from our Rowan trees make the best arrows as it has a straight grain but any straight grained wood will do just as well, so a fletcher will use whatever suitable wood is available. However my uncle does not make arrows from long straight sticks, as you may think, he makes them from the tree itself which has to be cut down and sawn into logs of just over a yard long, and like the longbow staves, the wood is stored and allowed to season. After the logs are cut and seasoned, using an axe, they are split into individual slats, roughly half an inch by half an inch making at least two hundred good arrows from a ten inch diameter log. These slats are then tied tightly together in bundles of about fifty and again left to season. He keeps a close eye on this final seasoning, untying each bundle now and then to rearrange the slats to keep them as straight as possible. Once he is satisfied that the slats will now keep their straightness, he can start to make them into rounded arrow shafts.

A quality target shooting arrow costing three farthings, will be about 36 inches long and have a diameter of about a quarter to three eighths of an inch. It must be smooth and straight, have an iron arrow head and will have perfect flights. He also makes unsmoothed less straight arrows for general use which cost half a penny.

Blacksmiths make the arrow heads from iron and my uncle buys two for a cost of one farthing. A normal type of head is shaped like a bird's outstretched wings with the bird's head forming the point and the wings forming the barbs. It measures roughly three to four inches from the point to the end of the shaft fitting and one inch across the barbs which are sharpened to a knife edge. Another type of point is the bodkin; which as you can imagine is shaped like a needle and measures about five inches long.

I have learned that there are four elements: Vital Spirit, Earth, Fire and Water.

However, there must be more to it than this, as the wind must be connected to vital spirit in some way because it affects the arrows in flight which brings us to the very important fletching......

Flights are needed to keep an arrow balanced as it flies towards its target through the vital spirit, that Brother Benedict calls air, which is what we breathe. These flights are made from large bird's wing feathers and as the largest birds in England are the Turkey and Grey Goose, these birds provide the flights for an arrow. The feather shaft is hollow and can be split down the centre leaving two feathery strips of which only the largest strip is used and as feathers fit neatly around a birds body they are right and left curved, therefore it is important that when making an arrow you use three left or three right curving flights, otherwise the arrow will be unbalanced when in use.

Three slices of a feathery strip about five inches long are equally spaced out around the rear end of the arrow shaft then fixed into position with horse glue, leaving the last inch of the shaft bare to allow the bowman to hold the arrow nock into the bowstring. Then thin fibres of hemp or flax are wound around and around the arrow shaft between the barbs, taking care not to damage or twist the rows of feather vanes. Then they are given a coat of linseed oil, making sure that no vanes are stuck together, finally the flights may be trimmed with shears to suite the archer preference.

Now we come to the bowstrings which can be made from various materials such as, leather strips, vines and linen, in fact any stringy material that will not stretch to any great extent or snap when pulled; even horse tail hair or animal sinew can be used. However, the most commonly used strings are made from hemp and flax fibres which are twisted together three at a time, exactly like plaiting a girls hair …….. Left strand over the centre strand then right strand over centre strand and so on causing the fibres to bind against one another.

Uncle James twists his own twines to make bowstrings using hemp and flax. He twists two twines of hemp with one twine of flax. Producing a bowstring with the combination of both materials adds to the strength which also has a resistance to stretching, resulting in a string diameter of one quarter of an inch, nobody knows however if it is the strongest or the best. As I grew older and learned more about archery from Brother Arnold, I was able to make vast improvements in arrow and string making but the longbow could not be improved on, as it was perfect as it was.

There always seemed to be battles all over the country but don't ask me what they are all about, all I know is that we fight the Welsh, we fight the Scottish and we even fight our own English men sometimes. I can't wait to grow up and skewer a few of the enemy with my arrows, no matter who they are. My best kills so far have been rabbits and birds but nothing bigger. I have however, shot at a dead pig that had been hanging over a fire to burn off its bristly hairs. It is said that shooting a pig is just like shooting into a man but shooting the pig got me in trouble because I put holes in the skin which was to be made into doublets, britches, arm braces and such like.

My brave brother John is now home from the north where he had been fighting the Scots and I asked him how many men had he killed but for some reason he didn't want to talk about it and it took quite a bit of persuasion to get him to tell me about his battles. I had already heard of a big battle we had won in September of last year at somewhere called *Homildon,* so I asked him if he had been there, and if he had, I wanted him to tell me about it.

John gave in saying "We were occupying a position in a valley at a place called Millfield which is on the river Till and we were waiting to cut off a strong Scottish army led by the Earl of Douglas; who were making their way home after raiding Northumberland. I was in the front of our army with the rest of the longbow men and we each had a quiver of twenty four arrows, of which it was said were twenty four Scotsmen's lives under our belts."

"The Earl's army" he said "would have to pass through Millfield on their way home; and when they eventually came upon us they halted alongside a hill called Homildon Hill. I don't know how many men were in our army, or in the Scottish army, but we had been told that they had at least twice as many men as us. Our army was commanded by the Earl of Northumberland and his eldest son Henry, who had the nickname of Harry Hotspur as he could not stop himself from wanting to gallop hot footedly into a battle."

"The Scots had halted less than two hundred yards away from us" John continued, "and we were ordered to shoot our arrows into this densely packed mass of men, who were unable to fall back out of range due to their heavy baggage train following up close behind them. Our arrows were repeatedly thudding into their ranks and it was a one sided fight. As our army slowly advanced towards them I lost all my fears, taking good aim with the last of my arrows. Thousands of Scots men were falling and the screams of dying men and horses was horrendous."

"But you still haven't told me how many you killed, yourself?" I asked

His only reply was the shrugging of his shoulders, so I guess it must have been a lot.

**

CHAPTER SIX

I felt as though I was not growing up fast enough and I was eager to start using a proper longbow, so my father has allowed me to use his which I have to slant across my body because of its length. I still have to hold the arrow in my right hand and I can now stretch the string 28 inches which gives me a pull of about 62 pounds (according to my graph) but I'm still a lot short of the of the ninety needed to be a good archer.

It took a long time for me to get Brother Arnold to teach me all he knew about archery as he had seen enough bloodshed and senseless killing of ordinary peasants in his lifetime, just so rich men with enough land and money already, could have more. Brother Arnold was another monk who had a bald head, so it was hard to tell his age but he must be at least fifty. The other monks prayed three times a day but not him, he was quite different, you would be lucky if he went to mass at all and he only went to confession once or twice a year. His main task was the tending of the grapes in the Abbey grounds and the making of wine. I knew that there would be no point in asking him questions about the secrets of wine making as it will only be more 'nose tapping' again; but he was proud of his skills and told me the basics of how it's done. He even took me into his vineyard within the enclosed walls of the Abbey.

"These walls are very important to the growing of grapes" he said "as they keep the wind off the vines and the sun's heat is trapped around them."

I had already noticed that it was a lot warmer in this enclosure which was about two hundred yards long and about fifty yards wide, where now, because it is winter, there are neat rows of bare vines stretching down the field.

Once I was able to convince him that my interest in archery was serious and that I wanted to be the best archer in the country, even better than Robyn Hode who I was not sure had been a real person or just a story; but I told him that someday I wanted to go to the Nottingham Goose Fair where all the best archers in the country went. This satisfied Brother Arnold and he agreed to teach me, saying that we could use the confines of the walled enclosure to practice. However before all this could happen, Brother Benedict wanted to send me to the counting house in London instead of having to make the trip himself.

I still had plenty of things to learn and was now only going to the monastery four times a week instead of six so he thought that the experience would be good for me, as my skill at counting the church donations along with the money from the sale of their wine, costing one penny per bottle, was good and with no mistakes.

I was told to ask my father, if he would allow me to go with Brother Arnold to change the Abbey's hoard of pennies, half pennies and farthings into nobles. My father had no objections but told me to watch out for thieves once I got to into London. Brother Arnold was going as the Abbey representative and as he knew nothing about reading or counting money, it was up to me to do the transaction. This I hoped, might be my chance for me to change my ill-gotten Noble.

We set off at first light on a Monday several days after the feast of my birthday, St Crispin's, along with six men at arms for protection. We had plenty of food comprising of: bread, cheese, salted fish, salted beef, two nine gallon firkins of ale, a dozen bottles of wine, along with four kegs of water and a sack of oats for the horses. It was expected that our trip would take four days. Four of the guards were riding on horseback, Brother Arnold was driving a cart pulled by two horses and I was sitting next to him with two of the guards sitting in the back, who now and then changed places with the rider's. I even got a chance to ride a horse, giving one of the horsemen a rest. In the cart were two chests, each full with little bags of small value coins. There was eighteen pounds in farthings, twelve pounds in halfpennies, ten pounds in pennies and twenty pounds in Groats.

I had hidden the Whittington man's noble in my boot, so all I had to do when we were exchanging the money was to count one hundred and twenty nobles for the small coins and sixty nobles for the groats and I was hoping to get my ill-gotten noble changed into small coins at the same time. Brother Arnold had made this trip many times so he knew the way to go once we got to into London, saying that the distance from Faversham to the counting house was roughly forty three miles, using the almost straight road...... Watling Street.

The plan was to ride as far as we could on the first day, rest up somewhere then have an easy shorter second days travel into London. We would then change the money and start back straight away and then stopping at another rest house, leaving a thirty eight mile ride back to Faversham in the last two days. Twenty miles a day is a good day's travel on foot, therefore four days with horses should easily cover the trip; this however was not to be the case.

The morning's travel was uneventful and we had passed *Sittingbourne* before eight am. Brother Arnold was very talkative as the cart was bouncing its way over the dusty road, telling me that he knew my grandfather and what had happened to my Great Grandparents. He also told me that before he became a monk he had been with Wat Tyler in the peasant's revolt. I had never heard of Wat Tyler, or the Peasant's revolt, so for the next ten miles to Chatham he told me and the two guards riding in the back part of the story.

"'In 1381, thirty years after the great loss of life from the Black Death" he said.

"Walter Tyler, was a person who had caught the plague and survived. He gathered around him peasants who started to demand more money for having to toil harder by doing two men's work but only receiving one man's pay as there was still a shortage of peasant workers to tend the land after the great loss of life all those years ago; what workers there were only received two pennies per day."

"What is more" he went on, "legally, under the Feudal System, peasants were not allowed to leave their present employment or to move away from the landowners property without permission and on top of all this, men were needed for the continuing battles with France, which was another reason for the labour shortage."

"Why are we always at war with France?" I asked.

"Don't interrupt" said Brother Arnold.

"To continue" said our driver, giving me a wink and a smile, "if people were unable to pay a poll tax of one shilling per adult to fund this war, their possessions such as farming tools or planting seeds were taken to the value of twelve pennies; which meant that a person may not be able to survive without the tools of their trade or the seeds for the next year's crop."

Bring back my hero, Robyn Hode I thought.

Brother Arnold continued with his story, "More laws were quickly passed, declaring that wages would not be increased and workers were obliged to toil harder for longer hours but the peasants found out that better wages could be earned in other areas, so they just moved away without permission. This was alright with their new employers, who were only too willing to pay more money rather than lose their crops but if the landowner found out where his serfs were working he was entitled to force them to return to their original jobs at the original wages, resulting in people like Walter Tyler starting to rebel against this Feudal System. Wat as he was commonly known, gathered around him men who wanted freedom from serfdom and have the right to work and live where they wanted to and receive a fair day's wage for fair day's toil. Wat moved into Kent, where I joined him" he said. "We had quite an army and captured Canterbury then moved on towards London also capturing Blackheath; and because we had such a large peasant army of about fifteen thousand men, young King Richard, was forced to meet with us at a place called Mile End, near Smithfield's in London itself."

One of the guards riding in the cart then asked "Is this when you decided to become a monk?"

"Almost" said Brother Arnold, "but that's enough story telling for the time being, we have covered about sixteen miles so we shall stop at that inn just ahead and have something to eat and drink."

How convenient to find an ale house, I thought.

Brother Arnold pulled the cart behind the inn and gave two pennies to one of the men to buy eight quarts of ale.

"I don't drink ale" I said,

Which brought laughter from the guards who shouted, "It's about time you started then."

Brother Arnold had been given five shillings to cover this kind of cost, so when the ale came, seven quarts were gone in a flash. I could only manage half a pint but Brother Arnold kindly helped me with the other pint and a half. Fortunately, there was a stream close by where I found a clear fast flowing spot to have a refreshing drink. The horses also drank from the stream and were happily chomping their oat bags.

The guards wanted more ale but Brother Arnold told them that they could use some out of our stock and drink it on the way because he wanted to cover at least another twelve miles before stopping; so we ate some bread and cheese, removed the feed bags, hitched up the horses and started off again.

I was a bit giddy from drinking the ale and was feeling sleepy but wanted to see the crossing over the river Medway, so I kept myself awake as we passed through Chatham towards the river. It seemed strange going over such a large bridge and I wondered how much trouble they must have had getting from one side of the river to Rochester before it was built? After crossing this wonder, I lay down in the back of the cart and the rocking motion soon sent me to sleep. I awoke when the cart stopped at a place called the Plough Inn in Dartford where we were going to spend the night. We had travelled thirty miles so there was only thirteen miles to go.

I had woken up with a raging thirst but no ale for me just water.

"WATER" the landlord bellowed, "nobody drinks water unless it has been boiled."

"Boiled water then please." I asked.

My father had told me not to drink any water in London as it was not pure but I had forgotten and anyway we were not in London yet, were we?

The landlord pulled his face at having to get it but soon cheered up when seven quarts of ale were ordered. We had been travelling for nine hours, for three of which I had been asleep; once the horses were fed and watered it was time for everybody to relax.

The money chests were carried into the inn and placed in the room in which we were all to sleep. One man was set to guard the horses for two hours, after which another man was to take over and so on until the morning. Included in the price of the room was a meal of bread, cheese, beef and ham and a quart of ale each for the men and more boiled water for me! All for two pence per person which I thought was too costly.

That's two pence at noon and two pence here for drinks, sixteen pence for the room followed by another round of ale at two pence; that's twenty two pence, leaving three shillings and two pence out of the five shillings allowed for the trip. When I mentioned this to Brother Benedict he gave me the nose tapping treatment as he said "don't ask too many questions the clipping money will cover any extra cost."

"What's clipping money?" I asked.

This resulted in more tapping of the nose, only this time he did the tapping on my nose! Which shut me up.

How's anybody ever going to learn anything? I wondered.

We arrived at the counting house in London well before noon the next day but for some reason it wasn't open for business. Brother Arnold and one of the guards went to find out what was happening and why the counting house was closed. It turned out that today, Tuesday, had been chosen for the Lord Mayor's Parade and that no trading was going to be done until Wednesday, the next day. We had been told that everybody should know that the Lord Mayor's Parade was always held on St Jude's day, the 28th of October, so we were forced to wait another day before we could see to our business and set off home.

Brother Arnold took us a short distance to the priory of Saint Bartholomew's where we could spend the night for a donation of one penny per person for food and lodging; as it was safe to leave the money in the Priory, the guards went into the town and I stayed close to Brother Arnold who took me to watch the Lord

Mayors Parade. I had seen coaches before but nothing as magnificent as the Lord Mayor's coach. I thought that it was made of gold and as it was no use asking questions anymore, I thought that I would have to look in the books back at the monastery to find out about the procession. The priory was run by Friars not monks and as you now know me, I just had to ask "Where do you have a dump and a pee?"

One of the Friars showed me to what he called the water closet where there was a hole in the floor, "this is the W.C. (short for water closet) and you squat down here and everything goes down into a brick trench called a sewer then rain water washes the human waste into the river Thames" he said.

It's no wonder people don't drink water in London!

"And what if it doesn't rain?" I asked, whilst pinching my nose.

His answer was "It always rains, sooner or later."

I found out that the Priory had a library just as big as Faversham Abbey's and with time to spare until Wednesday I asked if I may look at some of their books. It took quite some persuading by Brother Arnold to get the head prior to allow this as the library was only supposed to be used by the clergy and learned men. He told the head prior that it was my intention to become a monk and that I had been taking lessons at Faversham Monastery for a year and that I could read and write and was studying the scriptures. I gave him a quick sidelong glance without moving my head and he just winked; I thought that I was a good liar but Brother Arnold was even better than me, for who would disbelieve a monk!

Where do you start I wondered; I suppose that I should first look for a book about Wat Tyler and the peasants revolt but as there were so many books I had to ask the Friar in charge of the library to help me. He told me that there were two books on the subject, saying that one was to be found in the medical section and then he got the other one from out of a cupboard.

As I started to read I wondered if this was the same Wat Tyler that Brother Arnold had told me about because he was nothing like what this book was saying. There must have been another Wat Tyler I thought. The dates were the same but the book was saying that Wat was a trouble maker and that he was part of a plot to overthrow the crown, as well as the Catholic Church, by inciting a rebellion and telling the ungrateful serfs, who didn't know when they were well off, to demand greater wages.

The book went on to say how Wat had no control over his men and relating that it was a good job he was put to death in St. Bartholomew's Hospital and that the rabble were driven out of London. This didn't sound right to me, until I realised that it was the same as reading about a battle, where one side said one thing and the other side said something different. I believed what Brother Arnold had so far told me because there was still trouble getting a fair days wage for a fair days work.

Maybe I'll just have to wait and hear the rest of Brother Arnold's story, I thought to myself. After reading this book I now wanted to see what the other book said about Wat Tyler. Besides being a Priory, St, Bartholomew's was also a Hospital. The book however, turned out to be a short medical report.

It read:

Saint Bartholomew's Hospital, Smithfield's, LONDON. June 15th 1381

A forty year old peasant known as Walter Tyler was brought from Smithfield's market place at two pm, suffering from two sword wounds in his body and a knife wound in his neck. The wounds were not critical but as he was being treated armed soldiers entered the treating room, removed him from his bed and extended his neck wound to the extent of cutting his head off.
Signed ...... John Mirfield, Sergion, Cleric, Medica.

The next morning, two of the guards had not appeared and Brother Arnold said that we should wait and see what had happened to them. They turned up about eleven am which was a relief to us all, although they were a little worse for wear!

We all set off for the counting house where I was to do my bit. We arrived about 11am and there were guards and customers all over the place so we had to wait until everybody else had finished their business before our money could be exchanged. When it finally came to our turn the cashier was reluctant to change our money as it was getting near to closing time. However, he relented when he saw the size of Brother Arnold! The cashier was a tiny man with white hair and rummy eyes sticking out of a pale face; his hands were delicate looking and he had a goose quill stuck behind his ear. He must have been about forty five years of age but he looked over sixty.

With me checking, he began counting the twenty pounds in Groats, putting them into two separate piles for which he gave me sixty Nobles; which I then gave to Brother Arnold. Next came the small coins; we are going to be here for days and days counting this lot I thought but instead of counting the coins the cashier put all the farthings onto a scale and added some more loose coins of his own and wrote down 8d on a chalk board. I looked at Brother Arnold who only tapped his nose. Then the cashier weighed the halfpennies, added twelve more and wrote down 6d, finally the pennies were weighed with another four pennies added and was also written down on the chalk board, when he totalled this up the cashier said "One shilling and six pence to pay."

Brother Arnold had me count out eighteen pennies from another purse he had with him. I couldn't keep quiet anymore and had to ask why the coins were being weighed. The cashier could see that Brother Arnold was about to tap his nose again, so he took pity on me and said "These coins are counted by weight because some people clip a small piece off the edge of the soft silver coin then when they have enough clippings they sell the metal to a silversmith."

I had never heard of this and the cashier told me that it was not widely known which was just as well, as if people did know, then they would not want to own clipped coins. However, it made no difference when spending them and only the church and those in the know, which now included me, knew about it. That is why you had to pay the extra one shilling and six pence.

"Has the church lost this money then?" I asked.

The cashier replied "Well yes but as most of this money was from the church collection boxes, clipped coins are better than nothing."

With that I collected the Nobles from the cashier which went into Brother Arnold's bag. I hoped the cashier would not tap his nose at my next question.

"Why then did you count the Groats and put them into two piles and not weigh them?" I asked.

The cashier replied "I shall tell you as the rush of customers have gone. The Groat has a face value and not a weight value and if you look at each pile you will see that the thickness is different. All of the old thicker coins are being collected back into the treasury to be melted down and re-minted and made lighter and I don't doubt that this will be done again at some stage in the future."

I had seen plenty of Groats before but never knew they had different weights, so the cashier showed me a few which I could see were different in thickness.

The cashier then said "that is why I gave your monk the other seven pence"

"What seven pence?" I asked.

"There were twenty eight old groats" he said "and at a farthing a groat that's seven pence."

The puzzled look on my face told him that I didn't know about the extra farthings paid in exchange for the heavier coins and he quickly told me never to repeat what he had just said because ordinary people with one old groat would be coming into the counting house and clog up the place.

I promised, but my brain ticked into motion and I wondered what the profit would be if I had lots of old groats at a farthing a time and if the coins were ever to be made even lighter, well ……..

This may be worth remembering I thought.

Whilst the cashier was talking to me, Brother Arnold had gone out to give the money to the guards so this was my chance.
"Would you change this Noble for my father please?" I asked, crossing my finger.

"Will all pennies do?" he replied without a second thought.

"Yes" I gulped.

He gave me a sealed bag of coins containing eighty pennies and that was it; all that worry for nothing. As the years went by I always did my trading with this cashier whose name was Edward and we became a good friends.

**

CHAPTER SEVEN

We set off for home in the mid-afternoon, crossing over another building wonder, London Bridge. It was getting quite dark as we reached Blackheath and everybody was tired, including the horses; so after the usual stop over at an inn it was bed again with thirty miles to go. The next day we made an early start and it was decided that we would stop in Rochester.

Great, I thought. If we get there early enough I could perhaps spend some of my ill-gotten gain. I had asked my father for two shillings of my unspent reward money in case I saw anything that I wanted to buy in London but I had put this money in my hide out under the pig sty and took out the noble instead; all I had to do now was tell my travelling companions the same story. Brother Arnold asked me what I wanted to buy. "A short handled axe for me and a present for my mother" I told him. He then told me that the best place to buy these things was in Chatham because it was bigger than Rochester; so the plan was changed for my benefit.

The river Medway was crossed at one o'clock and a suitable inn was found, where we settled in for the rest of the day. One of the guards came from Chatham and knew his way around the town and he took me to the right place to buy my axe and waited whilst I had a look at what was on offer. There were a lot of long and short handled axes in the shop, most of them costing six or seven pence each but my eyes fell on a big butcher's knife which was priced at nine pence and it really took my fancy. All of the axes were good but the knife was more exciting and when the shopkeeper saw my interest in this knife he told me that it was made of the finest steel and was as sharp as a sword.

He said that he would add a leather sheath into the bargain if I bought it; *but nine pence!* I thought.

I had never spent more than a farthing before and this was a big deal for me so I eventually bought a good sharp axe for six pence. John the guard was now fed up with my dithering and wanted to get back to the inn for a drink of ale, so I was left to do whatever I pleased. I was now getting to like spending money, so what was I to get for my mother?

And I bought the best shoes on offer at six pence I also bought a pair for my sister at four pence. I was still thinking about the heavy knife which the shopkeeper had said was called a cleaver. The blade was nine inches long from the handle, two inches across and a quarter of an inch thick and it had a very sharp edge but the short handled axe had always been what I wanted. As time went by I kept passing the same shop and went in to look at the cleaver again which the shop keeper was willing to swap for the axe along with another three pence. Whilst still wandering around the shop I noticed a small saw, the blade was ten inches long and an inch and a half wide which folded into a hardwood handle and was priced at six pence.

Decisions, decisions, at the finish I ended up with one axe at six pence, one cleaver and one saw knocked down to the combined price of one shilling and two pence, which when added to the ten pence for shoes came to two shilling and six pence. I so was excited about my purchases that I ran all the way back to the inn to show everybody what I had bought but nobody was bothered, as they were all sleeping the afternoon's drink away and it was the same next day as we set off for Faversham. Four of the men at arms had rode on ahead with the nobles, leaving the rest of us to make our own leisurely way home as there was nothing left to be guarded; so with the horses clopping along and me driving, this would be my last chance to hear about Wat Tyler. However, it was one of the guards who asked to hear the end of the story.

"Where was I up to?" asked Brother Arnold, "Ah yes" he said, now fully relaxed in the back of the cart and supping on his last bottle of wine.

"I have already said that the King had met with us rebels at mile end haven't I? Well this was in the middle of June and we all thought that the trouble was over because the fifteen-year old King had promised that he would abolish feudalism and serfdom, so, like a lot of the rebels I started to go home."

After another big swig of wine Brother Arnold went on, "but a large number of peasants were out of control and went on a rampage and stormed the Tower of London, capturing and killing Simon Sudbury who was the Bishop of London. The rebellion had broken up" Brother Arnold continued "but after being stabbed with a dagger by the Lord Mayor, Wat Tyler was taken to Saint Bartholomew's Hospital where he died."

"And before you ask" he said "yes, the same Bartholomew's where we stayed on Tuesday night."

Brother Arnold then finished his story. "Everybody believed the King would keep his promise but he went back on his word and that's when I became a monk, because with Walter Tyler dead, who would lead the revolt?"

I said nothing about reading how Wat Tyler had really died.

My mother had been watching the road for us all morning and when we arrived at Oare she was so relieved that she insisted I went straight home which was fine with me. She was absolutely delighted with her shoes saying that red was her favourite colour and that they fitted her feet perfectly. Thanking me she said "I shall not ever wear dem, only fur best" my sister was also pleased but being a girl would not say if red was her favourite colour or not, I could tell that it was though, as her face gave her away and she had them on until bed time...... I am not even sure if she took them off then!

My father and grandfather had not been worried about me in the slightest as they knew what travelling was all about, having done a bit of it themselves in their time. They just wanted to hear all about it and about the wares that I returned home with. Neither of them had seen a folding saw before and asked me why I wanted it. I told them that I thought that it would be easier to saw a small branch off a tree, instead of having to chop it off like Uncle James did and as the saw folded I would not hurt my fingers on the sharp teeth.

"And what about the cleaver?" asked my grandfather.

"Well" I boasted, "not only can it do the same job as an axe but I shall also be able to use both hands on the blade to plane down longbows."

With my story told and a few pats on the back off father, it was time for food and a good drink of water;

telling myself that I would never travel again without carrying my own supply.

I was still puzzled about the peasants revolt and wanted to know what was true and what wasn't and knew that the best person to ask about it would be my grandfather, so on the following day I found him in my father's workshop sanding down a longbow and asked "did you take part of the peasant's revolt in 1381 Grandfather?"

He glared at me and snarled "Why what have you heard about me?"
This took me aback, as it seemed that he had something to hide.

"I've heard nothing about you grandfather, it's just that Brother Arnold has been telling me the story about Wat Tyler and how the peasants revolted against the landowners."

"Oh, that's alright then" he replied. "I'm a Freeman Leaseholder and I tended the land my father was allowed to rent because of his service to the young Prince Edward at Crècy; and as a Leaseholder I was not obliged to work as a serf.

"What service was that Grandfather?"

"I don't really know" he said "I think it was because he fought alongside the prince and it had also had something to do with him winning his spurs."

I noted to myself of two more things that I now needed to look up in the books, leasehold and spurs.

"Sorry grandfather, please go on" I said.

He was amazed at my politeness and continued.

"As well as the landowners, I too was having trouble finding people to help with my crops and was having to toil almost night and day but I was working for myself whilst other people were labouring longer hours without any extra payment, therefore a lot of peasants moved out of the area to find better paid jobs."

His story was the same as Brother Arnold's so I now learned the valuable lesson of...... don't always believe everything that you read!

"When people like Wat Tyler were prepared to lead a rebellion" my grandfather went on "the serfs were ready to follow and although I was in agreement with the revolt, I was not directly involved as I still had to tend to my own land, which some people didn't like me for."

"Most of the country's population were also in favour of change" grandfather continued, "and that's why Canterbury was so easily captured. However, there are always hotheads who don't know when to stop and more killing went on after King Richard had agreed to abolish the feudal system, giving him an excuse to go back on his word. The landowners themselves could see that change would eventually have to come and this is why the peasants are only now, slowly, starting to get freedom from this drudgery."

"That's good enough for me" I said.

Out of my wealth of two nobles, I had spent two shillings and six pence whilst in Chatham, which left me with ten shillings and ten pence or one hundred and thirty pennies. Then, if my plan was to work, I would be able to change this into thirty two old Groats, with two pence left over. If I then took these coins to the counting house to be changed, I would have a profit of eight pence which is over a week's wages for a farm labourer. Unfortunately, I soon discovered that most of the heavier groats had already been taken out of circulation, so that was the end of that plan…… well, the end for the time being.

Brother Benedict told me how pleased he was with my trip to London, asking if I would like to go again sometime, "yes please" I said.

He then said "when there is a sum of one hundred pounds or more another trip will be required, probably in six months' time."

Without thinking I said "I must get some old groats then."

"Ah" asked Brother Benedict "how did you find out about the extra farthing paid for old groats? I suppose Brother Arnold told you about it, did he?"

My face went as red as a beetroot and I had to confess how I had found out.

"Well" he said, "there is nothing to stop you changing any old groats you collect for yourself but you must promise not to tell anybody else about this, as we in the clergy only do it to cover for clipped money and I suppose you now know about that as well do you?"

"Yes" I replied, "but that's also a secret I shall have keep to myself."

All I ever seemed to be doing was asking questions but as my father once said, "If you don't ask questions you will never learn anything."

However, looking in books and reading what they say, saves me a lot of hassle from asking, so I read that there wasn't much to learn about the Lord Mayor's Parade except that a new Lord Mayor is appointed every year and a parade is held, which the Lord Mayor joins at the Mansion House in the City of London and goes on to the Royal Courts of Justice in the city of Westminster, where he swears his allegiance to the Crown and that his coach is not made of gold but is gilded.

On reading up about leasehold or rental this is what I was to learn:

Under common and civil law, land may be leased or rented by its owner to another party, which means person or persons. A leasehold or rented land may be granted to people who have given service to the crown and that various degrees of freedom as to the use of the land must be agreed with the landowner and that the cost of the leasehold or rent will be reasonably set by the landowner.

Now for my next noted question to look up in books; spurs, what's that all about then? Let's see now, my great grandfather was in the battle of Crècy with Prince Edward, so what does the book say?

The French cavalry could not break the English formations and after sixteen attempts took frightful losses. King Edward's eldest son came under heavy attack from the French cavalry as the battle progressed but the King refused to send help saying that he wanted his son to 'win his spurs' which he eventually did with the help of two archers who were fighting shoulder to shoulder with him.

One of the archer's was my great grandfather, the other was a man named John Clark and they were both granted English Tenancies; what a shame that my great grandfather had to die of the plague only four years later.

I was to learn that 'winning spurs' was to gain an achievement in battle I also learned that Prince Edward later became known as The Black Prince. This was because his armour had been treated with a chemical acid which caused the surface of the iron to turn black.

When I started my archery training with Brother Arnold, he didn't allow me to ride Floss to the monastery, I had to run all the way there from my home. I also had to pull together two wide spread low branches of a monastery tree, the running was easy and the pulling of the branches didn't give me much trouble either, well not until I was told that I had to pull them closer and closer to my body. Brother Arnold had said that if you want to be the finest archer in the country you must train your body as well as being able to shoot arrows. I can now run the mile from home in six minutes and the tree branches have been changed for a longbow.

I still see my friends on a Sunday at church but any spare time I now have is spent shooting arrows, riding

Floss or in the forest with my brother and sometimes with his friend Isaac.

Isaac is another giant of a man who is over six feet tall and has a big bushy red beard to match what hair he had left on his head but it's impossible to tell his age which I guess must be about forty. He is another person who didn't believe in washing himself, so it was always best to stay up wind of him. If I was one hundred yards down wind of him, I could pinpoint exactly where he was from the smell and could stalk him to within ten yards without him seeing me. I could also approach one of the many forest deer in the same way, only this time I couldn't get to within twenty yards of them because of their sensitive hearing. When I noticed their head and ears prick up, I knew it was time to shoot my arrow.

It was important that we had fresh meat to eat but it was sad that such beautiful animals had to be killed, so I made a vow that if I was not able to get to within ten yards of them, I would allow the deer to escape. However this was not the case with wild boar as there is nothing graceful about these animals, in fact they were dangerous to anybody who was passing through the forest, especially children as they could be attacked with a charge that was difficult to avoid; but when any feast days were coming up this was a good source of free pork.

Rabbits were a popular source of meat but catching them was very different from shooting arrows at them and although this was good sport an archer would be very lucky to hit such a small fast moving target. What you had to do to catch a rabbit, was to use a string noose which is spread around their burrow entrance, with the trailing end of the noose strongly pegged into the earth; then when the rabbit comes out of its hole, its neck is caught in the noose. This doesn't kill the rabbit, that has to be done by giving it a rabbit punch, which is by clonking it with a stick behind its neck.

Squirrels are also caught in the same way but this time the noose could not be laid on the ground. More than one noose was needed and they had to be made of a stiff yet flexible vine that was tied in several positions around its nesting tree, as you don't know which side of the tree the Squirrel is going to climb.

Isaac had to laugh at my tiny folding saw but could see its advantage over an axe when cutting things like arrows to the correct length, it would be of no use to him however, because he had to cut down trees with a two handled cross saw. I had seen Isaac cutting down trees before but I wanted to know how he could make a tree fall in exactly the right direction he wanted it to, because if it fell wrong, the tree could catch into another tree and not fall to the ground.

"This is how it's done" he said.

"I stand with my back to the tree looking in the direction that I want it to fall, then I turn around and chop a 'V' shape into it, about six inches deep and six inches wide then I get my helper, you, and we start sawing on the opposite side to the 'V' and as the saw cuts into the tree it becomes off balance and the weight of it makes it fall towards the 'V' cut on the side that I want it to fall. Cutting out the 'V' is just like when you pull a log out of the side of a heap and the rest of the logs fall down."

Isaac lined up an oak, chopped out the 'V' then we sawed it down, I was sweating hard but I enjoyed any exercise that strengthened my body. We were sawing for about twenty minutes and Isaac made sure that the saw cut was aiming exactly opposite the 'V' point. When the saw cut was starting to open up, Isaac pulled me well out of the way in case the tree bounced backwards as that sometimes happened when they were falling; but sure enough it fell in the direction it was supposed to without bouncing backwards. I was allowed to line up the next tree fall, chopping the 'V' so that when it fell down it dropped where I wanted it to.

My father has never sold the longbow that was used to measure an archers pull and he always checks that the original string setting was still nine inches, he also hangs a half hundredweight sack from the string; if the stretch is near enough twenty seven inches he can then use it to give people their pull strengths using his graph. He couldn't read or write so he needed a little bit of help at first to read the graph but he soon got the hang of it as all he had to do was to measure the archer's pull then trace his finger across the parchment to the corresponding pounds line. He would get a pint of ale for his trouble and of course praise for his clever brain.

As I was approaching the age of fourteen my pull, according to my father's skilful knowledge, is thirty inches. He doesn't need to read from the graph now as he knows the readings off the top of his head, telling me my pull was near enough seventy two pounds. I wondered if he would ever have to pay for ale again as his mates kept on trying to improve their pull strength and getting him to measure them; what's more, is that my father had put up a prize of a gallon of ale for anybody who could pull one hundred and twenty pounds.

Don't let Brother Arnold know about this, I told him. There again he wasn't so daft, as to pull one hundred and twenty pounds on his longbow, a man would have to pull the string back some thirty eight inches, which is more than most men can stretch their arms.

In between the body building and training, Brother Arnold was showing me what changes he had made to an arrow and it seemed to me that a monk's role in life was experimenting and improving things, as he had rows and rows of arrows made of different sorts of wood with different flights and dozens of different shaped points. There were shafts from a quarter of an inch to three quarters of an inch in diameter and a range of lengths from twenty four inches to forty inches but his pride and joy was a magnificent looking longbow. It was about seven feet long and set in a place of honour on his massive workbench which he told me had been made by my grandfather over thirty years ago.

Brother Arnold had not been an outstanding archer but his great reach and strength allowed him to shoot an arrow much further than most archers and he had regularly shot arrows over four hundred yards. Also standing on his bench was a six inches thick block of oak, with an arrow marked off in inches sticking into it. He had shot at this block with all of his strength from a distance of five yards and the arrow had penetrated three inches into this very hard wood.

I didn't appreciate the work he had put into his experimentation at the time but as I got older I was able to use his skill and knowhow without having to go through the same trial and error that he had experienced and in the future all of my tournament arrows would be made at his bench. Brother Arnold wanted me to do some trial and error; making bowstrings from all sorts of material such as Hemp, Flax and Jute. I thought I knew all about bowstrings but kept my mouth shut as there was always something new to learn. Brother Arnold had tried all types of fibre but was unable to come up with any strengths, so this was my chance to work out the best which turned out to be the same as what Uncle James used……. two hemp strands with one of flax. Due to my experimentation I found that this combination could take the strain of one hundred and thirty pounds before breaking. I also noticed that when a string did break, it nearly always snapped at the knotted loop that connected it to the longbow and I wondered how this could be avoided.

On my way home past Faversham creek, I said to a one of the fishermen who are always using ropes "I know that you put loops on your hemp ropes but can it be done on a string?"

"Bring a string along and we shall see" replied the fisherman.

In a flash, I was off back to the Abbey to get some and twenty minutes later there was this beautiful back plait on the end of my string.

The fisherman told me that the loose strands of a hemp loop are singed with a flame which sticks the strands in place but he could not do this with my string as the hemp and flax would not stick together with heat. I thought that linseed oil or bark glue would do this, so next day at the monastery I started practicing back plaiting my own strings from the plentiful loose ends scattered about. I wanted the loop to be one inch in diameter so I unbound some of the string's loose ends and made a curved loop from the end back into the string, but instead of tying a knot, I slackened the string binding then threaded the loose ends in-between the original plaiting. Doing this is not so easy, as you tend to go cross eyed but once you have got the first bit right it gets easier as you continue.

Before the fisherman singed the loose hemp ends together, he had rolled the loop under his foot to even out the plait, I could do the same with the palms of my hands then trim off the sticking out fibres and varnish the joint. Not only would this keep the strength, it would make the string look nice and neat instead of having a string with an ugly knot.

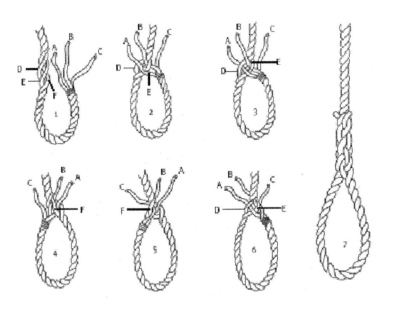

Diagram of Plaited Drawstring Loop Making

**

CHAPTER EIGHT

June 1409

Quite a lot has happened since I last wrote, firstly my grandfather had died in his sleep nine months ago and was buried alongside my grandmother in St. Mary's cemetery. This was a sad time for my family and there was great sorrow in Faversham and Oare, as he was one of the last survivors of the Plague.

William has gone off to Cambridge University to continue his studies and when he comes home on holiday he tries teaching me things such as Latin, which I thought was a waste of time.

The King has at last changed the weight of the groat, meaning that I can now put my financial plans into action. The face value of the groat is still four pence but the weight is now 60 grains instead of 72, not a lot of difference but enough to re-mint an extra groat from every five collected and although there are now very few of the first minted silver groats in circulation at a weight of 89 grains, two of these older coins and a little bit more silver added will make three new coins.

It was obvious what the King was trying to do……. his revenue will increase without him having to find or buy more silver and needless to say, the groat has become even more unpopular but the people couldn't tell you why, except for the fact that it was thinner and somehow they felt cheated.

And finally, Floss had given birth to a foal; but now let me tell you what has been happening since my first trip to London.

Knowing that I was collecting original groats and that I was changing them for myself on my frequent trips to London, Brother Benedict wanted me, at the age of seventeen, to take over the monasteries financial dealings for which I was to receive my first ever wages of one shilling a week. I was put in charge of two young monks, Brother Thomas and Brother John, who like all monks, were not allowed to earn any money as it was against their belief and up until now any money previously collected was not being put to any other use than to live off, travel or to give away to charity.

So what Brother Benedict could now see was that extra revenue could come to the monastery by lending the unused money at a reasonable rate of interest, just like the counting houses do. However, the monastery was not permitted to make a profit in this manner, therefore it was my job to loan money to potential borrowers, then donate the profit back into monastery funds; in this way they were not breaking with their faith. I could still do my own trading and when it became known that I was paying four pence for each old groat instead of three pence three farthings which was being paid by such people as the Whittington man before taking them to a counting house and making a profit for themselves, more and more old groats were coming out of the wood work. Even my father had been holding on to twelve old groats, for which I gave him the full payment of fifty one pence in pennies and halfpennies….well, it wouldn't do to make a profit out of your family would it?

I was amazed when my father and uncle James started building another dwelling about forty yards south of our home where Uncle James was to live once he had married Mary, whom it seemed was the girl he had got into trouble; she had a little boy also named James who we called Jamie. The wedding was not to be in the church but a civil wedding for some reason or other. When they came to live on the farm Jamie could be a bit of a pain but Mary was of great help to my mother. She was small with short cropped brown hair which made her look boyish. Mary wasn't very bright, quite thick really and you could not trust her to buy anything; the only thing she was good at was bartering but that was getting less and less, with money being a better way of getting things.

There were still problems for people journeying along the quiet country roads of England, as there were always robbers eager to attack any unguarded travellers which meant that you had to be well protected, especially when carrying money. It became my job to sort out the payment for an escort with Lord Thornbury, who was only too delighted to release as many men as required at six pence per day each. However, he was not too happy about having to deal with a young commoner such as me; but with a cut of the eventual build-up of profit and knowing that I could be trusted to keep my mouth shut, he put up with it.

It was difficult to separate what money belonged to the Abbey and what money belonged to me because as I was using the monastery as the changing house, I could have, if I had wanted to, done more trading for myself than I did for the Abbey; so Brother Benedict and I agreed that I would now receive two shillings per week and that all the groat profits should go to the monastery. This was fine with me as a bird in the hand is worth two in the bush, isn't it? And most of the old groats have been cashed in anyway.

I now go to London every three months but Brother Arnold, much to his disgust was not allowed to go along. What is more, I have the use a coach and two horses and can do the trip in two or three days depending on the weather. I was also going to Canterbury which is a lot nearer to Faversham and it had always puzzled me why Brother Benedict never used Canterbury to change his money in the past, until I discovered that you had to pay three pence to get a Noble changed into small coins and three pence to change small coins into Nobles, whereas in London you paid nothing.

It looks like I might have been wrong about the Whittington man.

The chests were now full with over one hundred pounds in small coins and groats, so I am going to London this coming Monday, which gives me and my helpers three days to sort out the money, the escort and the travelling expenses. Although making money meant a lot to me, it meant a lot more to my mother and sister. We had plenty of food from our farm and shelter cost nothing, apart from the rent of six nobles per year but good clothing and good shoes did matter and as the shoes I had bought for my sister on my first trip to London were now too small for her feet and worn out anyway, she needs at least one more pair if not more, as did my mother.

Yvette now at the age fifteen was turning into a beautiful young lady, she has a slim body and long blond hair flowing down her back, her face is as smooth and clear as baby's bottom and like all our family she was spotlessly clean. She even smells of flowers, not like a lot of the stinky people in Oare and Faversham. She is aware that her good looks can turn the heads of the boys in the town but if anybody was to try and take advantage of her in any way, they would have me to deal with.

Yvette could always wrap me around her little finger and knowing that I am off to London again and that it was reasonably safe to travel along country roads providing I had an escort, she wanted to come with me on this trip but my mother wouldn't hear of it. That was until…..silly me, suggested that they both come part of the way in my coach, stay the night at the best respectable Inn in Chatham, spend some of my money then be collected on the way back to Faversham. This soon brought my mother around, so now it was up to my father, he wasn't too happy about this but gave way to their pleading; somebody else was wrapped around, not one, but two little fingers it seemed.

"But they must only venture out in daylight and have a guard with them at all times" father said.

They would have Monday afternoon in the town then most of Tuesday until I picked them up on my return. When I mentioned it to Brother Benedict the next day, he had no objection to Yvette and my mother coming on the first part of the trip; so when Monday came along, my mother and sister waited eagerly at our farm whilst I rode to the monastery to collect the money and escort, leaving Floss there in the care of the monks. I was to pick up mother and Yvette whilst passing our home on the way to London but on my arrival at the monastery somebody had given the coach a good clean out and we had an extra passenger….. William.

William was still on his break from University and had heard about my sister going to Chatham, so he wanted to go as well. Besides this extra passenger there were two extra men at arms at the lord's expense. I was a bit worried that the journey would be too much for the ladies but with all the male attention they were getting the journey went well. Anyway, it was strangely disappointing when at noon we had to deposit our ladies at St. George Inn in Chatham, along with William and his two men at arms. I gave my mother and sister four shillings each to spend, saying, "You probably won't need all this money."

The replies were a sidewise snigger, from my mother and a "Hu don't you believe it" from my sister who had never spent more than a farthing in her life.

I don't know how much William had to spend but I'll bet it was more than forty eight pence.

For some reason that I need not mention, we had made the fastest return ever to Chatham, arriving well before noon the next day where more finger twisting by two women on us poor defenceless males produced one more night's stay at the Inn; on the grounds that those white wisps of cloud in the sky, on this glorious sunny day, might well turn to rain. William was no better and said that his father had agreed to pay any extra days wages, meals and lodging for all of the guards if we should be delayed.

Then he said, with his tongue in his cheek. "Just look at those clouds drifting through the sky, it looks like it's going to rain so perhaps we should stay over until tomorrow" which brought a nod of agreement from a certain young lady called Yvette; with that I had to supply another twelve pence to each of the ladies, who simply must have those hats, not to mention a few more bars of that violet smelling soap.

There was something different about William that seemed strange then it came to me, he was cleaner and less smelly. *Friend or not he had better behave himself with my sister!*
Yvette pretended that she was not enjoying all the attention being shown to her by our male escort as she was being quite coy and just wrinkled her nose up at any cheeky comments made by the men at arms but knowing her inside out she didn't fool me in the slightest she was loving every second of it. My mother was also being flattered and why not? She was still beautiful and kept herself in good trim. She also had flowing blond hair and also smelt of violets.
With all purchases made and all tummies full, it was time to explore the river Medway. My mother went to lie down until evening meal time, telling us that she was exhausted with all the shopping; so along with William and the prancing sister I went strolling along the riverside on this swelteringly hot with chance of rain, sunny afternoon. The very early start from London along with the nice weather was making me tired, so that when we sat down on the sloping grass bank overlooking the river I nodded off to sleep. After what must have been an hour later I awoke to find myself completely alone.

Where were they? They must have returned to St. Georges Inn, so I made my own disgruntled and angry way back.

They were there alright, William had a big grin on his face and butter wouldn't have melted in the other traitorous deserters mouth, Yvette that is; but fortunately for them my mother was just returning

from her nap, so least said soonest mended I said to myself. After all, what could happen in an hour? William could tell from the look I gave him that I wasn't pleased which broadened his grin even more.
It had rained in the night which gave us an excuse for tarrying but it had now stopped and Chatham was washed clean with a nice fresh sea smell coming in off the river as the coach, now driven by William, made its way back along Watling street towards home…. late of course due to the ladies wanting to look their best when they arrived home.

Everybody was in a festive mood and Yvette decided that she wanted to have a go at driving the coach, my mother also wanted to do the same. So with a little help from William and much laughter, the coach waggled its way along the dirt road with the horses unsure about what was expected of them. As we approached Oare, we were met by my father riding along the road on Floss, he was pretending to be worried about the extra days delay which pleased my mother but Yvette was sorry that her little bit of freedom was over. My father hadn't been worried in the least but he had to show willing didn't he? And his timing was perfect. *There must be something more to learn here about women,* I thought.

The coach had to stop whilst the two well-dressed gorgeous ladies did pirouettes for him but when he asked them how much change did he have coming things went a little bit quiet, then it was …

"Well, let's get along home then shall we?" from a young petite voice.

My father had saved me a trip to pick up my horse so there was no need for me to carry on to the Abbey with the money chests as William would take care of it, thus after unloading the many packages that mother and Yvette had and with a barely noticeable knowing glance between William and Yvette, the coach drove off with all of the soldiers friendly waving to the ladies as they left. I must admit, having the company of my mother and sister made a pleasant change for everybody but I had no intention of repeating the expensive ten shilling shopping spree, not to mention what it had cost my father.

For the rest of the day it was a fashion parade for all of us poor gullible men.

When all the excitement and thanks had died down, my father told me why he had picked up my horse from the monastery. Apparently, Floss was in season and had been allowed into the wrong field with the Lord's best stallion *Blackthorn*, who had serviced her. This made Lord John furious as he normally received payment for allowing his stallion to mount a mare. I wasn't too pleased myself but it didn't necessarily mean that Floss was going to have a foal. My father told me that in fifteen days or so, Lord Thornbury is going send his horse doctor to check Floss out to see if she was going to have a foal, if so the Lord would then be looking for compensation.

It was not my fault that Floss was put into the wrong field and nobody seems to know who did but if she was pregnant, Lord Thornbury will claim that the foal would belong to him, unless I paid him a servicing fee of six pounds. I knew that a Colt or a Filly would take about three hundred and thirty five days to be born and I also knew that it would be worth a lot of money, as Blackthorn had cost Lord Thornbury over one hundred pounds. The decision to settle the servicing fee was taken out of my hand as Brother Benedict said that the monastery would pay the six pounds because I was on monastery business and that Lord John normally charged ten pounds.

Amongst Grandfather John's meagre possessions was a dome shaped bottom of a broken bottle, my father was going to throw it away as it didn't seem to be of any use but when I asked if I could have it, he gave it to me. I seemed to recall seeing this piece of glass before and searched my memory for a clue as to why he had kept it but I couldn't remember, it was something to do with the sun I think. I knew that if you held it a couple of inches away from something and looked through the clear glass, what you were looking at looked bigger and if you turned the piece of glass over what you looked at looked smaller but it was not this that grandfather had talked about. I held it to my eye to look at the sun….. Ouch that hurt, don't you even think of trying to do this yourself. I was lucky not to have burned my eye out and then I remembered, my grandfather has said that he had used it to burn down his parent's dwelling during the plague.

How would he have managed to do that? I wondered.

Brother Benedict had told me that he would not always be there to answer my questions and that I must try and find out the answers for myself, so here goes……

I had nearly lost an eye and as everything looked bigger or smaller, let's see if it can make something burn, not my eye though.

Let's try the back of my hand…..yes, that was warm where a circle of light shone on to my skin and by moving the dome away from my hand, the circle of light got smaller and my skin got hotter.

That was enough on my hand, so I tried frayed linen, this didn't work as I couldn't get the circle of light to appear, what shall I do next?

Let's try the linen itself….. Brilliant, it's smouldering and by blowing on the smoulder I made the linen catch alight. I tried other materials and the best was parchment which set alight without having to blow on it. Great I can now make fire and my dome will always be with me but I shall still need to use flint when the sun isn't shining. When I showed Brother Benedict this strange item, he didn't know what I was on about, so it was nice showing him something for a change.

My horse Floss has given birth to a colt which I have named *Red* because he is not black like his father or chestnut like his mother; he looks more red than anything, so that's what I have named him. Lord Thornbury had kindly sent his horse doctor to help Floss give birth because she was carrying such a heavy foal and we had been watching and worrying that my pride and joy might not survive her ordeal. Floss kept us waiting all night so it was a relief when about mid-afternoon on the following day, Red finally dropped to the straw covered ground. I had wondered why Lord Thornbury was showing so much interest in Red until I found out that he wanted to buy him, he was offering a whopping ten pounds which was over a year's wages for a man at arms.

Red's father, Blackthorn is a thoroughbred and Floss is also well bred, meaning that Red was probably worth maybe as much as Blackthorn and we know what he cost. My father wanted me to sell Red but I had a better understanding of money than he did, so I decided to keep my colt no matter what I was offered.

After he was born, Red was soon on his feet and suckling to his mother, so all those who had helped with his birth departed to catch up on some sleep. Next morning mother and child were doing well and Red's coat was as smooth as silk, so they were left alone to get to know each other. Lord Thornbury raised his offer to twenty pounds and when I again refused, sent me a bill for two pounds to pay for the services of his horse doctor. I didn't like the way he was trying to get Red so I went to see Brother Benedict for his advice.

I could afford the horse doctor's fee but wanted Brother Benedict's opinion, as It seemed that Lord's and gentry could practically do what they liked, claiming it was their right and as most people were ignorant of the law, they took it for granted that what they were being told must be correct; but not me. Brother Benedict told me that as Lord Thornbury had freely offered the service of his horse doctor I should not be charged.

"But, however" he said "the horse doctor has to be paid by the owner therefore, the fee is payable by you." Lord Thornbury fully expected me to sell Red to him and that's why he had the horse doctor help with the birth and I must admit, if the doctor had not used his skills, my foal may not have survived. I was making a good living from my financial dealings, so I paid up.
Lord Thornbury thought I was getting a bit too big for my boots, which was only too obvious, as he was very

curt with me. When I handed over the doctor's fee, he growled and said "that colt is mine by right..... And whoever put your mare into the same field as my stallion should be made to pay a fine."

This worried me because I now felt that as Lord Thornbury had not ended up with Red, he would make efforts to find out who actually put the horses together, he could not claim off me as I was away in London and the servicing fee had been paid by the monastery and would you believe it, Lord Thornbury already had a name for my new colt, Redthorn, but when you think about it, all the names are linked; Thornbury, Blackthorn and Redthorn ... the cheek of it!

I must see Brother Benedict again, as his views are important to me and his advice is always good.

"Don't worry" he said "the church can get away with murder ... well, perhaps not murder but certainly with a gate being left open and as far as I am aware there is no proof of who left it open so now, nearly a year after the event, who could tell what actually happened? Leave it with me" he said.

That was the last I heard about it but I knew that I would have to watch my step with Lord Thornbury, as it was only too obvious that he was used to getting his own way and although he was not powerful enough to go against the Church, he was well able to give me trouble even though I had saved his sons life.

Uncle James' son always wanted to be in my company and kept hanging around me at weekends, much to my annoyance; but he was happy with the little bow I had made for him telling me, that one day when he grew up, he wants to be a great archer like me and Robyn Hode. I think young Jamie must be about seven or eight by now so it now became my turn to try and give answers to awkward questions.

"Uncle Cris, why does my father call me a Lollard if I am a bad boy by not getting on with my jobs?" he asked.

 Yes I thought, my father used this one on me when I was little.

"It's like this Jamie" I said. "A clever man named John Wycliffe, thought that the church was too worldly and that the Pope should not take part in world affairs. John Wycliffe used to be well thought of in royal circles and a few years before I was born, had translated the Latin bible into English but his ideas started to be seen as a threat to the church and the crown. He wanted the English people to change from having Roman Catholic Churches with Latin teachings, to churches with Anglican teachings using his Wycliffe English Bible, of which some of the texts read different from the Latin Bible. He had a lot of followers who agreed with his ideas but could not do it openly as they didn't want to be excommunicated from the church, so they became secretive and became known as the Lollard's which is taken from the Flanders word, Lollen; which means to whisper or mumble softly."

I had remembered all of this from what Brother Benedict had taught me and some people thought the Lollard's were just lazy people who were trying to form a church of their own and take the wealth away from the Catholic Churches and Abbeys.

"So stop lolling about" I said "and get on with your jobs!"

This was a simple answer to his question but there was a lot more to it than laziness, as the Lollard movement has now become very cautious and wary, but is still festering in the country. Some people say that every other man you talk to is a Lollard.

Jamie then said "'Thanks Uncle Cris, I shall stop lolling about if you tell me why it is that the sun moves across the sky?"

"This is the last question I am going to answer" I begrudgingly replied.

"The sun is like a leaf floating on a big pond, which the wind blows across from one side to the other then it sinks into the water."

"Oh" said Jamie looking puzzled, "so why doesn't it go the other way when the wind changes?"

The sooner Jamie learns to accept things as they are the better, as I don't know the answer to that one and I don't think anybody else does either.

"Alright then Uncle Cris"

I'm not so sure I like being put on the spot like this

"Go on then" I said.

"Well" Jaime continued, "I know its noon time when the shadow is on the noon mark when I look at your sundial but how did you get the noon mark in the first place?"

At last a question I can answer *(good old Brother Benedict)*
"I want you to look at the stars with me tonight" I said "then I want you to make your own sun dial."

The sky was beautifully clear as I pointed out seven stars in the sky, which he couldn't see at first, until I marked the shape of the stars on the ground, then he spotted them in the sky.

"If you were to join them up" I said, as I scratched a line joining up the seven marks on the ground.

"They look like the shape of my father's plough. Now, pointing to the last two stars on the ground, try to imagine that they are the plough's blade." Jamie looked into the sky and told me he could imagine the blade end.

"The next bit isn't so easy to start with" I said "but stick at it."

Where have heard that before?

"Now then" I said "I want you to mark a line along the ground from these two stars and break a stick the same length as the distance between the two stars that form the blade, then space the stick out along the line roughly five times and mark another star position on the ground, then look into the sky and do the same with your eyes."

After much looking and head scratching, Jamie found the star I wanted him to see.

"That's the North Star" I said "and whenever you are looking at this star you are facing north, as this star is the only one that stays still. Now, if we lay your stick along the ground pointing in line from your feet towards the North Star, we can come back tomorrow and I shall show you when it is noon."

The next day, Jamie was delighted when I stuck another stick upright in the ground at the opposite end of the stick where his feet had been, telling him that this end of the stick was pointing south. Jamie could now see that there was a shadow of the upright stick on the ground.

"When the sun's shadow from this stick is in line with the stick on the ground" I said "the sun will be directly south and it will be noon."

He must have watched the shadow creeping across the ground for ages, until he shouted out to me "it's done it."

We looked at his sundial then we looked at my sundial and both the shadows were in line with my mark and his stick, telling us it was noontime.

"But what about the other marks on your sundial?" he asked.

"They are the hours" I said "but you need to have a time piece to be able to mark these shadow positions and if you have a time piece you do not need a sundial!"

That got me out of that question.

I then told him that you had to take some things for granted as not everybody knows all the answers about everything.

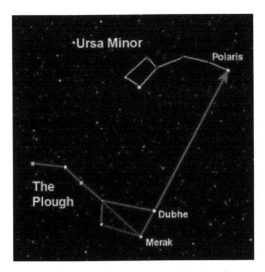

The North Star - Polaris

At the monastery all the financial dealing were running smoothly with my two helpers doing most of the work but I could not, for the life of me, think why anybody, especially young men, would want to become a monk. When I asked Brother Benedict about this he said:

"It's just that some people are not happy with the life they live or what they are obliged or forced to do by another person, so they wish to withdraw from the world and live a secluded life. However, it's not because they want to be lazy, as the work they do can sometimes be harder than in the outside world, for which I must remind you, they do not get any payment. They come into the monastery the same way as you have, to improve their minds, but sometimes they feel that a cloistered life is not what they thought it would be and go back into the outside world. So we like to call the monastery a growing up school where young men can decide what they wish to become before dedicating their life to the Abbey, whereas you came here as a Yeoman's son who was not seeking a monastic life.

So let me tell you why I became a monk. My name used to be Andrew Blenkinsopp and my father was an apothecary in London. During the great plague the people of London thought that rich people were keeping all the cures for themselves and my father was attacked by desperate parents who thought that he was depriving the poor of a chance to live; so they took all his medicines and gave whatever they stole to their children. However, a lot of the mixtures were poisonous and the thieves didn't realise that they were killing their own families."

When I was a small child, my father was still not trusted to treat illnesses, due to the deaths his stolen medicines had caused and we had to move away from London and start a new life in Canterbury. He had taught me how to read and write and I was lucky enough to go to Cambridge for two years to study chemistry but when my father died I had to give it up and come home to continue his business. However, alchemy was not what I wanted to do, so when my mother later passed away I gave up the shop and went into the monastery."

**

CHAPTER NINE

I was now negotiating loans out of the monastery funds to tradesmen who wanted to improve their workplaces and I have learned from Edward, my counting house contact, that loaning money is a good way of making a living, which is what money lenders do. But there were dishonest dealings going on. Not only with the lenders but also with the borrowers; the lenders took over a trade if a repayment was not made on time and then there were the borrowers who quietly moved away from the area taking their equipment with them without repaying the money lender.

In our case however the monastery will be more understanding if a repayment is not made on time and would be willing to wait a little bit longer; whilst the borrower would not want his family to get a bad name in the community and suffer the shame of the church if he was to leave the area. The church itself could also see that the community was benefiting from these loans and so they gave me their blessing. The church wanted to become a partner in the loaning of money, so we called our venture 'The Faversham Loan and Trust Company'. I was to be the director and receive a wage of four shillings a week, plus a tenth of all profits made. I could not possibly handle all this extra work and needed another man to help me, besides my two young monks but who can I get that's clever enough to do the job?

This was not going to be easy, as most people are uneducated.

William would have been perfect but he had another year to do at Cambridge, so I shall have to start looking for someone out of the area. However William was livid, telling me that he wanted the job and that he was willing to drop out of university; and would you believe it, his father had no objection either. As William was not the oldest son *(This was news to me, I didn't know William had an older brother)* he would not inherit the Thornbury Estate.

I had grown up knowing that it was always the eldest son who inherited any family titles or land, which my brother John often reminded me of; because to divide a property would reduce the size of an estate, and it could not be done with tenanted land as there could only be one master. Therefore I was second in line unless something was to happen to my brother, in which case the farm would pass to me. However, if John was to marry and have a son, I would then become third in line. This was one of the reasons I had no great interest in our farm and why my father was more interested in John than he was in me…. not that much more interested, but enough.

William would probably have to live off his brother or become a soldier or priest, which is normally what the gentry have to do. As for me becoming a priest, that would be a laugh but what's all this about William's brother? He told me that his brother had always stayed at the Royal Court in London and at the age of twenty four was an assistant to Prince Henry, who was our future King. Lord Thornbury wanted his son to be a director of the loan company but as much as I liked William, the idea and inspiration was mine, so I had no intention of having my nose pushed out at some stage in the future. I had a good reputation with the Abbey, the church and with the people of the Faversham, so Lord Thornbury can go and boil his head! But I knew that he was becoming my enemy and that I would have to watch my step in the future.

William was to receive a wage of two shillings per week paid out of my running costs, with the prospect of this being increased when he knew the ins and outs of trading, the same way as I had to learn.

Now as the grape harvest is in, I am able to start using the walled enclosure of the vine field to practice my archery again and was using this area to experiment with arrows to perfect my aim. I knew that there was no difference when using the right wing quills or the left wing quills of a bird just as long as all three flights curved the same way; but I keep both left and right flighted arrows in my quiver when shooting in competitions just to pretend that it did. I even wet my finger and held it up to see which side of the finger is coldest or threw a piece of grass into the air to see which way the wind was blowing, not all bunkum but it was surprising how it put the other archers off. I had learned all about the effects of wind when practicing on my father's farm and also how you had to aim at a higher angle the further you shot an arrow. Even Brother Benedict couldn't explain why things fell back to the ground, he just said, "what goes up must come down."

I made my own quivers out of linen and water proofed them with wax or linseed oil. I made the top cover out of stiff leather so that the flights were not crushed, as it's no use making an arrow with perfect flights then bunching them up and damaging them. The bottom of the bag was also made of leather to prevent the arrow points sticking through the linen and instead of having twenty four arrows in a quiver, I have twelve right curving flights in one and twelve left curving flights in another. It is also important that I protect my arms with leather braces because when shooting, the arrow flights can draw blood as they brush past them once the arrow is released.

Now that I'm nearly nineteen, my longbow pull strength has vastly increased and I can pull one hundred pounds, which is as good as Jack Smith who is built like a stone wall. He stands five feet four inches tall and has arms as thick as my thigh's. I'm six inches taller than he is but we are just as good as one other at target shooting.

There are now two other national archery competitions, the first being a twenty foot circle marked out with a rope on the ground, set at two hundred yards from the firing line with the centre of the circle being on the two hundred yards line. In this contest each archer had one minute to shoot as many arrows as fast as he can, the winner being the person who had landed the most arrows inside the circle. To make sure that every archer started to shoot their arrows at the same time, the order was shouted.....

Nock, draw, aim and release, with the sounding of a horn to end the minute.

However, the big problem when deciding the winner of this competition was sorting out which arrows belonged to which bowman. I always used flights made from the feathers of the Turkey because the monks breed these birds and the quills are readily available to me. Whilst all the other archers use the white goose flights and as the colour of the Turkey feathers are near enough red, that's how I got my nickname 'Red'. At two hundred yards I could shoot about ten arrows, all of which usually landed in the twenty foot circle as this is the distance of my practice range in the enclosed walls of the Abbey. Whereas Jack could only loose off eight arrows due to his build but it takes a long time to sort out the arrows all of which have different markings.

The second new competition was a long distance shoot where five arrows are shot by each archer, with the man who shoots the furthest arrow winning. There was no problem sorting out this winner as you just looked to see whose mark was on the furthest arrow. Jack is now winning this local distance shoot and his furthest arrow with the wind behind him reached nearly three hundred and twenty yards. My best shot with the wind behind me was two hundred and ninety yards but I am winning the two hundred yard competitions as Jack, being so stocky is not as lithe as I am and can't flex his body when he bends to nock his arrows out of the ground.

Jack wanted a colour to dye his flights, so that he could have a nickname as he was fed up with being called Smithy. He could try green as this was easily got from plants but at two hundred yard his arrows would be hard see against the grass.

"I rather fancy blue" he said "but where can I get blue dye?"

"Leave it with me" I said.

"Woad" said Brother Benedict. "Get hold of the cabbage like plant or buy the blue dye that is made from it."

"So what is Woad when it's at home?" I asked

"When the Romans invaded these shores" he said "the Britain's all painted their bodies with a blue dye which had been extracted from this plant, in a futile attempt to frighten them away. The plant is difficult to grow and is also poisonous, so I don't know if you will be able to get any." Replied Brother Benedict.
"I like the name blue" Jack said. "That's the colour I want to make my flights."

And so it came to pass, as they say in the bible, Jack got his blue dye, not from a cabbage however but out of a bottle. The liquid contents were made from the leaf of a plant called *Indigo* which as far as I know was first brought to England by the Romans. When the Indigo plant is soaked in water it makes a dark blue dye. It had been bought from an alchemist by William on his last trip to Canterbury at a cost of five pence which Jack repaid, so he is now able to colour his flights blue, which also became his nick name ... BLUE.

King Henry has now made archery a compulsive national sporting pastime, ensuring that the whole of the nation's male population are training for what we know will eventually be another war with France. Great events are financed by the Crown, the entry fees are quite low and the prizes are in cash. There are now three archery contests each year in Faversham: Mayday which has always been the time for our local archery competitions, then added to this we have the 3rd of July, which is Saint Thomas's day, or doubting Thomas day as we call it and the last is Saint Crispin's day, the 25th October. *My birthday*

The reason for using Saints' days is because they are holy days when people don't have to work, they also know when they are due. Most of the population don't even know what day of the week it is and as for knowing the date, well, it's a good job there is such thing as word of mouth. Peasants work for six days with Sunday being their day of rest, so this is the day they know best. This is also the only day I can spend time with my horses as I have found it easier to buy a spacious house in Faversham, saving myself the trip from Oare every day. This allows me to be at the loan company in just a couple of minutes.

Getting my meals was a problem at first but I can eat at the monastery whenever I want to however, I still preferred my mother's cooking; so going home on a Saturday night was something I really looked forward to. Living on your own seems strange after sharing one room with four other people all of your life.

Yvette was growing up fast and she was not happy with having to share her private moments with all of the family, so after visiting my house she asked if she could come and live with me so that she could have her own room and more importantly, her privacy. I could see her point of view and wanted to help her, so I asked my father if he would let her come and stay at my house to look after me. This did not go down well with him at first but after some argument and negotiation, he and my mother realised her needs but only gave their permission on the understanding that she still came to the farm and did her jobs.

Why, why, why, did I bother?

My house has become a building site with a wooden floor and one of the new-fangled water pump machines just outside the rear of the house. My house became so cosy that my mother often visited and stayed in my sister's room some nights. My sister also had a man cut a large ale barrel in half and put it into one of my four rooms to have a bath in….. Yvette certainly knew how to spend my money.

But I ask myself what good is money stuck in a locked up room? And if I was unable to use money to make a living, I could always go back to working on the farm; but there again, don't think I am silly with money as I am still quite well off.

I could see that my mother was envious of what my sister had made of her house, *not mine anymore, it seems*, so I suggested to Yvette that she should get the workmen that had been employed on my house to make the same changes and improvements to my parents' dwelling.

My horse Floss was like all mothers with their young sons and Red at the age of one was frolicking around her and nipping her tail until she chased him away. He was still a bit skittish when anybody came near him and it took a while for him to do what his mother showed him. Food was always a good way of making friends but Red would always go to Jamie without

having to be bribed with an apple. Red was still too young to ride and I had to warn Jamie that he mustn't get on his back until his legs were stronger, which will not be for another year as riding him too early could well damage his hocks, which need time to strengthen. If the weather was fine and the tide was out along the river Swale, I liked to ride Floss across the sandy shore and through the shallow water. Red loved these gallops and followed on without me having to bridle him, the sand and the sea were strengthening his legs and both horses knew what was coming when I took the saddle off Floss, as they could now roll in the sand. I always made sure that I had an apple for each of them just in case they got too used to the freedom. Then it was a quick wipe down with grass followed by a full grooming once we got back to the farm.

My brother John had returned from the north and was now working on the farm which would be his one day, so I thought he should stay at home instead of going back to keep the Scots from invading England. He and my father were not happy that I was not helping out on the farm and that the only time I saw to my horses was at the weekend, so I had to pay my father a shilling per week to employ a man to do what he thought was my work, which I thought was a bit mean after the money I had spent improving his farm house. I also had to pay him three pence a week to feed my horses.

Jack has discovered girls, who think his facial scar is heroic, which he says, he got fighting the Scots. I didn't think much of girls but my mother had laughingly said "dat will change soon enough, den vous will be like all de udder boys, anyway your sweetheart Catherine will be coming over from France soon."

"When, are you going to stop teasing me about that spotty girl" I moaned. "And she isn't my sweetheart!"

I haven't seen Catherine for a couple of years but she is coming to England with my sister after my family's next trip to France, so I might have to move out of my own house for a few weeks…..yuck.

**

CHAPTER TEN

The monastery had all the tools and equipment to make almost anything and there was a little iron foundry next to Brother Arnold's work place with a small charcoal forge, a set of bellows and an anvil where I have been able to make my own arrow heads without saying anything to Jack or his father. There is nothing wrong with making things for yourself but the monastery had a policy of not competing for work with the local tradesmen, so what Blue and his father don't know won't hurt them. Like everything else, it's easy when you have the know-how and the tools to do the job.

I had played around with clay from the river and had shaped arrow heads with my fingers, making the point at one end and squashing the other end over a stick to finish it off but you can't squash hot iron over a stick can you? Blacksmith Arnold, as was his name when in the forge, has shown me how to do it. Making the point was simple, you get a rod of iron about the same length and size as an arrow, push the first four inches into the forge fire until it got red hot and then beat it with a hammer on the anvil until you get the shape you want.

"But how do you get the hole in the end to fit the arrow shaft?" I asked.

"The best way to do this" Blacksmith Arnold said "is to make the hole first, then make the point."

He got a piece of rod made out of lead to practice with and whereas I had squashed the clay over a stick with my fingers, Blacksmith Arnold used the hammer and the anvil to flatten and spread out the end of the soft lead to look like the letter 'T' only with the top bar of the 'T' about three inches deep and long enough to wrap around the end of an iron rod which I was holding onto the anvil. Then he pulled the iron rod out leaving a slotted hole, "it's just like wrapping a strap of a wide leather belt around your finger" he said "then pulling your finger out."

We changed places and I had to do the same with the other end of the rod and although my hole was rough and not straight in line with the rod it was at least a slotted hole. Brother Arnold, *I can't get used to calling him blacksmith,* chopped just over four inches off his end of the rod using a chisel, then using a pair of tongs to hold the slotted end he beat the other end into a point which made the metal stretch to over five inches.

More practice on lead then it was time to make one out of iron. Lead could be flattened cold but to flatten the end of iron, it has to be heated in the fire until it is red hot, then hammered on the anvil; which is then wrapped into a slot as was done with the lead. With skill and careful forging the iron can be beaten into a perfect wrap, then the iron rod is re-heated and chopped to a suitable length with a chisel to make the arrow head, finally using tongs to hold the slotted end, it is re-placed in the fire and beaten into a point, such as barbed or bodkin.

The balancing of an arrow in flight, as I have already said, is done using feathers but I have found out that in competition shooting to get the same results every time, all of the arrows must be equally balanced; not just in flight but also along the shaft itself. This is done by placing each arrow across your finger behind the arrow head. If the head is heavier than the shaft then it must be changed for a lighter one and if the head is lighter, it must be changed for a heavier one until each arrow is balanced. Once this is done the arrow shaft is pulled out of the slotted hole dipped in hot birch bark glue, re-fitted into the head and allowed to set hard. Although this finger balancing takes a long time, it is worth it and gives me greater confidence when shooting, as after the first arrow has been fired, I am able to gauge where the remaining arrows will probably hit the target. However, this balancing is not important for distance or circle shooting because the greater accuracy is not required. I have three quivers of arrows ready for shooting in the October tournament. Two quivers of a dozen balanced arrows each, for target shooting containing birds right and left wing flights and one quiver of twenty four normal arrows for the two hundred yard and distance shoots.

At the final archery competition for this year there is an entrance fee of one penny for each event, which put a lot of the Faversham archers off, knowing that their chances of winning against Red or Blue were slim but there are one hundred and twenty five archers entered: eight from Faversham, four from Chatham, one from Sittingbourne and three from Canterbury. The rest are from Mercia and Yorkshire, which is often called the rydings, and there are also quite a lot of Welshmen. These archers had heard about the Faversham event whilst competing in Nottingham but they had never heard of St. Crispin or his brother as it is only Faversham that celebrated this Saint's day, and as this is the only event taking place in the country, they have come here to compete.

Now that the harvesting is over, they are allowed to make camp on my father's land which is close to Watling Street, where a wide practice range has been set up, with plenty of makeshift targets spread out across the fields. William and I took time off from our dealings, which gave me plenty of time to size up the opposition and for him to court my sister; whilst at the same time keeping her away from these interesting young men who seemed to have enough money to spend on ale. They had heard about Blue and Red and they had also heard about my right and left flighted arrows, so I hoped it would put them off.

Uncle James knew a few of these men, who he called vagabonds but not to their faces of course, as he considered some of them to be highway robbers and from the money that they had to spend he may well be right. The morning of the 25th of October was dull and overcast with a strong wind blowing and gusting in all directions and rain was coming down in buckets, which suited me fine because my personal trainer Brother Arnold was going to stand down range when the target shooting takes place to give me secret signals about the wind direction; quite like the secret signals my father gave to my grandfather's tug of war team.

It stopped raining just before noon and the first contest was the distance shoot. I knew that I had little chance of winning this event but couldn't have dropped out as people would have said he only enters contests he can win. There were about ninety archers entered for this event and the best I shot was one hundred and ninety yards.

"And the winner," shouted the head judge, "is Jack Smith from Faversham with a distance of two hundred and forty yards, for which he shall receive a Noble. Second with two hundred and thirty yards is Tom Eaton from Chatham with a prize of a Crown and third prize goes to Taff Evans from Wales with a distance of two hundred and twenty yards; who gets two shillings for his troubles."

There were ten prizes in all and I came last getting my penny back.

The next event is the two hundred yard shoot in which I am going to use my left hand at last and I have fourteen arrows stuck into the ground sloping slightly backwards towards me and spaced three inches apart. Then all I have to do is bend nock the arrow with my left hand, hold it against the longbow with my right hand then start to pull as I straighten up, aim, and shoot. English archers are expected to release ten aimed arrows in one minute but I plan to fire more.

All of the archers were going to compete in this event, so I was dreading the counting as there will be at least one thousand arrows in the target area and what is more, there are all sorts of coloured flights and it's not only me that has red fletching. When the order came, Nock, draw, aim, release, I was so tensed up that the minute was gone before I knew it and when I looked on the ground twelve of my arrows were gone. I was drawing and shooting without having to think about it as I had put a marker peg in the ground two yards in front of me in line with the centre of the target area, so that all I had to do was line my aim from the peg as I was straightening up to shoot.

None of the archers were allowed to go up to the target area and all of the arrows outside the twenty foot circle of rope were removed by the judges before the counting started; then those in the target area were being pulled out of the ground to be sorted out into colours and markings. If an arrow was touching the rope or was stuck into it, it was added into the score. Besides my red flights, I had painted a blue strip (using Jacks indigo) around the shafts, so that I could easily identify them as being mine. When all the arrows had been counted, eleven of them were mine and I won easily, collecting a Noble. Tom Miller came second with ten; it didn't bother me who won the remaining prizes and 'Blue' won nothing with only six arrows in the circle.

Now comes the main event, as far as I was concerned, the target shoot. Brother Arnold had been watching the wind which was still blustering all over the place and told me that at the shooting end of the field it was going from left to right but at the target end the wind was going from right to left. I had spent some time finding out about wind strengths in my father's fields and rated them from one to three, with one being no wind and three being the strongest. Brother Arnold had worked out a signalling system by attaching a small pennon flag to the pole he always had with him, so that I could see the wind direction where he stood and he had three arm positions up along the pole indicated the wind strength; which gave me some idea what the wind was doing at the target end of the field. I could work out for myself what the wind was doing at my end.

There were four judges from Kent and a senior judge from London who were appointed by the Crown to decide any disputes and to set any changes to the rules; and that the senior judge's word would be final. It was now three o-clock in the afternoon and the senior judge decided that all the shooting will be at targets set at seventy five yards instead fifty yards. Another change was that a score of 13 points had to be made by an archer with his five arrows, to enable him to go into the second round. This meant that we had to score at least four 3 point inners and one 1 point outer.

There were eighteen targets altogether which meant that with one hundred and twenty six entrants there would be exactly seven first round groups. We had to draw lots to see which group we would be in because those shooting first would allow the other archers to see how their arrows were landing and as luck would have it I was in the first group, Blue was in the fifth group.

I went through with the pretence of choosing right or left flighted arrows and with Brother Arnold's help scored 19 points but would you believe it, the wind dropped off for the fifth round and Jack scored 21 points! Quite a number of archers were shooting with the same arrows they had used for the twenty foot circle competition and it was plain to see the dog eared flights where other arrows had damaged them.

The wind was still up and down for the next hour and there were only thirty two archers that had scored 13 points or more, I of course was one of them. The number of targets were now reduced to twelve which meant that there would be a second round of three groups, two with twelve archers and one of eight; this time I was in the last group. Now we were getting down to serious shooting and the worst twenty two scorers will be eliminated; leaving a straight shoot off for the best ten archers, shooting at targets set at one hundred yards. I wanted the wind to be blowing strong all over the place and it looked like it was getting stronger but it was also starting to rain. *Just the job,* I thought, as I had four strings all exactly the same length with my special plaited back loops, which did not go unnoticed. The rain took its toll on the unprepared one string competitors. I was one of eight archers, as was Blue, that had got through with scores over 13 but there were four archers which included Tom Miller, who with a score of 11 points, were soon reduced to two with a shoot off; and Tom Miller was not one of them.

The rain had stopped but the wind was still blustering and Brother Arnold was still down range as we all lined up for the final. His flapping pennon was telling me that the wind was coming from the left side of the field and his hand was half way up the pole giving me the wind strength of two. Where I was standing it was coming from the right side of the field also at strength two, so I did my pretend bit by picking a left curved flighted arrow. I considered that the wind would blow my arrow one way then blow it back the other way before it reached the target; so I made a big pretence of aiming my arrow slightly to my right, into the wind, which everybody else would be doing. Then I aimed directly at the bull's eye and fired my first arrow. It landed in the bull, two inches higher than the bull's eye and what looked like three inches to the left of it, telling me that the wind strength was slightly different from where Brother Arnold and I were standing.

I glanced at my competitors' targets which showed inners, or worse, to the right of the bull; so I made a point of selecting a right flighted arrow and looked over to my secret guide, noticing that his hand was slightly higher on the pole, at strength three and that the wind was still blowing in the same direction at his end of the field. The wind at my end was still at strength two, so I took aim just below the bull's eye and from one hundred yards away it looked like I had hit a bull's eye. The shouts from the crowd confirmed this, which put a smile on my face as the arrow had just clipped the white disk at the top. I knew that all the other archers had been watching my shooting and had adjusted their aim with Jack and some of the others scoring bulls.

For arrow three the wind was the same at my end but Brother Arnold had slid his hand right down the pole and the pennon was just fluttering. I did some more kidding with my choice of arrow and aimed at the right hand side of the red bull. My arrow hit the bull, just missing the bull's eye by half an inch to the left and slightly low. Arrow four landed in the same place for another five points, *if the wind stays the same I shall aim that much higher and a little bit more to the right of the bull,* I said to myself.

Brother Arnold moved his hand as I was about to shoot arrow number five, so I slackened my pull pretending to alter my stance. The wind at my end had changed direction, starting to come from behind and it had completely changed direction where Brother Arnold was standing as it was now coming from the right side of the field at strength two. Working this out in my head, I knew that I should still aim to my right and that the same pull on the bowstring would make my arrow strike the target higher, so for my last arrow I chose a left flighted arrow and aimed halfway to the right of the bull's eye and about three inches lower than the centre line of the target.

The wind was still behind me and Brother Arnold had not moved an inch and the pennon on his pole was slightly flapping to the left with his hand at strength one; so nock, draw, aim, release…… and twang the arrow was gone. Every part of me was soaring through the sky with the arrow and with eager anticipation I held my stance, watching it fly towards the target. All of the other archers had finished shooting and there seemed to be complete silence around the field. I must have been in some kind of a trance, from which I was quickly aroused *when the crowd let out such a roar……..it must be another bull's eye,* I thought to myself.

Never, in all of Faversham's history, had two bull's eyes been scored at the same time and my last arrow was in the dead centre of the white disk, giving me a record score of 35 points and making me the winner. I received the prize of one Noble, making my total winnings thirteen shillings and five pence. Taff Evans came second and Jack came third.

Brother Arnold just sauntered off back to the monastery but I could see the wry smile on his face; so roll on Nottingham, which is reported to hold the best tournament in England. Hundreds of archers from all over the country take part and Blue and I are determined to go next year. This will be held on another Saint's day….. Saint Mathew's Day, the 21st of September.

Brother Arnold will be coming with us and we are planning to go on horseback. I shall be on Floss and Brother Arnold will be riding a massive war horse called Thunder, which is what is needed to carry his weight. Jack will be riding his nice ten year-old stallion called Striker. William also wants to come with us but someone has to look after the loan company, not to mention that my sister has got her claws into him and wants him to stay at home. I think her intentions are on marriage and from what I can see, he is not opposed to the idea himself but his father will be when he finds out! One good thing about Yvette, is that she has got William to keep himself clean.

**

CHAPTER ELEVEN

It is only two weeks to Christmas and my sister has decided (*who's the boss around here?*) that our family and Uncle James' family must celebrate Christmas Day with us in Faversham as Catherine will be here in England until the end of January when her grandfather will come in his fishing boat to take her back to France. A not so spotty Catherine is staying in Yvette's room, so at least I didn't have to move out of the house!

William was also invited to our celebration but his father wanted him to attend his banquet at the manor. As a respected member of the community I had been invited to this event myself and could bring a guest. William had mentioned this to my sister, saying that after the feasting there was to be a Grand Ball and that he wanted her to come as his guest. The two female heads of Yvette and Catherine got plotting, informing me that Catherine could come as my guest and we could move our celebration to the following day, the 26th which is Boxing Day; so called because boxed presents and bonus payments were given to the workers by the land owners on this day.

I was now, not counting William, employing three other people. Two on my father's farm, one to replace me and the other to take some of the workload off my father and Thomas from the monastery, who had jumped at the chance to come and work for me when he knew I was looking to expand. He was a great asset to the business giving me a direct link to the Abbey, whilst Brother John my other helper from the monastery, seemed quite happy to stay where he was.

It was now decided that our family's Christmas celebration was to be a day later and my mother's best friend, Lady Thornbury, was able to add two more names to the guest list….. My Mother and Father's! It went without saying that William had to escort two young ladies and my mother on a shopping trip to Canterbury to buy the much needed clothes for the banquet and Grand Ball.

Twas the day before Christmas and all through the house not a creature was stirring, not even a mouse; well not quite, as the house was now full up with my family! Snow had been falling for two days and was about an inch deep which had forced me to go to the farm and collect my parents, as once tomorrow comes and the snow keeps falling, we may not be able to use my coach. This turned out to be a good start to the holiday and my father, 'bless him' as Yvette said, had provided a keg of ale and a keg of wine. All I had to do was turn up and of course pay for the food. The three busy ladies were fussing around the house sorting out places to sleep and organising enough food to feed an army, when all at once William, Blue and ex-Brother Thomas, decided to show their faces; thus the sleeping arrangements ended up as, get your head down wherever you can.

My sister and I could speak French but Catherine could not speak one word of English and she wasn't in the slightest bit interested in learning it either. I now thought that she looked quite pretty, the spots had gone, and I felt quite jealous at the attention that she had been getting particularly from Jack, who was getting a little bit drunk and in a slurred voice asked me to translate to her how he was wounded in the face by a Scottish arrow.

"Tell her dat I 'ad been badly wounded in the face but would not leave der battle until I 'ad captured two Knights." Jack said in his slurred English with a touch of French accent!

Not likely! I thought "Jack is saying that he had slipped and cut his face and cried for two nights" I said, in my best French accent with a touch of tongue in cheek!

Yvette giggled behind her hand as Catherine said, "Pauvre petit garçon, mais je suis sûr que sa mère aurait embrassé mieux."

(Poor little boy, but I am sure that his mother would have kissed it better.)

"What did she say, what did she say?" slurred Jack

Yvette had to get in on the fun, mocking Jack, and said "Catherine says that she thinks you are a brave man and should be smothered in kisses."

With that Jack staggered into the bathroom and fell asleep in the tub.

Normally, I don't drink wine or ale but on this occasion I was the host so I couldn't get away with it and I woke up early on Christmas morning to find myself in my sisters room and sleeping next to Catherine, who was in the middle of the bed with Yvette on her other side. We were only half dressed but Catherine was wrapped around me like a vine, fortunately she was sound asleep so I slid slowly out of her grasp. Muzzy headed I made my way to my own room to see if my bed was free but my parents were fast asleep there, so the best I could do was to sit on a stool, rest my aching head on the kitchen table and nod off again. The next thing I knew was, "Merry Christmas," and "Joyeux Noel," from two smug little miss' who threw snow over me and dashed off to turf Jack out of the bathtub, which he didn't take kindly to.

My mother was up out of bed and was busily cooking what smelt like bacon, "not for me" I groaned and joined Jack and my father on my bed. I guess their heads were hurting too!

"Never again," I uttered, "Never again!"

Eventually I was forced to stumble into the main room. "Come on, come on" urged my mother. "We don't have long before we have to go to the manor."

It was only noon and the feasting wasn't to start until 6pm but my brain was not functioning right, so I had to 'get a move on' to go nowhere for quite a while.

I was trying to avoid Catherine's eyes and wondered how much she had remembered from last night but her face was giving nothing away, so I hoped that I had got away with sleeping on the same bed with her.

"How are you this morning Cris?" my sister whispered into my ear.

"How should I be?" I whispered back.

"So," she said, "you don't remember asking Catherine to marry you then?"

"WHAT! ... You must be joking?" croaks poor old me, shocked at her statement and with my head still hurting from the wine and ale. "She's a nice girl but too young for that sort of thing."

What are they saying?, I thought, as I watched Yvette chattering away to Catherine, who just shrugged her shoulders tossed back her long black hair and stormed out into the snow; which was now over four inches deep.

William, having tried to battle through the snow to bring a coach for the ladies, was only able to bring along three extra horses; on which they delightedly sat side saddle, gathering their long woollen cloaks around them whilst me (*still a little worse for wear*) and my father trudged behind.

Lord and Lady Thornbury welcomed the hundred or so guests that had made it through the snow; and so the feasting began in the great hall, whilst minstrels played in the background.
After the ladies shopping trip with William I had not seen their dresses as they had secretly hidden them away. We arrived at the manor where the two girls and my mother took off their cloaks.

Wow! My mouth dropped open and my eyes widened to twice their size!

It was unbelievable that Yvette and Catherine could look so beautiful. They were both dressed the same, in pink evening gowns with silver shoes on their feet, my sister had put her hair up on top of her head somehow; but Catherine's was flowing, shiny black down her back. I was just about to try a little bit of William's charm and complement them, when they shoved their noses sideways in the air and sat down to eat pheasant and drink Champagne. My mother also looked stunning and beautiful in her pale blue gown with matching shoes and she didn't mind my compliments in the slightest.

Whatever's up with those two girls, I just don't know, I thought. I really couldn't see what it was that I had done wrong until I remembered the alleged marriage proposal. I had heard that if a man had proposed marriage to a woman then refused to marry her he could be held in breach of promise; but could that be done if you are drunk? Catherine was ignoring me as we feasted on our grand banquet but if she doesn't want to speak, then that's alright with me.

After we had all eaten our fill and the tables had been cleared away, it was time for the dancing. I didn't know how to dance but the two 'non-talking' females did and they frolicked with William, who had learnt this social grace which was well appreciated by the selectively mute girls.

"Straighten your face and come and dance with your Fiancée," my sozzled sister shouted to me as she giggled and looked at Catherine.

It was my turn to snub them but like a lamb I relented, stood up and held this beautiful girl in my arms for the rest of the evening.

The only words I spoke were, "when you are old enough and still want to……."

I was not allowed to finish what I was saying as I was forced to stop talking by a long, long kiss, which was a relief.

Thank goodness that I'm not actually committed to marriage, that pair of madams were just taking advantage of my unusual drunken state. I thought to myself. Just as well I did the right thing in saying something, otherwise it could have gone on for quite some time!

Outside the snow was still falling fast and some of the guests were starting to make their way home before they got stranded. However, with such a short journey home for us, Yvette and Catherine showed no inclination to leave their first Ball and with so much dancing, it was not only my head that was aching.

The next day, Boxing Day, I had my own humble banquet and was delighted when a lot of my loan customers paid their respects and at any one time there must have been twenty people milling about in my house. During the night the snow had stopped falling and the sun was now making a gallant attempt to shine through the grey December sky.

Uncle James, Mary and young Jamie had arrived early, which cleared my conscience about putting them off on Christmas Day. As a gift I gave young Jamie the axe that I had bought in Chatham, as I didn't think I would need it any more. It was as good as new in fact it was even sharper than when I had bought it; and for the rest of the day there was no shortage of firewood as Jamie chopped away, pleased with his present.

New Year passed and it was soon back to normal, then before we knew it, it was the end of January and Catherine was on her way home. Our time together had been wonderful but did I want to be married? *I don't think so, not yet anyway.*

William however wanted to marry Yvette but Lord Thornbury was adamant and proclaimed that under no circumstances was his son going to marry the daughter of a yeoman saying that if he went against his wishes, he would cease to be a member of his family. My mother thought that this was a bit strange as she knew all about his wife Lady Beatrice Thornbury and how romantic it had been for a future English Lord to marry a French serf's daughter. Yvette was devastated and wanted nothing more to do with William if he chose to follow his father's wishes. I could see both sides of the argument and felt like 'piggy in the middle', as what man in his right mind would give up all those riches to marry a commoner.

I should have kept my opinions to myself.

My sister now stopped talking to me and moved back to the farm, which is how it remained until the beginning of March when I asked William if he would like to become a full partner of the company. I got no answer as he quickly vanished out of the office and jumped into our coach, only to return an hour later with a load of clothes, junk and a fiancée! They married a month later in Saint Mary's Church with his mother in attendance but not his father.

William had burnt his bridges as far as his family were concerned but I had gained a good business partner, as well as brother-in-law and with that, Lord John Thornbury ceased to have anything to do with Faversham Financing and as he was the Sherriff of Kent, he spitefully reported the Church and the Abbey's involvement in money lending to the Archbishop of Canterbury. The Archbishop had no option other than to stop them from being involved with this activity, even though he knew about all about it, but this only helped to make us more money because the outstanding loan repayments and the interest earned, stayed with the company.

Having chosen my sister over his father made William a romantic hero in a manner which helped our business to grow, as people respected what he did for love and wanted to lend money from us, trusting in our morals.

Now that Yvette is married she doesn't need to go home to work on the farm anymore so she stays with her husband and me in our house where we now have a cast iron fireplace with an adjoining oven. All kinds of improvements to houses were being invented, which my sister was taking note of; one of which was slate roofing tiles……. Oh alright then, that's not such a new invention, as slate tiles were common in Wales and on the roof of the manor and the Abbey but not on ordinary dwellings in Kent.

William and I were quite happy to allow Yvette to make changes to our house and although a slate roof was not as nice looking as a thatched roof, at least it would be fireproof and would be less likely to blow away in a strong wind nor would it make such a comforting home for birds and mice. Yvette thought that slating was the up and coming thing and as her workforce was increasing, she asked for a loan from the company to start making tiled roofs, which the thatchers in Faversham were not too pleased about and said that tiled roofing would never catch on. We could afford to take a slight loss if her dealings fell flat, so we started up her roofing company. Yvette was to be in complete control of everything to do with building work, William was to be in control of the financing and the paying of wages, whilst her trusted foreman Will Jackson, took charge of the workmen.

Jack and I were asked not to take part in the Doubting Thomas Day archery tournament on the third of July as nobody else would enter against Red and Blue, which I knew was bound to happen eventually, so when we were told that we were to receive a shilling each as compensation, we decided to try and make some sort of entertainment of our shooting skills……. but what?

"How's this for an idea?" Jack said, "It is well known about fire arrows so maybe we can we use this as entertainment... I know," he said, "I am right handed and you are left handed, so if we were to tie a piece of string between our two arrows and shoot them at the same time they should fly together, then if we had a flame burning at the points, it might look good."

"And what about this" I said, "If I remember reading it right, Robyn Hode* shot arrows into the drawbridge of Nottingham Castle in such a way that he could climb them like a ladder and cut the rope holding up the draw bridge, thus allowing his men to enter the fortress and capture it; we could try something like that."

"But Cris, I don't think any arrows will be strong enough to take our weight" muttered Jack, but there again, "if I was to make thicker bodkin arrowheads, say a half an inch in diameter and six inches long and you were to make the shafts to fit into them, we may be able to do the same as Robyn Hode."

It was worth a try, so we made a couple of arrows which was no problem but they were too heavy to shoot accurately if we were further than twenty yards away from the target. In the end we settled for thinner five inch long bodkin heads that would sink two inches into planking. We still needed to be at a twenty yard distance to get the arrows positioned correctly in the proposed target but now all we needed was a light person to put his weight on the arrow heads and not on the shafts which would break; but who have we got that's lighter than us?

"You can just forget it" said William. "I'm not risking my neck so that the pair of you can show off to the crowd."

"Think about it William," I said "you are already a hero for marrying my sister, so if you climbed the arrows and rescued her from the castle, you would be an even bigger hero!"

All it wanted was plenty of practice and when Yvette heard about the plan she said, "I could be Maid Marian and if William won't climb the arrows, then I shall climb them and rescue him!"

And that was it, poor William had no choice in the matter.

We then had to look for something that could be used as a drawbridge, the most obvious thing would be a hay cart but the flooring was too thin, so we ended up with a fifteen-foot long logging cart which had floor boards two inch thick. It was loaned to us by Isaac the woodsman, well perhaps loaned is not the right word, hired is more like it as he would have to use two horses to pull the cart to the common, so our compensation money from the tournament had to be paid over to him.

The cart's trace bar could be pulled back over the wagon when stood on end, on which, we intend to fit a pulley to lower Yvette to the ground and to make sure that the cart would not topple over we were going to prop it up on both sides with long slanting logs. Our secret practice sessions in the woods worked out perfectly, with William getting better and better at climbing the arrow heads and Yvette loved being pulled up and down on a seat attached to the pulley. The only problem that we had was getting the arrows out of the cart and the holes they left when we pulled them out; but you can't have everything can you?

My sister had made William and his men Lincoln green hats with large goose feathers stuck in the side of them and made a coned hat with a long ribbon tied from the point for her to wear.

The 3rd of July was nice and sunny day and the cart had been positioned the day before, with a ladder set between the wheels for Yvette to climb up to a platform built at the top. The play-acting was to be called 'Robyn Hode to the Rescue' and we were due to perform after the archery contests had finished.

Every town in Kent had contests on Saint Thomas' Day so there were only fifteen senior local archers competing in Faversham and all three events were won by my friend Tom Miller who lives and works with his father at their flour mill on Beacon Hill, west of my father's farm.

"Robyn, save me, save me," shouted Maid Marian from the newly fitted turrets made by one of her workmen. "The wicked Sheriff of Nottingham is forcing me to marry him."

"Stay where you are and I shall come and rescue you" shouted William as he fully engaged in the pretence that he was Robyn Hode.

With that the crowd shouted, "Save her Robyn, save her." They had all heard the story-tellers speak about the love story between Robyn and Maid Marian so they were all ears.

William then shouted to the audience, "My merry Men will use their arrows to make me a ladder in the drawbridge." This was our cue and we ran to within fifteen feet of the cart, where I shot an arrow into the cart twelve inches from the ground then Jack shot an arrow twelve inches higher and twelve inches to the left of mine. Then it was my turn again, this time shooting twenty-four inches above my last arrow, then Jack's turn and so on. The crowd were loving it and cheered us on, letting out a roar as each arrow embedded itself into the cart.

William was getting a little bit stage struck and before we had gone halfway up the cart he started climbing…… this wasn't in the plan but it only added to the danger excitement for the crowd. We knew that 'Robyn Hode' was safe from our arrows that were hitting the drawbridge above his head, but Jack had made a dummy arrow bodkin out of lead which hit the cart four feet above William and bounced off, making the crowd gasp as it fell past him. After shooting seven arrows each, plus the dummy one, William climbed over the top of the cart and waved from the turrets to the cheering crowd, whilst holding a smiling Maid Marian with his other arm.

Yvette then shouted, "But how are you going to get me to the ground Robyn? I don't think I am brave enough to climb down your ladder."

"Don't worry Marian," called out Robyn in a loud voice, so that the now silent crowd could hear what he was saying.

"Merry Men, bring up the lady's seat," he shouted over to me and Jack.

With that, I threw a rope up to William who pulled up the block and tackle and fixed it to the trace bar, then we fixed the seat to the pulley and Maid Marian was lowered to the ground by Jack to the load cheers from her audience.

William then climbed down the arrows and hugged his wife, to which all the women in the crowd put their hands to their mouths and went...... "Ah, bless him."

What a great success this turned out to be, Jack and I were cheered by the crowd but William and Yvette got an even greater cheer and much hand clapping........well everybody blubbers at a love story don't they?

Jack and I had perfected our act of shooting two linked arrows at the same time and had wrapped the arrow heads in pieces of linen that had been dipped in birch bark glue and resin which burned nicely; but the string joining the arrows had to be changed for a thin wire and the arrow shafts were now forty inches long, so that our fingers didn't get singed. It had taken us quite a while to work out how to present this act and although it was not as good as the drawbridge rescue, we ended up straddling a one inch diameter upright pole at a distance of fifty yards and setting its large linen flag on fire.

Later that month tragedy struck……. Lord Thornbury had been returning from a very important Royal gathering in London that had something to do with a new war with France. He had been riding along with an escort of four men at arms when he was attacked by a large band of robbers at a notorious danger ambush spot on the London side of Sittingbourne. One of his men had been killed in the fight and Lord John had an arrow lodged in his side. Two of the robbers were killed and the rest of them ran away, dragging a man who was wounded in the shoulder, with them.

Lord Thornbury made his peace with William when he and his mother rushed to his side in Sittingbourne. He told William that he was sorry that he had disinherited him and asked to be forgiven, which William willingly did. Two days later the manor had a new Lord John Thornbury who had arrived at his father's death bed a couple of hours before he passed away.

This was the most serious robbery and killing ever made in Kent and after the funeral in Westminster Abbey, Prince Henry asked for his father's permission to root out all the robbers in the county. He set up innocent looking travelling coaches with armed men hiding in them, to tempt robbers into attacking, then on a bugle call other men at arms would gallop forward to help the men hidden in the coach, killing or capturing the villains. Prince Henry then had known danger spots cleared of trees and bushes for two hundred yards each side of the roadway to prevent further ambushes. This was implemented in notorious danger spots around the country.

People in Faversham and Oare were wondering what changes the new Lord would make and were pleased to hear that the feudal system was to be abolished and that serfs could now have more say in what work they chose to undertake. This made no difference to the amount of wages paid per day but the hours people had to labour became shorter and the farm hands were given Saturday afternoons off with pay; and if there was any extra work to be done more payments were agreed.

On several occasions, Brother Arnold had been to the Goose Fair in Nottingham so he knew the way, saying that it would take about ten days to travel the two hundred miles but to allow for any delays we needed to set off from Faversham two weeks before Saint Mathew's Day, which he reminded us would be on Sunday the 21st of September. Therefore, on Sunday the seventh our little party which now included Tom Miller set off for Nottingham. Tom had won all three events in July and felt that he was good enough to join us on our trip and would be riding a twelve-year old mare called Dobbin.

It had always puzzled me why Brother Arnold was not as pious as the rest of the monks and why the Abbey had allowed him such freedom from worshiping God and it was Jamie's question about the Lollards that provided the answer……. The Lollards it seemed were trying to take away the Catholic Church's power, wealth and influence in England and create a separate hierarchy by reforming the Catholic Church as the Church of England. The state had already executed and imprisoned some Lollards, one of the first being a man named John Badby who after refusing to renounce his Lollardy was burnt at the stake for the crime of heresy. Therefore the Catholic Church had to be prepared to combat Lollardy which was becoming more and more threatening to the state.

If however the King was to sanction this Lollard reformation, then civil war may well break out but as it stands King Henry is a confirmed Catholic and has imprisoned or killed known Lollard heretics who had already caused unrest and an uprising could be expected at any time. There was nothing unusual about monks taking up arms to defend themselves and that's why the Abbey had Brother Arnold in their midst. They were paying his travelling expenses for the month that we shall be away from Faversham so that he could talk to other monks and get their views on the situation. Brother Arnold had set a price of two pence per day for expenses, so a noble each in small coins will be more than enough to cover the cost.

We spent the first night at the Royal Oak in Chatham, where everybody except for me had a half pennyworth of ale, so I was quite happy to take the first watch guarding the horses, Whilst doing so I heard a bit of a ruckus coming from the bar room, it seemed that Brother Arnold was being insulted for being a monk but with Jack's help and a bit of fisticuffs, this argument was soon sorted out. Monday night was spent with the priory friars at Saint Bartholomew's, after which, it was all new territory for me. We were still travelling along Watling Street and spent our third night at Saint Albans Abbey which is built on top of a hill overlooking a river called the Ver.

At our present rate of travel, having now covered a third of the distance, we would be in Nottingham on the sixteenth of September….. Five days too early, therefore we could afford to take things a little bit easier. Brother Arnold decided to stay over another day at the Abbey to discuss the problems regarding the bad feelings towards the Catholic Church, then he would be able to report their views back to Faversham Abbey. This gave us the chance to go into the town on Wednesday which was market day. It was only a short walk down the hill to the market place where our three new faces in the community stood out like sore thumbs; and we were invited to spend our money in Ye Olde Fighting Cock's Inn.

Jack went missing for an hour and when he came back he told us with a smile on his face, that he had taken the landlord's daughter for a stroll along the river; which five minutes later got us slung out of the Inn. There wasn't much difference between this market and Faversham market, so after buying some corn bread and cheese we collected our weapons and spent the afternoon practicing archery in the fields beyond the Abbey. There were no targets to shoot at as we didn't want to damage our arrows, it was only distance practice.

"And the winner is" I shouted, "sneaky Brother Arnold." Who had used my Longbow and five of my arrows!

"Second, with an arrow fifteen paces shorter, is Blacksmith Blue, third is the Jolly Miller, five paces shorter still and last but by no means least, is Red Crispin, who needs no fun taking out of him, thank you very much."

**

CHAPTER TWELVE

On Thursday we took it slowly along the Roman road and camped for the night at a place that was supposed to have been a Roman site just outside Leighton-Busar, then towards the end of the following day we camped alongside the river Ouzel where we all had a swim, including the horses. I had brought a bar of lye soap with me and persuaded everybody to use it which made a pleasant change. The sky was a bit cloudy and it looked like it was going to rain so we took shelter in a barn that was close by, it had plenty of hay for the horses to feed on and for us to make comfortable beds but having used up all of our food supplies, we would probably have to go hungry until tomorrow. Brother Arnold went looking for the owner of the barn and turned up an hour later with the farmer. They were carrying hot chicken and barley broth in a large cauldron as well as corn bread, cheese and a gallon of apple cider, for which we paid six pence. We also paid two pence for enough oats to last the horses for three days.

One good thing about travelling with a monk is that most people are willing to help and trust you, so the farmer was happy to leave us in his barn for the night. We ate some of the food and started to settle down to sleep when with a flash of lightning and a crash of thunder it started to rain and just my luck, the barn roof was dripping just where I was lying. I moved my bed to under a small haywain where I was quite content. The rain pattering on the barn roof reminded me of being snug and warm in my bed at home which was a joy to my ears and within a couple of minutes I was fast asleep.

The following day was a fresh sunny Saturday morning and as the rain had stopped I took another cold swim in the river before thinking about food to sustain us on our journey. My companions had seen my fire lighting dome in action before but it was always a sight to behold as the small circle of light set fire to a piece of parchment and we soon had a fire going in a clearing to heat the last of the broth, which we ate with what bread remained. The farmer had asked us to leave the pot in the barn and we could take away as much hay as we wanted, so after grooming our horses we were on our way again. It must have been about mid-day that Tom noticed a Windmill to our right which he said he would like to have a closer look at, so it was decided that we should have an early day and spend the night in the village close by, which turned out to be called Bugbrooke.

The flour mill named Heygate was owned by the Bakers Arms and the owner was only too happy to introduce us to his brother who worked it. Whilst Tom was comparing notes with the miller, the rest of our little band settled down to a meal of freshly baked wheat bread and local lamb joint; which was covered with finely chopped mint herb leaf collected fresh from the nearby Hoarestone brook. It had been mixed into a sauce with apple cider and was very tasty. I even had a pint of the locally brewed ale, which didn't taste too bad either. Most of the villagers had gone to the market three miles away in Northampton and the place was ghost like, until they all started to trickle back as it began to get dark. Saturday night out must be the big event in Bugbrooke as the Bakers Arms was full of people giving us advice on how to travel the twenty five miles to High Cross, then turn right at the crossroad towards Leicester. My main concern was to make sure that there was no landlord's daughter for Jack to take for a walk along the brook!

During the evening Jack got very talkative and said, "Cris, why is it you don't seem interested in girls?"

This took me back a bit, so I replied, "It's not that I am uninterested, it's because there are only two girls I know, my sister and her French friend, who take a regular wash and change their clothes and the smell of an unwashed body just puts me off."

Jack then said, "But too much washing takes the natural oil out of your skin and you can get sick."

"Rubbish," I replied. "Who told you that?"

"Well" he said, "if Lords and gentry don't often wash themselves, it must be right."

It would eventually be in France that Jack found out that cleanliness is next to godliness.

I had always said never again to ale but after my first pint in the afternoon and then the next one that night, it was better still for the third; after which I went to bed feeling that all was well with the world and everybody was my friend. However, it was a good job that our monk had taken charge of the bill, or we would have departed Bugbrooke broke. Our overnight stop cost us three pence each and one penny each for the horses.

We were about one hundred and twenty five miles on our way with something like seventy five miles still to go and during the night in the Bakers Arms, we all seemed to bond closer together. Jack and Tom had lost their reserve with Brother Arnold, who was a man of the world after all, and not the stuffy religious self-righteous person that they had first thought. Jack even found out that our monk was interested in girls!

So bright and early on the Sunday morning, after seeing to the horses and stocking up with food and drink, we were on our way again with one week to go before the tournament and a twenty five mile ride to High cross ahead of us. There were no dwellings anywhere along this flat landscape and later that afternoon we reached the crossroad, which Brother Arnold told us was another old Roman road named 'The Foss Way' that stretched north to Lincoln. We had passed through some small rain showers and were anxious to dry off, so we turned right and camped a mile further north where there was a large forest and soon we had several fires going. Jack and Tom went hunting for meat whilst Brother Arnold and I stayed with the horses.

"How did the talks about the Lollard's go, at Saint Albans Abbey?" I asked.

"Pretty disturbing" he replied. "Most peasants in this area were not bothered one way or the other, until they had been made to believe that they would be better off with a change of religion as they would not have to make church donations anymore and some people........ as you may have noticed, have started to be a little bit insulting to us monks. However, they're scared to say too much and risk being excommunicated."

"So what do you think is going to happen?" I asked.

"As long as King Henry supports the Catholic Church" he answered, "everything will just simmer along as it is and if anybody tries to make trouble, they shall be severely dealt with."

Jack and Tom came back empty handed but while they were away I had set rabbit snares and squirrel traps, managing to catch one nice rabbit and two squirrels. This was all new to my friends but Brother Arnold had caught animals in this way before and whereas I knew how to gut and skin them, he showed us how they were cooked out in the open. He had us collect some large stones, which he placed into a hole that he had dug and moved one of the fires over them. Once the pile of stones were heated up, he removed the fire and half of the stones then placed the two gutted squirrel's on the stones that remained in the hole and replaced the stones taken out over them. They were then covered with leaves and earth, to keep the heat in. This was then left for two hours so that the squirrels cooked between the hot stones. In the meantime we roasted the rabbit on a spit over the other fire. We had all eaten rabbit before but only Brother Arnold and I had eaten squirrel meat. The smell was absolutely mouth-watering as they were pulled out of the stone oven.

It was raining on and off all night and we took it in turns to keep the fires going, which helped to keep us dry and warm in our makeshift shelter. The horses had their backs covered with waterproofed linen and seemed happy enough chewing on the bags of oats and some straw that we had taken from the farmer the day before. Monday came and we had a short fifteen miles ride to the Abbey of 'Saint Mary de Pratis', in Leicester. Brother Arnold spent the afternoon in talks with the monks who were experiencing the same lack of reverence that the Saint Albans brothers were being subjected to, whilst the rest of us went for a stroll along the river Soar. We learnt that this river led all the way to the river Trent in Nottingham, twenty four miles away, meaning that we would arrive on Tuesday night. Brother Arnold then decided that it would be better for us to stay at the Abbey until Friday, where the cost would only be one penny per day. This now gave us two whole days to rest the horses and explore the town and best of all.......only Brother Arnold was allowed to stay in the Abbey, we had to stay in the Grey Friars priory a short distance away, giving us complete freedom to do what we wished.

Tuesday morning was spent with Tom looking at the north mill as well as the Guild hall, which had been built the same year that I was born and then it was back to the priory for bread and cheese. I am not a drinking man, sorry.........I was not a drinking man, because we spent the afternoon in the Green Dragon Inn, which is right next to the market place, then it was back to the priory where once again we ate bread and cheese. Then the Green Dragon again, then to bed. No sore head for me the next day thank goodness but I did wake up late, when the sun was high in the sky.

Never in my life had I stayed in bed so late in the day unless I had been ill. Jack and Tom were missing, so I went into the library and browsed through the books, finding one all about the city of Leicester. I knew that we had a parliament but read that the first Earl of Leicester, Simon de Montford, had led a famous revolt against King Henry III in 1265 and forced him to grant the first English Parliament. I was just putting the book back when Brother Arnold rushed in to the library saying that everybody was looking for me as it was market day and that there was to be an archery contest on the fields just outside the south gate.

Jack had entered me for the target contest which was due to start right away.

"Why isn't Jack entering for himself?" I asked, but Brother Arnold let Jack give me the answer.

"It's because a person can only enter one contest" he said, "I am doing the distance shoot and Tom is doing the two hundred yards shoot and the entry fee is only a penny."

There must have been hundreds of archers milling about, some of whom, like us, were on their way to the Nottingham archery contest. The contest was money for old rope because we all won a piglet.

What do you do with three little piggy's that go to market?

We bartered them for a free night of ale and wine for four men in the Green Dragon and the landlord's other Inn the Angel, which was on the far side of the market square. Brother Arnold had put on a cap and ordinary peasant clothes and became one of the boys but at the end of the night it had still cost us six pence to buy drinks for some of the loser's.

"Never again and I mean it this time" I said, as three 'sots' and a wino monk woke up next morning in the back room of the Angel. "If this goes on, we shall have no chance of winning anything at the Goose Fair."

So we made a pact that there would be no more drinking until Monday night after the Nottingham tournament was over. Thursday was spent in sore-headed meditation for us all, except for Brother Arnold, who seemed no worse for wear.

I had not seen Floss since the evening before market day but she had been well-looked after in the priory stable by one of the friars named Tucker. Friar Tucker complimented me on having such a fine horse and that he would be sorry to lose her tomorrow but lose her he did as we set off on the last leg of our journey. We passed out through the north gate of Leicester and crossed the two bridges over the *Soar* and followed this river to Nottingham. We arrived in Nottingham at 4pm on the Friday having crossed over the River Trent at a place called West Bridgeford, and Brother Arnold took us another couple of miles to Lenton Priory where we hoped to lodge until the fair was over.

That must be the castle we are passing on our right. I shall have a look at that whilst we are here. I promised myself.

As it turned out, it was a good job that we had arrived two days before the contests began because Nottingham was starting to fill up with people wanting somewhere to stay and the priory was only able to make room for one of their own plus one other. So, the not so sad Tom and Jack went to look for somewhere else to stay, which suited them fine but they were reminded no drinking until after the tournament.

I was to meet up with them at the Castle later on, whilst Brother Arnold held his talks with other visiting monks from around the country. Tom was waiting for me when I arrived at the castle but I couldn't see any arrow marks in the gate and he took me the short distance to where he and Jack were staying, which was at the rear of a blacksmith's shop, lower down the hill and about half a mile away from the priory.

Jack was busy helping the blacksmith with shoeing of the many horses that had lost their plates on the cobbled streets around the town and because of his help, they only had to pay a penny per day for their food and lodgings. The blacksmith's name was Robert and he was another giant of a man and about the same age as Brother Arnold. He had massive shoulders and was obviously an archer, we later found out that he had never lost the distance shoot in Nottingham since it had been introduced. His best distance had been almost four hundred yards, which he admitted was with the wind behind him. Jack had taken a sneaky look at his arrows and noticed that he was using what looked like poplar shafts with hardly any flights at all, which were sticking out straight from the shaft, with no left or right curve in them and the points were made of what looked like lead.

It would be a waste of time asking him how he made the feathers lie straight, as the nose tapping would only start again, so it was up to Jack to discover how this was done. Oh no! The blacksmith has an eighteen year old daughter named Jane who looked like she could shoe horses herself. She was about five feet four inches tall, plain looking with brown hair that was cropped nearly as short as a man's and surprisingly smelt of cherries.

I had a sly glance at her and wondered what my chances would be but only had eyes for Jack, with his facial scar from a different Scottish battle this time no doubt.

Jack was showing very little interest in her as a girl, which I think she liked.

"Right then Jack" I said, "it's up to you to find out the secret of how Robert is able to take the curve out of the feathers, so use your charm on Jane."

"Not I" he said, "get Tom to do it."

"Not me" said Tom, "do it yourself."

"Not me either!" I said.

Nottingham looked about as big as London and the town was spread out on hills sloping away from the river Trent whilst the castle, which overlooked the river, was built on a cliff. There were very few trees to be seen and I wondered where Sherwood Forest was to be found. The meadows east of the castle were flat, so this area is probably the site where the archery contests would take place.

Stalls were already being set up for traders who were living in brightly painted houses on wheels and Jane warned us about these people she called Gypsies who travel the country from fair to fair in caravans.

"These people steal children away from their parents and will cast spells on you if you don't buy something from them, so we always buy some wooden clothes pegs just to be on the safe side." she said.

When I got back to the priory, I told Brother Arnold that the others were staying with a blacksmith archer named.........."don't tell me," chirped in Brother Arnold. "Robert Smith I'll bet? He's an old friend from years ago. I hope you didn't tell him who I was?"

"Well no" I said, "I just told him that I was staying at the priory with a monk."

"Of Course, I wasn't a monk when we were fighting the Welsh." he said.

The next morning, with only one more day to go before the tournament started, the meadows look just like a town, with colourful gypsy caravans and all sorts of mechanical rides which went round and round, up and down, or backwards and forwards; and further over to the south of this colourful encampment was a vast open area of fields where, as I had thought, was the place where the archery tournaments would be taking place.

"Don't say anything" said Brother Arnold, as three men and a girl walked towards us.

"Good morning Cris" the blacksmith said to me. "And good morning to you Brother.......don't I know you?"

Brother Arnold said nothing at first he just smiled and said, "So you don't recognise me then?"

"Bob" said Robert laughingly, "BOB, it can't be, can it? Yes it is, you old devil..... Oops sorry, so this is what you have been up to all this time."

"Bob eh," I muttered to the others when we were left to fend for ourselves as the old friends disappeared into the crowd.

Jane was sticking to Jack like a leach and he didn't seem to mind one little bit, he even had the same look on his face that he had had when we were thrown out of the Fighting Cock Inn, in Saint Albans.

Jack had got the secret about the straight flights out of Jane on the promise that we would not alter our arrows until the tournament was over and had left Nottingham. He also found out that the points were made from a mixture of lead and zinc. Jane had also told him about arguments between the gypsy traders and the city councillors regarding the right to hold a fair in Nottingham.

Apparently the councillors wanted to keep all of the business for themselves and not allow the travelling gypsies to hold a separate fair and whereas the council called the fair 'the goods fair', the travellers called it 'the goose fair' because of all of the geese that they had brought into the city for sale.

Jack and Jane then decided that they wanted to be alone, so Tom and I walked over to the archery ranges which looked five times wider than Faversham common and at least three times as long; and then we spent the afternoon looking at men fishing along the river Trent.

On parting, we agreed to meet up early next morning to register for the tournament and it was then that we heard that the archery contests had been extended from two days to four, to allow for the additional two hundred yard and the long distance events. Jack had made a promise to Jane but I hadn't, so when I got back to the priory I asked if I could borrow a kettle and disappeared with it full of water into a copse behind the priory, where my trusty dome started a fire. I boiled the water until steam was coming out of the spout, then after what Jack had told me, I held a goose quill in the steam and started to straighten out some the feathers that I had collected from those cast by the many geese in the market place.

Success, the steam softened the grizzle and the feathers could then be smoothed out straight but as it happened we would not be able to steam the flights on our arrows because this needed to be done before they are attached to the shaft.

Registration started at 6am the next morning and as there were over three hundred archers competing, we could only enter two of the three contests. This is when I became aware of how people who could not read or write made their mark and when a person makes their mark it is taken as their signature.

But how does anybody else know the mark or even know who the mark belong to?

My father made his like an 'X' but people like the Whittington man know what my father looks like so the face has to match up with the mark. It took three people to match the mark with the Nottingham contestants, the man himself, a person who can say who he is and a scribe. Everybody can say their name even if they can't write it and so the contestant says his name to the scribe who writes it into a book.

A lot of people take their name from the jobs that they do, so if two or more people have the same name, then next to the contestant's name the scribe will write where he comes from; with Blue it was, Jack Smith from Faversham, whereas I signed my name. There were plenty of men with the name Bowyer and plenty with the name Jack or John Bowyer but only one Crispin Bowyer and Tom was Thomas Miller from Oare. The contestant then has to make any secret mark that he wanted next to his name in the book, such as a cross, a tick, a circle, or anything that he can always recall. He is then given a small flat painted coloured stick as proof of registration. If he is lucky enough to win a prize, he is then given a different coloured stick but to claim his prize he must go back to the same scribe with somebody who knows him, say his name and make his mark on a separate piece of parchment which the scribe then checks against the mark in the book. If they match, the stick is then exchanged for the prize.

I obviously chose the target and the two hundred yards competitions, each of which had an entrance fee of two pence. Unfortunately, due to the large number of entrants, a lot of helpers were required to assist the judges and who better than the monks, which included Brother Arnold, so that looked like the end of my secret helper.

**

CHAPTER THIRTEEN

The first event will be the two hundred yards shoot commencing at noon, only this time instead of a twenty foot circle, two long ropes had been laid across the field; the first set at one hundred and ninety yards from the firing line, whilst the other is set at two hundred and ten yards.

Therefore after receiving a two inch long yellow stick for the target shoot and a three inch long yellow stick for the two hundred yard event, I went looking for my friends. Brother Arnold was easy to find because of the long staff he had borrowed from the priory but the other two were not so easily found in the crowd; and it was only on my return to the blacksmith's forge that we met up again. Tom had entered the same events as me whilst Jack had chosen the distance shoot instead of the two hundred yards, having received a four inch long yellow stick to add to his two inch yellow stick. Robert's wife Anne, welcomed us all into their house where we were treated to a breakfast of ham and eggs.

"Come on in me ducks and get tucked into this lot." she said.

Jane was fussing about Jack, who had that well known look on his face and I wondered if he would get out of Nottingham without an angry father chasing him.

Brother Arnold, having been in such crowds before, pulled out of his habit the three Lincoln green Robyn Hode hats we had used for the Saint Thomas's Day Maid Marian rescue and although Tom's hat was a little small for him, he became a merry man. There were no feathers with the hats but the ample number of goose quills lying about, soon put that right; not only could we see each other but the crowd could also see us, and they loved this little gesture to their local hero. We took turns at being Robyn Hode, whilst Bob as Friar Tuck was a natural favourite with everybody.

As we arrived at the range for the two hundred yard contest, each archer had to surrender his yellow stick and have his arrow marking's recorded to make sure that they were all different, so it was 1pm before we could start the competition. All of the archers were spread out in a line with their arrows sticking in the ground in front of them; the wind was behind us and the sun was on our left side. Then at the command of nock, draw, aim, release, a great cheer went up from the crowd. I didn't need a marker peg this time and when the bugle sounded the end of the minute I had fired fourteen of the twenty arrows stuck in the ground.

I had been too busy shooting, to notice what was going on around me but Jane and her mother told us that the sound of the arrows flying through the sky sounded like a strong wind blowing through the trees and the flying arrows looked like a great flock of birds crossing the sky. Only the judges were allowed forward to check the score and after about half-an-hour the arrows that had fallen short, none of which were mine, were brought back to the waiting contestants. Then the overshot arrows were being brought back, *none of mine yet, I hope I don't have any.*

There was one to start with for Tom and one for Robert, then one, no two more for Tom and one more for Robert. Oh no! And one for me. When it came to the final count, there were ten archers who had thirteen arrows in the target area and I was one of them.

Brother Arnold said, "You should have seen the state of the arrows, there were some stuck into others, some that had collided on the way and fallen well short and some that had their flights torn off."

I knew what he was talking about because a few of my returned arrows had received damage to the feathers and shafts.

There were ten prizes to be won so I was sure of winning something. The first prize was to be three nobles (one pound), the second prize was two nobles and so on down to the last prize of one groat.

It was then back to the twenty foot circle for the shoot off so my marker peg was needed, and I was determined to release more than fourteen arrows.

"And the winners" shouted the main judge, "with fifteen arrows each" … *I had shot fifteen arrows*, "are Glynn Flint and Christopher Bower, who share first and second prize."

That's not me is it? Yes it is, he has shouted my name out wrong, what's half of five nobles?

"And the winners shall receive" concluded the Judge, "two nobles three shillings and four pence each," giving between us, a gilt painted stick and a red painted stick which we had to present at the same time to collect our winnings. Tom came sixth and I couldn't care less who the other winners were. I had had a suspicion that Glynn Flint would do well in the target contest, having noticed how good his arrows seemed. They looked balanced and well cared for, just like mine were, so I considered him to be my closest rival when it came to the target contest.

Jack came with me to claim my prize and Glynn Flint took of all people, Taff Evans who I had not seen since last year at the Faversham tournament. Taff had been hurt in the shoulder and was not taking part in any events, *was he perhaps a robber after all, as Uncle James had said,* which made me wonder if he had been involved in the death of Williams's father?

Tomorrow morning will be the distance shoot and as I was not an entrant I was allowed to celebrate my victory along with Brother Arnold, who was in disguise again.

We were to meet up with my new Welsh friends at an Inn called 'The Trip', which was built into the rock beneath Nottingham Castle and when we arrived, it was full of rowdy drinkers. Robert and his family, along with Jack and Tom, were already there and Robert told us that the full name of the Inn was 'Ye Olde Trip to Jerusalem', which he said, was supposed to be the oldest Inn in the country. He then told us that King Richard I, or Richard the Lion Heart as Robert called him was supposed to have drank there, or at least some of his men had, before leaving on the crusades to the holy land. He also claimed, as most people in Nottingham did - with their tongues in their cheeks - that Robyn Hode had existed.

Soft Jack had proposed to Jane during the night and I wondered if he realised what he had let himself in for. It looks like he shall have to do a runner when we leave on Wednesday or Thursday.

"Jack you silly ass, why have you told Jane you will marry her?" I asked,

"Why not? we have a lot in common and she will do anything I want her to do." he replied with a wink, "and anyway, she shall be waiting for me to marry her the next time we come to Nottingham." then with another wink, the next time we come to….. "If, we ever come that is."

The sky was overcast for the distance competition and it looked like it might rain. The wind was coming off the river which made no difference to the long distance event. Robert won, with a distance of three hundred and forty yards, Jack came second with three hundred and twenty five yards and a man named Guy Jones from Mercia came third. I shall not be drinking tonight unless I fail to get through the first round of the target shoot this afternoon, in which case, the drinks will be on Robert and Jack.

At last the target competition, which is what I have been waiting for. There are two hundred and eight contestants ready to shoot at twenty four large straw discs, set two yards apart from one another and fifty yards from the firing line. Meaning that there will be nine heats, with the ninth having sixteen entrants. Each straw target has a completely unmarked twelve inch round red parchment disc attached and as all of the iron pointed arrows will go straight through them, the holes they leave will be counted. Then after the first twenty four archers had shot, the red discs were to be changed for the next twenty four and so on until every archer had fired.

I was in the fifth heat and was trying to study what the other four heats had scored, but it was impossible to see the holes left by the arrows.

Each archer was allowed to shoot one of his five arrows as a sighting shot after which he could go up to the target to see where it had hit, he then had to get four arrows out of his five into the red disc to qualify for the next round. Those with four bulls were to hold on to their red parchments until round two, and I could see that less than half of the archers from the first four heats were holding their parchments. Tom had his red parchment as did Glynn and Jack, Robert had not scored four bulls, so he was out. Then after I had shot there were six holes in my red disc, so somebody had shot at my target instead of his own. I only needed the four so I was into round two, as were over one hundred other archers. As all of these heats had taken up most of the afternoon, round two was to commence the next morning.

It was 4pm by the time I returned to the priory, so after making a fuss of Floss I rode her along the river Trent with the intention of having a swim, but as there were so many people camping alongside the river, I rode further east, where I found a secluded spot and left Floss tied to a tree. Floating quietly on my back in the water I heard the sound of someone jumping into the river only a few yards away from me; and then a woman's voice taking an intake of breath and a screech at the cold water. She noticed me straight away and let out another screech of surprise.

"You have no right to be here," she bellowed, "this is my swimming place."

Being completely bare I was out of the water in a flash and into the bushes, which brought laughter from the woman.

"Sorry" she chuckled, "I didn't see you there, you startled me, but you have a nice bum."

I could see that she was completely naked and when she noticed my eyes goggling at her, she leisurely got out of the water and started to dry herself. Her skin was quite dark and I could tell straight away that she was a gypsy, as she had large rings in her ears.

"Well," she huffed, "Have you had a good look at Carlotta then, or should I do a little dance for you."
"Sorry," I said, "you are the first girl I have ever seen without any clothes on."

"Thank you for calling me a girl," she said, "but I am twenty six years of age, so hardly a girl."

Her hair was black and curly and she looked beautiful; but she didn't like me asking her if she was a gypsy.

"I hate being called that name" she said, "we are not gypsies, we are Romanies."

"Sorry," I said, "I didn't know."

"If there are any problems or any thefts are carried out," she complained, "it is always the Romanies who get the blame; and what people say about us stealing children is just an excuse for them to scare their offspring into behaving themselves."

Carlotta told me that her father was the leader of some of the traveller, and that I would be welcome at their camp at any time. Then it was my turn to give some answers. She had never heard of Faversham but was all ears when I told her about the October archery contest which her clan might be interested in.

"So, what do you do besides archery?" she asked.

"I run a counting house and loan company. " I said, trying to impress her, but I knew straight away that it was the wrong thing to say, by the look of disgust and a toss of the head that only a women can do.

""Huh…. and I thought that you were a nice man," she uttered, "none of you money people will change coins for us, as they think we have stolen them."
This time my hackles pricked up and I replied, "I shall only be too pleased to change your coins for you."

Carlotta and I made our way back towards Nottingham when we were attacked by four men with hoods over their heads, I noticed that one of them was holding his shoulder in a funny way, "Is that you Taff?" I shouted.

Carlotta was off like a shot but the robbers grabbed Floss' reigns and the man I took to be Taff, stabbed her in the withers.

"It's a pity you recognised me," said Taff, taking off his hood as I was pulled out of the saddle. "I was only going to hurt your arm to make sure you could not shoot tomorrow but you have now changed the situation so you will now have to go missing, permanently."

Was I scared, was Crispin scared? Too true he was.

"Listen," I whined, "if you let me go, I won't say a word to a soul, I promise."

The other three men still had their hoods on and as it was only Taff I had recognised they were willing to let me go, but Taff was having none of this. Whilst they were arguing, a band of Romanies came galloping to my rescue, there was no fight and the robbers were soon disarmed.

I had been expecting Glynn Flint to be amongst them once there hoods had been removed but I didn't know any of the other attackers. Floss was squirming on the ground with blood pouring from her neck and one of my rescuers said, "It's no use trying to save your horse, I shall have to put it down."

I knew that he was right and just nodded my head. Carlotta had saved my life but Floss was gone, my faithful horse who had been with me all these years.

I wanted to grab Taff and stick a knife into him myself but the four men had been taken away by the Romanies. Carlotta told me as we walked back to her caravan that the man who had put Floss out of her misery was her father.

"If we had not saved you," she said, "then we would have been blamed for the attack but I am afraid that you may not be seeing those men again."

When her father returned, she asked what had happened to the four men and he told us that a man with a damaged shoulder had fallen into the river Trent and that his three friends had seen him fall but they were too late to save his life.

Tuesday morning was wet and windy and most of the archers had heard about poor Taff's accident but not about the ambush, or about Floss. However, Glynn came up to me and swore that he had nothing to do with it, saying that Taff Evans had gambled a lot of money on him winning the contest, which is why he must have decided to put me out of the competition. He then informed me that the three other robbers had told him all about it and had decided to leave Nottingham as a sign of respect to Taff Evans.

Yes, I thought, *getting going, whilst the going was good*.
I went to the Romany camp to thank Carlotta's father Rodolfo, for rescuing me and to pick up my Saddle; but nothing was said about the drowned Welshman. However he wanted to ask me about the box of coins he had in front of him.

"I think money lenders try to cheat us," he said, "we can't get our nobles changed into smaller coins without having to pay six pence each; and we don't even try to change these groats as we don't wish to get cheated."

Carlotta had obviously told him that I would exchange his money and he had collected coins from all of his people. There were over one hundred nobles, and hundreds of groats, a lot of which were the heavy coins, which I told him were now worth four and a half pence each, along with lighter groats now worth four pennies and one farthing each.

He told me that the best offer he had been given was three and a half pennies for each groat. "So if you give me four pennies each for them," he said, "that will do."

I would have been willing to pay the full price but he was happy with four pence. So I told him that I would get these changed for him, at no cost, on my way back through London if he loaned me a horse and provided an escort.

Glynn Flint then rode into his camp trailing a horse that had belonged to Taff Evans and with an ashen face told me that this horse was now mine. He didn't know its name but as Taff is a common name for Welsh people, he thought that this would be as good enough name as anything. He then said that he had also decided to withdraw from the contest in respect.

He had been followed into the camp by some of Rodolfo's men who were carrying a lot of camping gear, so it was obvious what was happening and I felt sorry for Glynn and hoped that I never did anything to cross these Romany people.

The target shoot was about to restart but there was no sign of Jack and nobody seemed to know where he or Jane were; but they must be together so I wasn't too bothered and handed in my red disc as proof of being in round two. There were now twelve normal targets, set four yards apart with a firing distance of seventy five yards. Only this time there will be point scoring, therefore this afternoon the best thirty two scorers shall go into round three.

Quite a lot of archers had shot at the wrong targets yesterday, so it was not clear if all of today's competitors had actually scored four bulls on their own. However, with fewer targets, spread wider apart, the chance of this happening again seemed unlikely. Jack turned up just in time to shoot but he looked like he had not slept all night, (there was no sign of Jane, so she must have gone straight home to bed).

There were flags flying all over the field so I didn't need Brother Arnold's help in knowing the wind direction. I was to shoot on target number twelve and very nearly shot my first arrow at number eleven, but just managed to correct my aim in time. Even so, I stuck my marker peg into the ground as I walked forward to see where my first arrow had passed through the target, scoring an inner on the left side of the bull's eye, which was alright because the wind was coming from the right. The sky had gone dark and a light drizzle of rain was falling as we finished the round. I had scored three bulls and two inners for 21 points, easily making the cut into round three; and was given a blue stick as proof of staying in the contest. Jack shot like a novice and was out but Tom was still in. The remaining rounds of the competition will be with eight targets, set at one hundred yards but it had now started to rain hard and black clouds were making it hard to see the targets, so the final rounds have had to be abandoned until Wednesday.

I collected my new horse Taff and took him for a ride along the river to find Floss' remains but there was no sign of her whatsoever. The Romanies must have disposed of her body….. And would you believe it? I was ambushed again, only this time by Carlotta, who looked ravishing.

She was dressed in a bright red swishing skirt that had an inch of white silk hem, her low white bodice was open at the front to reveal a hint of bosom, which made my eyes pop out of my head! And as much as I tried, they kept wandering to this bare flesh, which didn't go unnoticed by this vixen who kept flicking her ragged hair off her face.

With a throaty chuckle, she said "come with me," and took me into a clearing where a tent had been erected, I was forced to tie my black stallion under a tree and was marched inside the tent. It was just like meeting in the river, all over again…..

Later, much later, Carlotta said, "I knew you would come here to see what had happened to the body of your poor horse. Well my father has had it taken away and I wanted to see you to let you know how sorry I am and maybe comfort you a little. I have put up what is now your tent, which was once owned by your attackers; they only had themselves to blame and people don't mess with Romanies and try to get them in trouble."

When she saw what I was thinking, from the look on my face, laughingly she said, "Don't worry, you were not messing with me and I won't be telling my people our secret anyway."

I was then instructed to go to the priory and let them know that I shall be testing out my new camping equipment for the night, which was done in double quick time…… and what a testing out night it turned out to be.

**

CHAPTER FOURTEEN

On a cloudless, windless, Wednesday morning thirty two archers shot in round four, then sixteen, of which the poorest eight were out, leaving me and seven others in the final round commencing at noon. The winning prize was to be six nobles, second four nobles, third two nobles down to the eighth prize of one groat. I already knew that drinking and archery didn't mix, but you can now add women to the list, as I should have won easily.......

Three people shared first place with a score of 21 points, Guy Jones and Fred Hitch, both from Mercia..... And a shameful Crispin Bowyer.

I collected four nobles, making my total winnings six nobles three shillings and four pence; but who cares about winning or why there was no shoot off to decide the winner? I was in love and had no hesitation in telling Carlotta that I wanted to marry her.

"Oh, no, no, no," he cried, "that's not possible, my father would never allow it and I don't think you would like what he would do to you if he knew we had been together."

"We can run away," I pleaded.

"Please, please don't even think about it," She cried, "you will be going home tomorrow, let's just spend our last night together and remember each other's love."

And so after our last glorious night in the tent, I reluctantly left her and made my way back to the priory where I received knowing glances from Brother Arnold.

Having departed the Priory on Thursday morning, we met up with Jack and Tom at Robert's smithy where Tom had a crying girl clinging to him, pleadingly saying "please come back to me….. You will, won't you?"

Jack had somehow managed to dump Jane and Brother Arnold was waving to someone I couldn't see.

I had arranged to collect the coins and my Romany escort at Rodolfo's camp along with my new camping equipment but Carlotta was nowhere to be seen. Two men named Carlos and Roberto are to come with us as far as London, then return to Nottingham with the small value coins. Carlos was about fifty years of age and Roberto appeared to be less than thirty, both of them were well built apart from around the shoulders, so they were obviously not archers; in fact I don't think there was a Romany archer in the tournament.

Thursday night was spent in Leicester Priory where my escort set up camp in the south fields. Friar Tucker, who had looked after Floss, said how sorry he was to learn of her death.

On the way to Nottingham, we had taken our time travelling but we now intended to cover thirty miles per day which is not too strenuous on the horses or the riders, providing you have short periods of rest, and that you did not exceed four or five days of travelling at this speed and as I had no love for Taff, the extra pace was alright with me.

So on Friday, we set off at this increased rate of travel and by late morning had passed the camp site where we had cooked the squirrels, then turned left on to

Watling street and travelled a further fifteen miles before camping for the night near a small Hamlet called Long Buckby. Saturday was spent travelling to Stony Stratford, which was been busy with market traders. Brother Arnold and I were lucky to get the last room at the Cock Inn, whilst Jack and Tom managed to get a room at the Bull Inn. My escorts had met up with other Romanies and arranged to join us at the Cock at 6am on Sunday morning.

As the two Inns were close to each other, we all met up later in the Cock and it was now getting to be a bit of a habit for Brother Arnold not to wear his habit because he was fed up with having to defend the Catholic Church, finding it easier to be called Bob and not get any earache. We then moved on for drinks at the Bull, where we learned of the rivalry between the two Inn's, apparently each tried to better the other, with 'padded-out' stories, which the locals called a load of old 'Cock and Bull'.

At the Bull, Bob told the market revellers of our trip to Nottingham and they wanted to hear all about our success at the Famous Goose Fair, which, when we returned to the Cock, had been completely changed and exaggerated with Bob Arnold scoring the maximum of fifty points in the target competition...... what a load of Cock and Bull!

But we were surprised to learn about where one of our nursery rhymes originated...... Apparently, the Cock Inn hired out horses to ride to Banbury Cross (*to see a fine lady upon a white horse*), as the rhyme goes.

Sunday morning turned out to be rainy with flashes of lightning, followed by the sound of thunder and we had a dismal wet day plodding along to Saint Albans where the sleeping arrangements were to be the same as last time, But as soon we arrived, Jack got me to loan him my tent so that he could go off on his own for the night, saying before he went, "if I am not back by the morning, you can pick me up at the Fighting Cock Inn." so with my agreement, he rode off to see the landlords daughter. *How does he get away with it?* I wondered.

I couldn't complain about Taff as we were now getting used to each other and although he was not as sleek as Floss, he was stronger and carried my extra equipment without any trouble, so I felt confident that he could travel forty miles a day if I asked him to. He enjoyed the grooming and even pushed me gently with his head, to remind me to put his feed bag on.
At the Abbey, Brother Arnold relayed the comments of the monks at Leicester and the friars at Lenton Priory regarding the Lollard's, which I thought seemed to be a little bit of over reacting but I must admit that monks were not as welcome in the community as they used to be. The next morning Jack had not returned to the Abbey, nor was he at the Inn as we passed through the town.

Tom said, "You all go on and I shall wait here for him, then if we don't catch up with you, we shall see you at Saint Bart's priory in London."

I was anxious to get to the counting house before they closed for the day and with twenty five miles to go, it would be cutting it close.

Brother Arnold said, "You and your two men go on ahead and I shall wait with Tom."

With that, my escort and I set a fast pace to London where we arrived before closing time, with an hour to spare. But with so much money to change, it took some persuading to get my friend Edward to make the transaction, however I promised to make it up to him.

There were one hundred and twenty nobles, which changed nicely into forty one pound bags of pennies. The groats were sorted out into three piles, one hundred and eighty old heavy groats, for which the interest will be one halfpenny each, one hundred and twenty four of the next minted groats with an interest of one farthing each and two hundred and eighteen new groats for which there was no interest. There were five hundred and twenty two coins at four pence each, amounting to eight pounds in bags of pennies and one hundred and sixty eight loose pennies.
When I carried the bags of coins and the loose pennies out to Carlos and Roberto, the relief on their faces was unbelievable.

Carlos said, "even though you are friendly with my people, you were still not trusted with our money and Carlotta would have been in real trouble if you had tried to cheat us."

I didn't know what to say to this and felt sorry that these Romany traveller's had so much distrust in other people, but what could you expect when no trust was given to them. With that, they bade me farewell and rode away, whilst the interest….. Ten shillings and one penny was mine.

Edward had one hundred and twenty one pennies ready for me when I went back into the counting house and he said, "Goodbye then Cris, I shall not be seeing you again."

"What do you mean?" I asked.

"The counting house is retiring me as they say I am too old and I leave at the end of October," he sadly replied.

This got me thinking, so I asked him if he had any family.

"Only my wife, we have never had any children," he replied.

My brain was ticking over now, and I asked, "Do you have a house of your own?"

"No" he answered, "we rent a place from the counting house but we shall have to give this up at the end of October."

For a long time I had thought of offering Edward a job but didn't think he would accept.

"Edward, do you want to stop working and if not, what would you want me to pay you if I offered you a Job in Faversham?"

In no time at all I had an experienced asset who would be joining the loan company, at two shillings per week and furthermore, I found out that his wife is a baker which fits in nicely with another idea that had been running through my head for some time. I told Edward how to get the Dover coach that stops in Faversham and where to find me, saying that I would have somewhere ready for them to live on their arrival. I was so pleased about having such a knowledgeable man joining me, that I gave him all of the profit from the Romany groats saying, "Come as soon as you can and give me what change is left when you arrive."

Brother Arnold showed up on his own at Saint Bart's priory, telling me that there was no sign of Jack when he had left Saint Albans but that Tom was going to wait for him and that they would see us back in Faversham.

"What did the landlord have to say?" I asked.

"What didn't he say? You should be asking. He was fuming, having been up all night searching for them," he replied. "He even picked on me as being a bad influence on you all!"
Well, at least Jack is probably safe and will turn up eventually, that's if the landlord doesn't get to him first. I thought.

The next day, with only forty three miles to travel, we decided to stop at St, George's Inn in Chatham for the night and make a leisurely journey home on Wednesday morning. We had just crossed over the River Medway, when 'STAND AND DELIVER' was shouted out as two rouges and a maiden jumped out in front of us.

"I knew that we were ahead of you" shouted Jack, as the three pretend robbers surrounded us.

"But I am sure you must be wondering who this girl is? Please meet my wife Helen."

"Helen" bawled Brother Arnold, "Helen, your wife" he bawled again, "is this, the girl from the Fighting Cock Inn? If it is, you cannot possibly be married."

"Well" blustered Jack, "Helen has been thrown out by her father and we are going to get married as soon as possible."

Helen was only sixteen and she was the prettiest girl I had ever seen, apart from Carlotta and the other two, that is. Tom quietly told me that Jack had spent the night in my tent with Helen and that he had waved to him from behind the Inn an hour after Brother Arnold had left and that they had all sneaked away.

"And, her father just let her go, did he?" roared Brother Arnold. "Thrown out my eye! You have taken her away from her parents haven't you? Your story is a load of old cock and bull."

Jack had no answer to this and meekly nodded saying, "Helen told me that she would kill herself with shame if I didn't take her with me, so what was I to do?"

"I'll tell you what you will do" shouted Brother Arnold in disgust, "you will stay here in the tent with Tom tonight and Helen will stay at the Saint George Inn with me and Crispin. Then, tomorrow, I shall personally take her home to Saint Albans and if you don't agree, I shall have you arrested for abduction."

The Inn was only half a mile away and as we were eating our supper, Jack turned up with Tom, promising that he would take Helen home himself and ask for permission to marry her. This was agreeable to Brother Arnold, providing that Jack returned with written proof off her father. With that, we were all happy to be reunited again and spent the rest of the evening putting the world to rights. Jack and Helen rode west the next morning and the rest of us rode east. It was to be another two weeks before we saw either of them again, all happily married with a certificate to prove it.

At noon, Tom dropped off at the mill, I rode towards my brother's farm, whilst Brother Arnold went on to Faversham monastery. As I approached the farm, Jamie was riding Red around my brother's fields and when he saw a man riding a black horse he came across to see who it was, when he got closer he anxiously shouted, "Where's Floss?"

There was no way that I could soften the blow, so I told him about the hold up and how Floss was killed. He burst into tears and started to console Red, so to get his mind off the tragedy, I quickly changed the subject.

"Anyway, what are you doing riding my horse without my permission?" I demanded.

"Well, well" stammered Jamie, "I thought that he was missing his mother and he loves galloping, so that's what we've been doing every day."

Red was looking fit and his coat was reflecting the light so I could see that he was being well-looked after but Red was more interested in Taff than me, the ungrateful animal. Jamie was looking into my face to see if I was really angry and when he saw that I was smiling, he turned on me and asked "what's this thing you are riding on then?"

"Cheek," I said, "this is Taff, I have brought him all this way from the middle of the country and I've a good mind not to give him to you now."

That changed his tune….. "For me, mine, me, my own horse, do you really mean it?"

My big mouth, what was I saying? I hadn't even thought of what to do with Taff now that I was home.

"Yes," I was forced to say, "This is my thanks to you for looking after Red until now."

"Until now?" Jamie uttered in shock, "Are you taking him away? If you are, I don't want that thing." Pointing at Taff and then he ran off leaving Red with me.
When I arrived at the farm, my brother introduced me to his girlfriend Nell, who I knew anyway. She was the same age as me, but twice as big, and like Jack's girl in Nottingham. I'm sure she could shoe horses and I'll bet she can plough a field with the best of them…… still whatever takes your fancy.

There was no reason to stay at the farm, so after telling everybody about my success in Nottingham and what had happened to Floss, I left Taff in his care, asking him to get Jamie to come and see me the next day, then rode Red into Faversham.

When Jamie finally arrived, I said, "If you don't want Taff I shall sell him to the glue factory."

This was not true of course.

"Oh, I can't let you do that, it looks like I had better save him then." Jaime said, with the slightest of smiles that he tried to conceal.

The amount of change that had occurred since we left Faversham for Nottingham was tremendous. First of all, I was expecting to find that my parents had gone off to France but due to the uncertainty of another war, the French had stopped all English people entering France, and those that did would be treated as spies. This meant that I may never see my French grandparents again and what is more…. never see Catherine again either.

William had been welcomed back into the family by his brother, the new Lord John Thornbury and my sister is now living in the manor, which thankfully saved me having to find a house for Edward and his wife who arrived in the middle of October and are now living with me.

Edward had returned five shillings of the money I had left with him and told me that the counting house had let him leave two weeks early. His wife Anne was so grateful that I had come to their rescue that she grabbed and hugged me as soon as she knew who I was.

"The counting house had no conscience in getting rid of my husband after all the years of good service he had given them." she said.

Edward had told her that I had ideas about baking and she was eager to know my plans, so I said to her, "get settled in for a couple of weeks, then we can meet with old John Baker and talk business." but being a woman, she had it sorted out by the end of the week without any help from anybody including me.

Yvette had made Will Jackson her business partner and even though she was young, she has a good head on her shoulders and was learning fast, with lots and lots of help from her extended family, she was even learning to read a little. Her new partner Will Jackson, who had been with her from the start, could see that building houses out of stone, along with roof tiling, was in demand and he was willing to take control of all the work, with my sister taking half of the profit. I had been expecting a little bit of resentment from Thomas, the ex-monk, for bringing Edward to work for me but he was only too pleased to welcome him on to the team, as we now called ourselves.

Anne was in her element caring for us at the house and she took charge of all the household needs. Her meals were delicious and the wheat bread made in my cast iron oven melted in the mouth.

"And we have our own fresh water, of all things, just by pushing up and down a handle!" she said, "what luxury."

Edward more or less took over the company and was able to do more with the finances than I could ever do, so I was quite happy to let him get on with it and now, because he was living outside of London, he started to get a little bit of colour in his cheeks and a bit of fat on his body.

Because we had such close connections with the church and the Abbey, people were coming as far away as Whitstable to get improvement loans and we were lending money on trust alone. However, Edward pointed out that we were only making small loans and should be careful if any large loans were asked for, which the borrower may for one reason or another be unable to repay. I didn't think that we would be lending large loans but you never know what lies ahead, so I left it in his capable hands.

I had seen bakeries in the various abbeys and priories I had visited, where they were using large cast iron ovens; and it was obvious to see their advantage over stone or clay ovens, where you first had to light a fire in the oven to get it hot then remove the fire and replace it with the items to be baked. Not only was this time consuming, it often dirtied the food, whereas with a cast iron oven the fire is separate from the baking area, therefore nothing gets dirty and no time is lost changing from one to the other and back again.

John, the Baker, was over sixty years of age and as he was the only bread maker in Faversham he felt it was his duty to continue making loaves for everybody but as soon as Anne had arrived in Faversham, she had offered to work for him and he couldn't employ her quick enough. I met with them and asked if they would like to form a partnership with me, using a large cast iron oven which I would buy? Saying that if they agreed, we would take a third share each of the profits and that Edward could handle the bakeries finances.
John was only too pleased to have the community liability removed from his shoulders and the partnership was sealed with a handshake from John, and a weepy hug from Anne, who was already used to using cast iron ovens. The bakery was in the next building to my house, with about a ten yard gap in between, which I intended to build on to expand the business.

"Now then partners, why do bakers only make corn bread for sale and not wheat bread?! I asked. "As wheat bread is lighter, fluffier and nicer to eat."

John and Anne looked at each other, smiled and nodded.

"Well partner" said John, "as you know, we normally only sell bread on market days and it has to last for three or four days; but with wheat bread, we add yeast to the dough, to make the loaves rise and go fluffy but the yeast causes the bread to go mouldy after a day or two and people don't want to waste their money.

"The wheat bread won't get a chance to go mouldy if we make it daily and sell it straight away." I replied, "And instead of making one big corn loaf for a farthing you could make two smaller wheat loaves for the same price."

They could see the sense in this, so on the following Monday, John and Edward took the regular Dover to London coach to purchase an oven, whilst Anne looked after the bakery. The oven arrived in the middle of November and my sister's men fitted it into the extension that had now been built across the gap between the two buildings. Within a fortnight, one hundred loaves a day were being made but it was obvious from the demand that we would have to expand even more very soon.

John's main task was to ensure that Tom delivered the sacks of flour and that Isaac delivered the wood for the fire, whilst Anne made the dough and baked the bread......

**

CHAPTER FIFTEEN

Jack had told me that on his return to Saint Albans, Helen had gone into the inn alone then five minutes later her father came running out looking for him."

I thought he was going to attack me," laughed Jack, "but he was only making sure I was still there and had not galloped off, anyway," he chuckled, "her father was only as big as a shrimp and although he and his wife were not pleased at losing their daughter, they could see that she was happy and that they had little choice in the matter as she had told them that she would run away again if they would not agree to the marriage; by the time of our wedding, her parents had got used to the idea of having a blacksmith for a son-in-law." He said.

"And what's more," he went on, "my father-in-law told me that this was the first time that the Fighting Cock had ever run out of ale!"

And so, a new Mrs Smith, became a baker's assistant whilst her husband got on with blacksmithing.

Business was booming and with Christmas approaching we had to quickly buy another oven to keep up with demand.

Lord John was not married, so William was still first in line to inherit the manor, whilst I was first in line to inherit the farm but not for long, as my brother was to marry Nelly in the summer and they could well have a son, making me second in line, which suites me, as I am not sure that I want to be a farmer anyway.

The Christmas Day banquet at the manor this year was organised by Lady Beatrice, with some help from my sister but for me, it was not as enjoyable without Catherine to dance with and Yvette was taking charge of our festive Boxing Day arrangements. On New Year's Eve she was going to have a manor banquet of her own and it was to be a fancy dress party; if you didn't dress up you wouldn't be allowed to attend.

I couldn't help remembering last year's Christmas festivity and my thoughts went back to waking up with Catherine wrapped around me. It's almost eleven months since I had last seen her and if she had been in England now, I am sure that I would have asked her to be my bride. I wondered how she was getting along and how she was feeling, or if she ever thought about me?

On Boxing Day my house was crowded with the addition of my brother and Nelly. Edward and Anne were there, as was last year's 'bathroom sleeper' and his wife. We even crowded in Lady Beatrice and her son Lord Thornbury, who thankfully knew nothing of my troubles with his father. He even said that it was a better party than their Christmas Day banquet; but I'm sure that he was only trying to please my sister.

On New Year's Eve, Brother Arnold turned up at my sister's fancy dress party dressed as a Roman Centurion with all the trimmings, and looked certain to win the men's first prize, until William showed up in a Viking outfit with horns coming out of his helmet and spindly white legs jutting out of his sheepskin leotard.

I'm glad I was not having to judge the winner, as they both tried to look fearsome. The judging task was to be undertaken by two people: Queen Boudicca (Yvette), who was responsible for picking the male and female prizes, whilst the other was Queen Matilda (Lady Beatrice), who came from *Boulogne* in western France, where the real Queen Matilda of England had once lived. (It was Queen Matilda who along with her husband King Stephen had founded Faversham Abbey, built in 1148 with stone from the local quarry).

I was dressed as a Cobbler for obvious reasons, whilst Jack and his wife came as knights, dressed in outfits of shiny silvery material that were made by Helen, to looked exactly like armour, even to the extent of tying the pieces together with leather straps and tin cups clanging together to make the right sound. This was so funny, that they won both the male and female prizes….. A bottle of brandy for Jack and another bottle of brandy for the other knight.

"Not fair, not fair" we all shouted, so a ladies prize had to be quickly found or else we were going to poor water over the organiser, who vanished and returned with a bottle of French perfume for Helen.

Jack now had two bottles of brandy, which were soon emptied by persons unknown, and if anybody had wished me a Happy New Year….. I don't remember, as it was back to never again, never again as I nursed my sore head the next afternoon. (I don't know what had happened to the morning).

Friar John and Friar James……my father and uncle, had slept in a cupboard at the manor but their understanding wives were in my room, whilst Edward the Confessor and his wife, slept in their own room. I was in the bath, never again…..*or have I already said that?*

"Isn't it good to be back to normal?" Anne said, at the beginning of the New Year, as she cooked ordinary food to see us off to the Bank, which Edward had informed me we were now to call the counting house. Anne had already been up for eight hours and was into the sixth batch of twenty loaves, which Helen was watching over whilst she saw to her men. The first batches of loaves had already been sold to people who wanted their bread hot and Helen had introduced Jam, made out of strawberries and other fruits that had been preserved from the summer, using a 'nose tapping' recipe she had learned from her mother.

It was hard to keep old John from doing too much work but he was up at four every morning to re- kindle the oven fires; and he seemed to have a new lease of life. He had lost his wife to an unknown illness ten years earlier, which caused him loose interest in living but at the New Year's Eve party dressed as King Arthur, he had drunk with the best of us and was even seen making eyes at Lady Beatrice, who on this one occasion had allowed him to call her by her Christian name.

There is now no need to ration bread, as with two ovens, there is more than enough to go round but John, along with Anne and Helen, had to work very hard before market days because the bakery still had to make corn bread for the people who could not get used to wheat loaves; so each evening before market days, we employed Nelly and Uncle James' wife Mary, to help make corn bread and from then on, I left them to it. In fact I was having less and less to do, due to all my willing and loyal teams doing all the work, therefore, after being the best man at my brother's wedding and having helped with the harvest at the end of Summer, I realised that a life of leisure was not what I wanted.

I didn't want to be a farmer but needed to do something interesting and useful and having employed my sister's company to build an impressive building across the square from the Anchor Inn, with 'Faversham Bank' carved in stone over the entrance, I was left twiddling my thumbs.

So what am I going to do?

I don't want the trip to Nottingham Goose Fair this year, neither does Jack for the obvious reason that he didn't want to run into Jane's father; but Tom Miller went, and came back with the two hundred yard prize and the girl who had been pleading with him last year…..Jean.

Jack wanted to know about the blacksmith's daughter but was too ashamed to ask. Tom had already told me about Jane and we decided to have a bit of fun with Blue.

"Did you see Jane whilst you were there?" I asked.

Jack's ears pricked up when Tom answered "as a matter of fact I did, she was bouncing her baby girl on her knee"

Jack nearly fell off his stool!

"Oh" I said, giving Jack a sly look, "did she ask about anybody?"

"No" said Tom, "she was too busy with her three-week old red-headed baby and couldn't get rid of me fast enough…….. Before her red headed husband came home!"

I received a clout across the head and so did Tom as we doubled up laughing.

I was feeling more and more useless at having less to do with everybody getting on with the work without my help, so it was back to Brother Benedict … sorry Abbot Benedict to find the answer. It was not so easy to see my mentor any more, as he was now busy running the Abbey but as usual he came up with a solution.

"Why don't you become involved with politics?" he advised.

"Politics? I know nothing about politics." I replied.

"What's to know?" he said, "people in Faversham know and trust you and would welcome a commoner looking after their interests because you know what's fair for the ordinary peasant."

I could see his point of view, as I didn't trust the ruling classes either.

"But they would never allow me into their ranks, would they?" I asked.

"Well you shall never know, if you don't try," he said.

"What a brilliant idea" said William, when I mentioned it to him, "and you are just the man we need. My brother was only saying last week, that somebody in the town should look after the welfare of the people, now that there is no feudalism and that serfdom has been abolished."

This was too much of a coincidence for me and I felt sure that I was being set up by the Abbot and Lord John Thornbury.

"Why don't you come with me and talk to my brother" said William, "to hear what he has to say and to work something out?"

Lord Thornbury admitted that he had talked with the Abbot and when my name had been suggested he had readily agreed with the choice.

"And" said William's brother, "if you take on the job, you shall receive a payment of nine pounds five shillings per year paid out of the taxes."

After a quick calculation this worked out to be over twenty seven nobles, and calculating again, it worked out to be near enough six pence per day.

"All you have to do is make sure that the town's people understand what their taxes are used for and that they are spent wisely." he said.

"But what will I have to do?" I asked, "And don't expect me to agree with everything you or the King say."

"That's the whole idea" chirped in William, "if you accept any proclamations, then the people who trust you will also accept them."

"Well, I shall not do anything unless the people of Faversham and Oare are happy for me to speak for them," I muttered.

"What I shall do?" said Lord Thornbury. "Is ask the priest if I can talk to his congregation on Sunday and put the suggestion that you become the Alderman for Faversham."

Alderman Bowyer, that sounds important I thought*, and it may stop the gentry pushing people about, but what am I letting myself in for?*

Saint Mary's Church could only hold about two hundred worshipers and the population of Faversham and Oare must be well over eight hundred people, of which there will probably be six hundred adults over fifteen years of age; but there was no way a meeting could be held in the church involving everybody at the same time. The priest, Father David, who was in favour of Lord John's suggestion, said that he would spread the word to his congregation that next Sunday as the morning and evening services would be for adults only and Lord Thornbury will put his ideas forward regarding a commoner representing them.

Due to the abolition of serfdom, Lord John had made himself popular with the people of Faversham and on Sunday morning there must have been three hundred people crowded into the church, anxious to hear what he had to say.
 "Ladies and Gentlemen…..Ladies and Gentlemen," he said again, once the murmuring had died down.

"Thank you for allowing me to talk to you on this beautiful day," this brought a laugh as it was thundering and lightning outside.

You could tell that Lord John was used to talking to a lot of people but I was a bag of nerves, knowing that I would have to follow with my well-rehearsed speech, worked out with William and Abbot Benedict.

"As you are aware," continued Lord John, "the feudal system has been abolished in England, allowing the people to have more say in what is happening in their lives." which brought a few nods of approval and some tittering from the listeners.

"And although there has been little trust between the peasants and the landowners in the past (more tittering went on) the King wants you, the people, to have one of your own to look after your interests in the town."
Everybody then started talking amongst themselves about this comment and it took Father David five minutes to bring order to his flock.

"Brethren" he shouted, holding up his arms and gesturing for silence. "Brethren, brethren, I want to thank Lord Thornbury for bringing in these changes, which I am sure, will benefit all of Faversham and I would like to suggest that Mr Crispin Bowyer become your first town representative."

After another five minutes of muttering father David went on, "we have to start somewhere and as most of you know Cris and the good work that he has already done with his bank loans, I therefore propose that we elect him as Alderman for Faversham and Oare."

I was watching the faces of the crowd and there were no scowls or shaking of heads, so I felt more relaxed. When he was allowed to continue, father David said, "If there are any people here, who think that Crispin

Bowyer is not the right person for the job, will you please put your hand up."

Two hands were raised and everybody laughed..... It was my mother and father, who were only teasing.

All that was required now, was my well-practiced speech, and not to be outdone I said too loudly, "LADIES AND GENTLEMEN"

After the merriment had died down and Jack had shouted 'get on with it Cris', receiving an elbow in his side from Helen for his trouble, I repeated, "Ladies and Gentlemen, I am lucky to have had lessons at the monastery which have allowed me to improve myself, *no comments or murmur's, so far good,* and feel sure that I know what will be fair for Faversham in the future. I should like to thank Lord John Thornbury for this opportunity to act on your behalf and feel sure that our community can look forward to a better way of life and freedom from drudgery. Therefore, without further ado, I accept the position as Alderman for Faversham, thank you for your support."

People don't normally clap their hands in church but they did this time; and after a repeat performance on Sunday evening, my position was confirmed.

But it was Lord John Thornbury who didn't know what he had let himself in for because Alderman Bowyer made him hand over all the present tax money that he had received from the town, which at one shilling per adult for this year amounted to thirty three pounds five shillings; which, before I became involved, had gone elsewhere with not a single penny ever being spent on improvements to Faversham. I was expecting an argument about this but Lord

Thornbury passed the money straight over to me and to my utter dismay, he also handed over the future responsibility for collecting the tax as well.

This money had nothing to do with rents payable to the landowners, of which the landlord paid a certain amount to the Crown, therefore Lord John was only too happy for the taxes to be spent on the town. After my wage had been taken out, I had twenty four pounds to spend on Faversham, which was now combined with Oare.

There were two things that needed sorting out straight away…..human waste and the rubbish, but unlike London which has sewers, most people in country towns 'dump' in a hole in the ground; and ever since the plague, parliament had been trying to find other ways to dispose of this waste, which was contaminating the rivers and the underground supply of drinking water, causing outbreaks of sickness.

Farmers could make compost heaps out of dung and spread it over their fields but Faversham town's people now needed to have this waste taken away, but who in their right mind would want to go around collecting human waste?

Well it takes all sorts to make a world and I discovered that there were two men with a cart living on the Gravenly marshes, that would willingly collect the dung from Faversham and dump it into the outgoing tide of the river Swale that flowed out into the English Channel, at a cost of four shillings and six pence per week. So it was agreed that I would give them three nobles, in advance, at the beginning each month, if they would start as soon as the town was ready.

What was needed now was a dumping box for each dwelling, which three of my sister's carpenters made. Within just a few weeks, we had four hundred wooden thunder boxes with rope handles and lids that folded over a bum seat at a cost of three pence each to make. Town's folk could collect one each and take to their dwelling free of charge, what is more, a lot of the town's people started to build their own little out houses to put these boxes in.

The total cost came to seventeen pounds for the year and without going into too much detail, the system worked reasonably well, but some people still preferred the hole in the ground. However, they were eventually persuaded by their neighbours that until the land had been cleared of human waste, which was filtering into the underground water system, my future plan of putting hand water pumps around the town to replace the existing wells could not start.

I was now left with seven pounds to clear the town of all the discarded rubbish and trash.

With Lord John's approval, I paid Isaac one noble per day out of which he was to employ six men to get rid of the discarded rubbish; and a lot of the town's population turned out to help fill twenty cartloads of trash and old building material, which over a three day period was all tipped into the quarry where the stone had come from to build the Abbey.

This left me with six pounds to last until the next tax collection.

I was feeling very pleased with my changes and bylaws, which were obviously needed, and people now took pride in the town. The fronts of houses started to get painted and the town was beginning to look neat and tidy.

Alderman Bowyer can do no wrong, I thought.

But I soon found out how wrong I was because this was when my problems started. There's a difference between helping people and telling them what they should do and so there was some resentment and argument when on April 1st 1412, it was time to start collecting the shilling per adult in taxes.

This was the part of being an alderman that I didn't like and no matter what I did, or tried to do, it was like trying to get blood out of a stone.

Lord Thornbury was of no help, as being new to the manor he had never had to collect this money. Father David tried to be of assistance by telling his congregation how the money was being spent; but if the people didn't have the money, how could they pay?

I certainly wasn't going to take their possessions away from them, and it wasn't that these people didn't want to pay, as how could they when they were living from hand to mouth?..... So I came up with the idea of getting those who owed taxes to borrow the money from my bank and pay it back over thirteen weeks at a penny per week. This involved more work for me, well more work for Thomas really, but the extra penny payment for each adult covered his additional work, as I have now made him the town clerk at an additional wage of a shilling per week.

This method of payment became so popular in the town, that once the shilling plus one penny was repaid, my town clerk was collecting people's taxes in advance, spread out over the year. They were only too glad to pay an extra penny and not have the worry of having to find this large amount of money in one go when the tax was due.

And now that the thunder box collectors were being paid monthly I still had a surplus of money, which allowed me to have water pumps fitted in three positions about the town, where there had been deep wells. Not only did this do away with having to wind a bucket up and down, it also meant that cleaner water could be brought to the surface without any dirt or rats contaminating it. Eventually, all the water wells were filled in and replaced with a hand pump in every position and I was enjoying watching the town flourish. However it was not my responsibility to settle any disputes between the towns' folk, so when people came to me with their complaints, I told them to take their problems to the Sherriff, who as you know is Lord Thornbury. However, Lord John was in London more than he was in Faversham and these disputes were festering, to the extent that violence was becoming a problem. So something had to be done to put things right.

William was the only person who could act for his brother but he was reluctant to become involved in what he called petty disputes.
"It may be petty to you, William," I said, "but if someone was to take a possession of yours and say it was theirs, and you were not big enough or strong enough to take it back, you would want somebody to do something about it wouldn't you?"

"But why me?" he moaned, "Why would anybody take any notice of me?"

"Because you shall have your brother's men at arms to force them to." I replied.

"Well, I shall have to see what John says when he comes home." he mumbled, "but in the meantime if you send the person who is complaining to me, I shall listen to what they have to say."

William wouldn't have decide whether to cut babies in half, like Solomon proposed in the bible, but he was usually successful in solving most problems once they were highlighted.

Lord John was only too happy to have his brother take this burden off his shoulders and made William the Magistrate for Faversham, with the responsibility to decide on all civil cases, other than murder and crimes against the Crown. For this responsibility he would receive a payment of twelve pounds per year out of Lord Johns own purse. He was also to impose any fines or punishment against an offender, not the stocks of course, which had long ago been done away with; but they were still standing, in place close to the Anchor Inn, where small children could often be seen putting their heads and hands through the holes without lifting the bar.

William was being given more and more responsibility by his brother and my sister asked me if I would mind letting him give up his partnership in the loan company, saying that her husband would never want to let me down, after all I had done for him; and she thought that he was working too hard.

"Did William ask you to see me about this?" I hissed. "No, no" she pleaded, "and please, please, don't ever tell him I talked to you."

Edward had been completely running the bank and I had been thinking of making him a partner, but how was I to bring up the subject without hurting Williams feeling? So this could be my chance.

"I want to call a full meeting with everybody, next Saturday when the bank is closed." I announced, "To see where we are up to and to see what everybody has to say regarding our future."

I had already put Edward's mind at rest, in case he thought that I was going to get rid of him, I even hinted about promotion, and although Yvette and Anne were not bank employees, I wanted them at the meeting to support their husbands.

Holding a meeting with only six people present, is a lot different than three hundred people in a church and I was fully relaxed as I sat down with everybody wondering what I was going to say, including me.

"I don't want any formality," I said, "but as you know, William and I are putting less time into the business and I want to know what you all feel about things, but don't worry if you think I won't like what you have to say, as I am sure it will be beneficial to us all."

SILENCE….. You could hear a pin drop, then……

William angrily said, "Yes it's true, I am doing less so if you want me to resign, I WILL."

This is not going well, I thought.

"William," I said, "I was thinking more in terms of expanding and offering promotions to Edward and Thomas, as I want to give them more reward for their excellent work. And perhaps employ more people as well, that's why I wanted you all together before I mentioned it" … giving Edward a slight wink.

This was a relief to William, who then proposed that Edward should be made a partner and that Thomas be made manager.

"What a good idea." I said.

After this, the atmosphere became more relaxed and everybody started talking at the same time, with Edward saying that he could get as many bank people as I wanted from London.

"As many people as 'you' want," I joked. Which, brought the tension down a bit more.

I could see that Yvette and William were glancing at each other but it was my sister who said, "Why don't you let William concentrate on being a magistrate and still be part of the bank?"

This was just the opening William needed.

"No, that's not fair," he said, "now that I know the bank will not need me I am prepared to resign, as I have more than enough to do as it is."

With that sorted, we all trundled across to the Anchor Inn to celebrate.

As managing director of the Bank, I had no involvement in the day to day running of affairs and it was only major decisions that needed my attention such as loans of over twenty pounds; one of which was for twenty eight pounds, asked for by my friend Tom Miller, who wanted to build his own house and a new and larger windmill on his father's land at Beacon Hill.

"What's wrong with the present mill?" I asked.

Tom told me that he wanted to build another mill because he could then grind corn in one mill and wheat in the other. I had no problem with this as I needed the flour and corn that he and his father ground for the local farmers. Not to mention that Yvette's company would get the building work; so the loan was granted at an agreeable interest rate of ten per cent and as it turned out, after building a new and larger windmill close to the old one, farmers from out of the area were giving him and his father their harvests to grind.

Now that the town was cleaned up, what was needed was someone to keep it that way, so I asked Isaac if he would like the job.

"But Cris," he moaned, "I have a job already, so why would you want me to do another?"

"I know that you often employ men when you are logging." I replied. "All I want you to do is to take charge of two men, who are to go around the town collecting any ongoing rubbish. I would also like you to buy a horse and cart for them to use for the collections."

"Cris," he moaned again, "You know that I am no good with money, it takes me all my time to sort out my own wages. I know how to handle men, and looking after a horse would be no trouble, but I don't know anything about paying wages. Anyway, I work for the manor."

"If I see Lord John to get his agreement, all you have to do is organise the men." I said, "I shall do the rest."

"And what are you prepared to pay me?" he asked.

"How does three pence a day sound, plus a penny a day for looking after the horse, as well as two pence a day each for your two men?"

His reply was, "you go and see the Lord, and I already have the men and can soon get a horse and cart!"

I was well aware that Isaac had men who were always asking him for work and I had already got permission from William's brother, Lord John, so that within a week Faversham had a refuse collecting service.

**

CHAPTER SIXTEEN

OCTOBER 1414

More things have happened since last year; my sister Yvette has given birth to a boy whom she has named William, after her husband, and her baby is now second in line to becoming the lord of the manor in Faversham……unless, that is, Lord John gets married and has a son.

Young Jamie is now learning to read and write at the monastery.

The King had died in March 1413 and his son was crowned Henry 'V' the following month, which had little effect on peasant life but what had affected the peasants, was the heavy rains in the summer of last year, which caused a crop failure. This resulted in my friend Tom Miller, being unable to meet his repayments to the bank because he had no harvest to grind. However, I was willing put his debt on hold, without adding any additional interest to the loan. The crop failure had caused a famine across most of Kent and the baking of bread fell away to almost nothing; there was no hay or oats to feed the animals nor were many vegetables saved from the rain sodden land.

When I asked the Church (in my capacity as Alderman) for their help to buy the essential food supplies from the farmers of Surrey and Hampshire, who did not have to suffer the weather blowing from across the English Channel, they were reluctant to part with their stored money; but because the Abbey funded some of the cost, the church was shamed into doing likewise and some of the suffering was eased. Not all of it however, because as there were no crops to harvest, the peasants had no jobs to go to, therefore they had no money to pay the increased prices for what food was available.

Besides using up all of the tax money I had also used some of my own funds to save a disaster, so I had a little bit of catching up to do to put the books right. Thankfully though, that is all behind us now. I was really amazed that the church, with all of its wealth, had to be forced into helping the starving population of Faversham….. *Could there be an argument for the Lollard's after all?* I thought.

I went to the Nottingham archery contest again this September gone, along with Tom and his wife. Taking a new longbow with me made out of a perfectly straight stave which had been part of my father's supporting weathering frame that must be years and years old. It's the best longbow that I have ever made and I have gone as far as possible with improving arrows, which I consider are also the best I have ever made. They now have four straight flights, instead of three curved ones, and the feather barbs are cut closer to the shaft making less friction as the arrows pass my protective arm bracer, which gives them greater accuracy.

After a pleasant journey in my coach, we arrived at Jean's parents' who whooped with joy at seeing their daughter again, having heard about the famine on the east coast of England the previous year; but they didn't know how this had affected her, especially as Tom was a miller. We were immediately invited to stay at their house during the tournament.

There were plenty of Romany travellers about but no Rodolfo or his daughter, who was now married to Roberto (one of my escorts' to London).

I had been looking forward to seeing Carlotta again to renew our….. 'Friendship' but was glad that she had kept our secret.

I had no interest in the distance shoot, won again by Robert the blacksmith, nor was I entering the two hundred yard shoot, in which Tom came second with twelve arrows. All I was interested in, was the target competition and was in the last eight for the shoot off, having scored five bulls in the next to last round, so I felt sure I could win. I knew three of my rivals, Tom my friend, Fred Hitch from Mercia and of all people, Glynn Flint, who had dropped out of the tournament when we had last met. I believed that he had nothing to do with me being ambushed and we became friends, especially when we became joint winners…… well at least 'I' was one of the two best archers in England.

I knew that our new King, when he was the Prince of Wales, had been in a battle at Shrewsbury in July 1403, where Welsh and Mercian archers had blotted out the sun with arrows; one of which had struck him in the left side of his face. This injury would normally have been fatal but Henry, at the age of sixteen, bravely refused to leave the field of battle. The arrow head was lodged in his cheekbone and had to be painfully removed, leaving him with a ghastly scar. It was generally believed that his father had usurped the throne from his grandfather's first cousin Richard II, who had then died in mysterious circumstances and that his father became Henry IV of England, but after a prolonged illness which he thought was brought on by his stealing the throne, he died. Whereupon the Prince of Wales, at the age of twenty six became King.

After his Coronation as Henry V, he restored lands to the sons and families of the men his father had executed for treason. He also gave pardons to those who had opposed his father's claim to the throne, providing they swore allegiance to his own reign. Those pardoned however, were made to pay a modest fine which went into the treasury funds that made him popular with parliament. Our new King had even knighted some Noblemen whose fathers had been executed, but there was still some opposition to his right of inheritance. However this was not done openly but was simmering in the background which eventually came to a head. As you will see later in my story, Henry therefore decided that he would try to avoid a conspiracy of rebellious Nobles by raising an army to reclaim his lands in France.

Henry had convinced the Country and the church that his claims to the crown of France could be fought as a holy war, having quoted Saint Augustine's writings of scriptural justification (for the waging of war) but the interpretation was an excuse for the King to motivate the people, not that much motivation was needed.
I don't know the rights and wrongs of who owns a country, and having tried to read up on it, I found that it was too difficult to understand; so I hoped that William knew more about it than I did.

"Well," said William, "it's quite complicated but I shall try to keep it as short as possible. As you will no doubt know, no inheritance can be passed down to a woman or to her children, so when Charles IV of France died in 1328, his nearest male relative was his nephew Edward III ... the King of England. But Edward was the son of Isabella of France, who was Charles' sister and she was his only direct relative, therefore, as I have just said, she could not pass the claim on to her son and the next male heir in line was Philip of Valos who became Philip VI of France. At first, Edward accepted Philip as Charles' successor but nine years later, when he had a strong army, he decided to challenge his claim to the Throne of France and this is why we have been fighting the French ever since."

Lord John Thornbury is not often in Faversham as he is now a courtier to the King, spending all of his time in London, preparing for a decisive war with France and William has been attending to all of his brother's commitments in Kent. I knew it was only a matter of time before we continued the dispute with France, therefore all of the training and tournaments across England over the years, has given King Henry a strong army of archers, so when that time comes I am determined to be a part of it.

It is now the middle of April 1415, and I have learnt from William that King Henry, having been on the throne for two years, had gathered all his lords and noblemen to a great council held at Westminster. This was to tell them of his intention to invade France and reclaim his lands and that they should start raising an army.

"The King," said William, "has entered into contracts with peers, knights and others who have committed themselves to providing companies of men of an agreed size and composition. The persons who intend to form these companies are to be called captains and the men chosen to serve under them shall be called their retinue. A typical retinue will be comprised of thirty men at arms and ninety archers, for which the crown agreed to pay the total amount of wages to the captains. The captains, have signed indentures which shall last for twelve months commencing on the 1st of July 1415, and the first payment for the retinue shall be paid on this date three months in advance and the next three month payments, as well as the following three months will be paid together, at the end of the year."

As a banker, I already knew what the army payments were to be, but the normal soldier only knew what he would receive, and even though my payment of six pence a day will be far less than a man at arms I was still satisfied as I didn't really need the payment as an archer nor was I obliged to join the army, as there was no feudal system anymore, meaning that the English people could not be forced to fight for the King.

All Lords, Dukes, Earls, Barons and Knights shall fight as men at arms and their payment, at a daily rate shall be as follows:
Lords and Dukes shall be paid two nobles, Earls shall be paid one noble, Barons and Knights shall be paid four shillings, ordinary men at arms shall be paid twelve pence and mounted archers shall be paid six pence per day, finally archers with no horses shall receive four pence per day.

All men at arms will have to supply their own weapons and armour, and all archers will be expected to have a longbow, a quiver, knife and sword. Arrows will be supplied by the King, although like me, they will probably take some of their own. Out of their payment, the soldiers will have to pay one penny and a half per day back to the captain, who has to provide the food and drink for his retinue. Therefore, I shall be given the sum of one pound fourteen shillings one and a half pence in advance, for ninety one days.

To raise the money needed to send an army to France, parliament had passed a law requiring further taxation but this time it would be repaid. The amount for Faversham was the same as the tax collection (thirty three pounds five shillings). The King was also receiving loans from his Nobles and merchants, one of who would you believe was Richard Whittington to whom, my father sells his crops, and who was the subject of our rags to riches stories which I always thought were fairy tales; but I never connected Richard Whittington, who had been the Lord Mayor of London several times, with Dick Whittington and his cat.

At the age of twenty four I still hadn't been in any battles, so, when the word came out that archers were being recruited to fight in France, I jumped at the chance and went into Faversham to join a retinue. All of the local men including Blue and Tom had made their mark against their names and I signed my name.

I was to become an aid to the compiler of the retinue and in so doing confirmed my suspicion that nearly everybody was called John, or John changed to Jack. I knew all of the archers who had signed up from Faversham and soon learned the names and faces of the men who were from Sittingbourne and Whitstable that were to be in the same retinue as me. All over the county, men were signing up with any person who would indent to raise a retinue, and in Faversham, men were signing up with an Earl named Sir Gilbert Umfraville, who was known as the Earl of Kyme, which is somewhere up north..... I think.

I had never heard the names Umfraville or Kyme, but with tongue twisters like this, it was easier for everybody to call him the Earl of Kent. I am not sure if there is a real Earl of Kent but if this was a mistake, it was only made by our men, and Sir Gilbert was happy to leave it that way; therefore, the Earl of Kent was entitled - Captain of the North Kent retinue, with a force of thirty men at arms and ninety archers. My uncle James, due to his past experience at warring, was made a junior captain of thirty archers and automatically I became his second in command. Thomas Easton from Sittingbourne was also in command of thirty archers and as he was aware of Jack's skill with the longbow, so he made him his second in command.

The Duke made Fred Hitch, who I knew from Nottingham, the third junior captain but I never saw any of his thirty archers.

(I found out more about these missing men once we arrived at Southampton)

Thomas Easton was a well-known archer and had fought in many battles along with my father and Uncle James, but he was getting on a bit, and at fifty two years of age had given up competing in tournaments. He had lost the edge, due to his eyesight which was failing him, but he was well respected as an experienced leader. The whole of Faversham was on edge with the anticipation of not knowing what to expect in the future; but targets had been permanently set up on any spare land for archers to practice on.

My father was doing a good trade selling longbows and he was getting orders for twenty or more from some retinue captains, who perhaps wanted to have a stock of them in case any got damage or lost but the orders were only for the cheaper ones that had not been sanded down. Uncle James was also busy, making arrows that will be sold to the crown. Only this time he had been ordered not to round the shafts off but to leave them square, which made it a bit awkward to fit the three flights, until he took it upon his self to round off the last six inches. Furthermore, he was not to attach arrow heads because these would be made and fitted by the King's blacksmiths who would coming on the campaign.

Edward and Thomas have been making bank loans to the families of the men going to France, who would then repay the money once they have received their wages in Southampton, on July 1st and Thomas is coming with us to a place called Fareham, wherever that is? Then we will bring the repayments back to Faversham in a small cart that I have had made by a specialist in Canterbury. It has secret panels built into the sides so that money can be concealed from prying eyes.

I have even had, a not so secret compartment, built into the bottom of the cart that will not be difficult to find, which should satisfy any thieves should it be robbed. The cart will carry two money chests and I have made sure that everybody knew that they were empty, but secretly, I had other plans for getting this money back to my bank. I wanted to borrow Taff to pull the cart and made an agreement with Jamie promising him that if he loaned me his horse, I would, on my return from France, allow him to be the proud owner of Red. Jamie couldn't make the deal quick enough and Poor old Taff, who nobody seemed to love, was recruited to come to France.

It is now the middle of June and we have mustered along the Roman road, south of Faversham, with our horses, weapons and equipment. The hustle, bustle and excitement from the crowd was unbelievable, as besides the men who were about to set off for Southampton, there were all of their families and most of Faversham wishing us well. My brother John, who has to stay at home to tend the farm, was giving me last minute instructions for the tenth time, which I had also received from my father….. don't forget to be on your guard at all times, especially in wooded areas, never trust anyone, not even your friends as they will rob you when you are asleep….. Take care of your feet….. Try to keep yourself and your bowstring dry.

Yesterday we had all crowded into Saint Mary's church to hear our last Sunday sermon, receive the blessing of the church and to make our confessions and now that we are about to set off, Brother Arnold, who almost had tears in his eyes, said his farewell and that he wished he was coming with us. It seemed that we would never get started on the first leg of our journey but we managed to set off at eight am on the Monday, one hour later than planned. Jamie was more upset at saying goodbye to Red than he was to us and shouted to his father, "See you in two weeks' time then."

This nearly gave the game away, so I gave a quick glance to Uncle James and whispered to him, "Jamie will have to come with us now, as he cannot be trusted with the secret."

He nodded to me and shouted, "No Jamie, you've got it wrong, you won't see me in two weeks, it's Thomas that you will be seeing and its four weeks anyway as it will take two weeks to get there and two weeks for him to get back." "But how would you like to come with us and look after the horses?" he asked.

"Wow" said Jamie, with a beaming face, "do you really mean it?"

'That's a good idea," I said, "then he can be company for Thomas on his return to Faversham."

With that, Jamie borrowed Red and galloped off home for the few possessions he wanted to take with him.

As half of our thirty archers are on foot we shall be marching, hopefully, at twenty miles per day. Taff will be pulling my cart, whilst two other horses will be pulling the supply cart. After travelling a couple of miles along the London road, we eventually managed to get the trailing children to turn around and head back home, allowing our little army to relax and get on with the foot slogging. I was riding on Red and Thomas was driving my cart with Jamie sitting beside him, who you just cannot please, as he wanted to be riding Red with me in the cart!

Nobody knew the way to Southampton but we were first going to go along Watling Street to meet up with Thomas Easton and his archers at Sittingbourne, then head south for Maidstone, which was a town well-known to most of us, then ask our way as we went along. There were a lot of opinions regarding the total distance we shall have to cover but it was generally believed to be about one hundred and thirty miles.

The Duke of Kent had left for London several weeks earlier, taking his men at arms with him as well as Fred Hitch and also I suppose, his archers, but I didn't see any of them as they left. All I saw was the Duke's armoured men and his servants; we were to join him in Fareham and look for his banner when we arrived. Every town and village we passed through gave us a warm hero's welcome and the food and drink provided by the Duke was hardly needed. Some of our men were even given roofs over their heads whenever we stopped for the night, but I had my tent with me which I shared with Jamie and Thomas. Our journey took us through, Maidstone, Tunbridge and East Grinstead and we eventually arrived in Chichester on Saturday….. Six days after leaving Faversham; having travelled over one hundred miles, but there was no hero's welcome in Chichester, nor was there any free food or drink.

With a week to go, before we were expected to arrive at Fareham, Thomas Easton and Uncle James decided that, with only about a twenty mile march ahead of us, we could rest up and make camp on the outskirts of the town, at a place called Fishbourne. Just for a couple of days, and as it was, inevitable that more money had to be loaned to some of the men to purchase ale.
Chichester was full of soldiers travelling to Southampton but the town was fed up with all of the rowdiness and would be glad to see the back of us, even though we were going to fight the French for them.

"What do you mean, fight the French for us?" roared the landlord of the Fountain Inn, when he heard talk of this.

"When have we ever gained anything from fighting the French? We have been continually raided by them and have never received a penny for our troubles. It's only the rich of this country that benefit from these wars, not us common folk who have to do the fighting." he bellowed, with nods from all of his regulars.

I recalled that this is more or less, one of the reasons why Brother Arnold had become a monk and I wondered, *is it right or wrong to fight and die so that other people can get rich, in fact what am I doing fighting the French, when I am half French myself?*

And the landlord was not finished yet.....

"We send armies over there to rob and kill the ordinary peasants and they do the same to us, so who gains? Not the poor people that's for sure."

It was obvious that there was bad feeling in the town, as fist fights and brawls were breaking out all over the place. I was aware that a lot of the towns and villages along the south coast had periodically been raided by small parties of Frenchmen, who plundered all the peasants possessions and killed anybody who opposed them; which is what my father had been doing when he was wounded in their country, so it was no wonder that they felt bitter. I still wanted to test my bravery against the French and to back out now would be classed as desertion so I'll just have to only kill rich people and not rob the poor.

Fortunately however, not all of Chichester's ale houses had the same opinion as that of the Fountain Inn and our business was given to the many welcoming innkeepers who were only too willing to take our money. Jack and Tom wanted me to go into the seedier area of town but as usual I was not interested in smelly females and wandered off on my own along the estuary.

Was there something wrong with me? I wondered, as I strolled along the waterway towards the harbour. I don't like to drink a lot of ale and my friends were starting to think that I am not interested in women. Well that's not true for a start! It's just the smell of an unwashed body that I can't stand. I am a red blooded male, as I had already proved with Carlotta, so when I see a nice girl I am no different than any other man, until I get up close to her. I can't blame Jack or Tom for being males….. But don't ever, let me catch William doing this sort of thing! After all he is married to my sister.

Come on Crispin, stop feeling sorry for yourself.

More money was being borrowed from Thomas and it looked like some people would be handing over their entire wages once they were paid. But don't blame me for making a small charge on these loans because that's how I make my living and Thomas still has to be paid, not counting the cost of his and Jamie's upkeep.

The Duke had made it my job to purchase supplies for both groups of archers as we journeyed to Southampton and despite having been given five pounds to buy fresh provisions, what food and drink we had acquired was now almost used up, with only two nobles, in small coins, to last us until we reached Fareham, where my responsibility was supposed to end.

It was now Thursday and I suggested to our leaders that we get a move on and travel the last leg of our journey which would give us a couple of days to find our retinue and get settled in. I was not in charge of our little army but Thomas and Uncle James agreed with me, so I went into Chichester the same day with the supply cart and spent the last of the money on bread, vegetables, meat and ale for the final march to our mustering point. On our arrival at Fareham on Friday, we had to pass through a crossroad where a group of guides were directing people to their respective retinue camps, and we were told to travel south along the river Hamble towards a place called Peel Common which overlooked the river Solent. We were to look for the Earl of Kent's banner, which I have seen before, and know that it's a large flag with a yellow five-leaved flower on a red background that is covered in small yellow cross signs.

What a gathering, I had never seen so many people in one place at the same time since going to Nottingham, and all of the fields along the coast between Portsmouth and Southampton were full of soldiers, who were either milling about, sleeping, cooking or gambling….. Not to mention smelling!
I now understood the importance of banners, as a large flag is easily recognised above the heads of a host of people; and we soon found our mustering point. Most of The Duke of Kent's men at arms were already there and had chosen a good campsite on a rise overlooking the river, but there was still no sign of Fred Hitches thirty archers, and I was beginning to wonder if they ever existed….. He was there but his men were nowhere to be seen.

My responsibility should now have ended but I was met by my sister's husband who had been waiting on and off for several days for the remaining part of the Duke of Kent's retinue to arrive. William was one of the Duke's messenger riders and had been in his service ever since the retinue was formed in Faversham; having travelled with him and his men to London then on here to Porchester Castle where the Nobility were staying. He told me that I was to travel the mile distance around the river to the castle the next day, where I was to assist in gathering the retinue's payments that will be paid out the day after that … Sunday the first of July. I was also to meet up with the Duke, who, William said, had a special job for me.

"What special job is that?" I asked.

William only smiled and replied, "Wait and see… but I think you will like it."

Well, as you can imagine, I was wondering what was in store for me as a dozen men at arms escorted me and Thomas to the castle. Jamie didn't want to be left out and the cheeky so and so rode Red, whilst I had to ride in the cart along the dirt track road. At the age of fifteen he was too young to go to war, much to his disgust, but I felt proud that he could read and write, so I let him get away with it.

Porchester Castle is at the end of a promontory, overlooking Portsmouth harbour with the sea coming right up to its formidable walls, which has provided a strong defence against French raiding parties in the past. King Henry was in residence, as I could see his banner depicting the golden lion of England and the fleur de lis of France flying over the fortress.

"The King wants me to form a special force of three hundred of the finest archers in England." said Sir Gilbert Umfraville, when I met up with him speaking to me in French, with a distinct Aquitaine accent. William has told me all about you and your skill as an archer and I know that you are educated and that you speak French like a native." He said.

"Oui Monsieur" I replied, in my Norman accent.

"Well" said Sir Gilbert, "I have chosen you to recruit these men and train them. I think you are the man we need, so what do you say?"

"But how will this, affect payments?" I asked, "Will these men get an increase in wages?"

"Two pence a day." replied the Duke. "That's why the King wants this special force setting up as soon as possible, so that the payments can be made straight away. You yourself will receive one shilling a day as an archer at arms and your selected men will also be paid this extra amount tomorrow. Furthermore, every retinue captain has already been told that he must release any chosen man, whether he likes it or not, and that if there are any arguments they will be settled by the King himself."

It was also important that all of my special archers had a horse each and Sir Gilbert informed me that mounts would be loaned to my men from the Kings stable until such time they were needed in France. I couldn't leave it at that, and the Duke finally agreed that I could appoint six men at an additional two pence per day to be in command of fifty archers each.

**

CHAPTER SEVENTEEN

Tom, Jack and Fred Hitch were obviously the first three of my special archers and this was when I found out about the missing thirty archers from our retinue. I don't know if other retinue captains were doing the same as the Duke of Kent, but Sir Gilbert had indented for ninety archers when in fact he only had sixty. The other thirty men were his household staff, who he should have been paying himself. It was not my place to question this business but I wondered if the King knew about it? This was probably the reason why my father had received orders for so many cheap longbows, as scrawny servants, clerks and other hangers on were walking about toting longbows across their shoulders.

Whilst these negotiations were taking place, I had asked Jamie to watch out into the harbour for my father and the Faversham fishing boat which I had secretly arranged to meet. Jamie already knew of my plan for getting the loan money back to Faversham, hence the reason we had to bring him along with us, as I intended to put the repayment money on board this boat on Sunday night and have Thomas sail home to Faversham with it. The boat turned up as expected, having sailed around the coast past Dover.

"We have already been here a day and it has taken us all this time to find you." My father said. "We have delivered our stock of oats and flour and found out that you were at the castle."

These supplies had been ordered by the Duke, from my friend Tom, whilst he was still in Faversham, which meant that I only had to pay a minimum fare of six pence for Thomas' return trip to Faversham, and now Jamie of course. Word soon spread about the special force of archers and men were coming from all along the coast to join up, one of whom was my joint winner from Nottingham….. Glynn Flint. Another was Guy Jones also a contestant from Nottingham, both of whom did not have to prove themselves to me and I immediately made them section leaders, this left me with one leader to find; but firstly, the payments had to be made to the army, which to my surprise, was completed in a couple of hours because the retinue captains and I had collected the money on Saturday.

I met with my five lieutenants, as I now called them, to decide how to select our force and although I was in complete charge, it was my intention to involve my little team in all decisions. Fred Hitch was relieved that he didn't have to lie anymore about his non-existent archers.

First of all, it was essential that each man could pull ninety pounds and prove that he can shoot ten arrows in a minute, of which five had to hit the target set at thirty feet. The testing began on Sunday afternoon, using four longbows that we had tested in the same way as my father's longbow. As the light was starting to fade on that long Sunday afternoon, we ended up with three hundred and fifty men who could pull the required thirty two inches or over, of which sixty men pulled well over one hundred pounds and they were instantly signed up as long range archers.

In the meantime, Thomas and Jamie had collected the repayments owed to the bank, which were placed in the chests ready to be sneaked aboard the fishing boat that night, along with both of them. Well, that was the plan….. But now as the chests were stashed away and it was time for the boat to depart, Jamie and Thomas wanted to join the army. I was willing to allow Thomas to come along as my helper and would continue to pay him and supply his victuals, but we had to lock Jamie in the boat's hold so that he would be forced to return to Faversham with my father. I told the captain that once it was known he was carrying the bank funds, he may well be pirated therefore he must not, under any circumstance return to Peel common. So I was much relieved as I watched the boat sail away, allowing me to concentrate on sorting out the finest archers from those chosen.

Now that the soldiers had money in their pockets there was a carnival atmosphere all along the fields between Portsmouth and Southampton with feasting, drinking, gambling, robbery and violence. Local merchants were taking advantage of our needs by selling wine and ale at double the normal prices, so it won't be long before a lot of the men will have completely spent what wages they had received. All that night there was complete havoc around the camps with several murders happening as the violence got out of control and as expected, my cart had been attacked but hadn't been damaged.

More men were coming forward, in the hope of being chosen for the special force and we now had ninety men who could pull over one hundred pounds. These men were formed into the long range distance archers, which I have named Blue section commanded by Jack, alias 'Blue'. I wanted to make sure that complete discipline was instilled in all of my men and introduced a keep-fit program where every man, including my lieutenants, had to run at least a mile every morning and if a person was unwilling to do this, he would no longer be a special archer. I left it to Jack to decide what his men would have to practice but I wanted each of his men to reach a distance of at least two hundred and eighty yards in non-windy conditions.

On the Monday, Tom Miller, Guy Jones, Fred Hitch and Glyn Flint continued selecting men, which now there were over three hundred to choose from, not counting Jack's ninety men. However, before the final selection, all of the men had to agree to carry out any orders without question. I still didn't have my last lieutenant and I am sure that certain men kept trying to pull thirty two inches on our testing longbows. I knew that it would not be so simple to get the men to keep clean and Jack was no better than the rest at washing his body or clothes, so I just hoped that eventually I could prove that washing and keeping clean was not harmful.

One hundred and fifty men who could hit a target, shaped like a man, seven times out of ten at fifty yards were eventually chosen as the finest archers. From the men still trying to enlist, the last sixty were formed into what became Tom's golden corn colourer section, to fulfil the total number of men I was allowed to muster. Jack had ninety men with blue arm bands, Glynn had fifty men with red arm bands, Guy had fifty with green bands, Fred's fifty men had Black, and Tom's men had Yellow. I was able to have these arm bands made in Southampton at a cost of five shillings, which I paid for myself and they became a status symbols which everybody wore with pride and it looked like I wouldn't need a sixth lieutenant after all. There were eighty men all of who were able to ride but had no horses, so these were reluctantly provided by the Duke and although their mounts were not the best of the bunch they were better than nothing. Some of my men were showing resentment at having to train every day because the rest of the army were just lolling about and generally doing nothing; but once they were told that they could do the same by giving up their two pence per day and go back to their retinues, they all settled down to steady training and keeping fit.

Four days after the army was paid, Uncle James came to see me about a wretch of a youth (Jamie) who had jumped ship before it had sailed. He had been caught drawing food rations from a retinue on this side of the river Hamble near Southampton and had only been discovered when a captain collared him drinking unpaid for ale. Jamie admitted that he had escaped from the fishing boat as soon as he was locked-up and had disappeared out of sight. I was forced to pay six pence for his stolen food, so it looked like I was stuck with him. There was no point in being angry with him as I would have done exactly the same….. But what was I to do with this whelp?

It was William who solved the problem.

"There's a position in the King's personal retinue, for a stable boy to look after some of the royal mounts." he said, "as one boy has a broken leg having been kicked by rouge horse, and I know that Jamie is good with horses."

"So Jamie, what do you say to that?" I asked.

"I want to stay with you and be one of your chosen archers." he sulkily replied.

"You are too young," I repeated for the hundredth time, "so the only way you will get to France is to work for the King…..you tell him Uncle James."

"Jamie will be with the baggage train," he said, "and working for the King would be the safest place of all, as he shall leave a strong guard on his possessions."

I was not convinced that this was a good idea, but if Jamie's father said it was alright, who was I to argue? But as it turned out, this arrangement was to prove useful to me. Besides William feeding information back to me from the royal court, Jamie could do the same; so Jamie became part of the Kings retinue and joined three other young boys, all with six horses each to look after, but there were over three hundred horses in the King's stable, and Jamie was looking after some of the less valuable steeds.

He got to love this job and had discovered that the horse that had broken the boys leg was a thoroughbred, which was thought to have gone bad, but the stallion named Lightning, had a cut mouth and only needed a special padded bit, as an ordinary metal bit kept on rubbing the sore which was not being allowed to heal. This wound had never been noticed before and when the King's master of horse discovered Jamie's natural ability with horses, he doubled his wages to two pence per day and put him to work with his own charges.

Towards the end of July there were ugly rumours going about that King Henry had been killed. If this was true, there would be no invasion of France and the army would have to repay the wages they no longer possessed. Fortunately, the King had learnt of a plot to kill him and immediately arrested the three ring leaders - Richard of Conisburgh, Henry Scrope and Sir Thomas Grey.

William told me that there were some Nobles who wanted to remove Henry from the throne and replace him with Edmund Mortimer the fifth Earl of March, as they felt that Edmund had a superior claim.

"Edmund, had been the presumptive heir to Richard II" said William, "and Henry's father had kept him in custody to prevent a revolt" William said. "But, our new King, on his accession, had released Edmund and restored his estates, so that when the three ringleaders disclosed their plan to Edmund, shortly before it was to take effect, Edmund told Henry of the assassination plot."

"Henry doesn't want his people to dwell on his father's usurpation" William continued, "so he has put out the story that these Nobles were Lollard's, thus hiding the real reason for the planned murder, but keep this to yourself" he concluded.
The Lollard movement was still festering in England which I had no intention of joining, but I was uncertain about a lot of the people I knew, including my brother John, who was on call to be part of a retaining army that would remain in England ready to combat any attempts of a takeover whilst our invading army was in France. Therefore, on the third of August, the first of the plotters, Sir Thomas Grey of Heston was hung drawn and quartered. This being the sentence for treason that was carried out on a commoner. He was strung up, partially hanged and then before actual death, was cut down from the gallows and carried to a table where his private parts were cut off and burnt

before his eyes. Then his stomach was cut open and all of his innards drawn out, followed up by the chopping off of his head and the cutting up of the rest of his body.

William, who had to witness this execution said, "Sir Thomas was doing the rope dance with piss running down his twitching legs and when removed from the gallows was choking away, trying to scream as he was cut up then ripped apart. The other two plotters, Richard Earl of Cambridge and Henry Lord Scrope of Masham, being of the upper class, were beheaded two days later." He said.

The training of my men was complete and I could rely on them to do exactly as ordered, which put me in mind of my grandfather's tug of war team where everybody pulled together and took orders from one man, which was how I intended my men to behave, with each man relying on his comrades. I was even getting some men to wash themselves as we rested after my river crossing training.
The fording of a river was dangerous for an army because all the enemy had to do was wait on the far bank and then attack the men as they waded across, so it was essential that my long range archers covered their crossing from the nearside bank, even if it involved shooting over their heads. There must be at least twenty thousand men camped along the Solent, most of who were English and Welsh, however the King had brought over from France five hundred men at arms from his lands in Aquitaine.

Leaders of retinues had been told to spread false rumours that our army would be landing at Calais, this being the obvious choice due to our stronghold there, so it was likely that there were probably French spies mingling with our men who were trying to discover the King's intentions. Not many people knew where the actual landing would be, including me, but my guess was that we would land close to Eu, then march on to Paris. If this was to be the case, I was worried that my French grandparents would be in danger, even though King Henry had given strict orders that none of his French people were to be harmed unless they put up a fight. But I didn't put much faith in this, as who knows what an invading army would do if they are set loose, when you consider that they could rob and kill their own men whilst still along the shore of the Solent.

**

CHAPTER EIGHTEEN

The army has been kicking its heels for six weeks and I just couldn't understand why it was taking so long to set sail, until William told me that King Henry had been awaiting the outcome of an attempt to invade England by the Scots, which had been repulsed by Sir Robert Umfraville (the uncle our captain). But, at last, we set sail for France in the afternoon of Sunday the 11th of August; once the King had sailed in the royal barge to his ship the Trinity Royal, which was festooned with all manner of Pennons and royal banners.

Things had been hectic, with the frantic last minute loading of what must be over a thousand ships carrying, siege engine's, carts, horses, cattle, sheep, pigs, barrels of ale and all that is needed to keep an army on campaign; along with cooks, bakers, stonemasons, carpenters, wheelwrights, tunneller's and blacksmiths, plus all sorts of tradesmen. There were also a considerable number of surgeons to attend the expected wounded, which has bolstered the army's confidence in our King. We even have priests and monks to attend to our souls. Sailors had been using large derricks, pulleys and winches to hoist the heavy equipment on board the ships, along with animals that would not climb the gang planks.

They also loaded, massive cannon that will fire huge stones, which only German mercenaries know how to shoot. I only hoped that they don't go off when I am about, as having seen a few practice shots they looked more dangerous to the handlers than the enemy, not to mention the loud noise that they make as they are fired. I was sailing on the Pelican, which followed the King's ship out into the English Channel.

About five thousand men have been left on the shores of the Solent as there was not enough room for them on any of the ships, Thomas my helper is one of them as well as Taff and my cart, but I figured that boats returning from France for more supplies will pick them up and convey them across the channel; and to make sure I get them back I have asked Thomas to load the cart up with horse fodder so that it would be shipped across to me. Jamie is on board the King's ship along with William and his brother Lord John Thornbury and now that we are afloat, word has filtered down that the fleet is sailing more or less directly south to the river Seine.

My knowledge of the French coast is pretty good as our family always travelled to Eu on boats heading towards the Seine, so I figured that we were going to have a march of about one hundred and twenty miles to Paris, but as the river meanders snake like north from the estuary past the town of Rouen, marching on the that side of the river would increase the distance. Therefore, I thought we would land on the south banks and have a straight march to the capital city.

I must give the King his due as before we sailed any traveller's that had been to France had been asked to give what knowledge they had about the French coast line to his planners, which is why I thought the landing might be at Eu, as my information had been taken down in great detail, but now that I think about it, there wasn't much secrecy shown by the planners, so there must be French spies at court as well as amongst the army.

Sunday night was spent sleeping wherever we could on deck, having been ordered to only eat food that didn't need cooking and not to start any fires on the ships. But as usual some people would not be told, thinking they knew better than anybody else, resulting in a boat close to us catching fire and almost sinking. On Monday afternoon we could see the shores of France and the fleet of ships arrived off the coast of Normandie around five pm that evening. The King's flagship anchored in the river estuary whilst the smaller boats lay just off the coast, ready to be run up onto the northern beaches of the Seine the next morning.

When dawn broke, there was no enemy to be seen and the men just couldn't wait to get onto dry land, but we had been ordered that nobody was to disembark until the King had gone ashore alone. We later learned that Henry had waded through the shallow water in full armour and fell on his knees praying for a victory over his enemies, which gave everybody a morale boost….. As the King had intended. After which, I was one of the first to wade towards the shore along with red section led by Glynn, and fifty men at arms to make a beach head, but as there was no opposition the signal went out that it was safe for the army to land.

From past experience, I knew that the sea would leave a salt residue in my clothing, which once dry would scratch my skin. So I found a fresh stream and soaked the salt out of them and washed my body at the same time, using some of the lye soap that I had brought with me, then sat half naked in the sun whilst my clothes dried.

The army had already started the mammoth task of unloading the boats and I was pleased that my duty was to protect the beach head; but this didn't last for long as I had to take my turn helping with the unloading, whilst Jack's Blue section and other men at arms did the watching. The water was about a foot deep where the landing boats had ground into the shingle beach but as the men stepped into the water, to wade ashore, they thought that the land was rocking underfoot causing them to lose their balance and fall over creating a lot of merriment and laughter.

King Henry had repeated his orders that the local population were his subjects and that there was to be no stealing or looting of property and that no harm was to be caused to his people, unless they were armed or put up a fight. There was to be no theft from Churches and the army must show discipline at all times.

The unloading took three days and the shore was littered with stores and siege equipment but now that the landings are complete, Henry has sent his Heralds to a walled garrison close by, called Harfleur, inviting them to surrender, which was as expected refused.

My men were too valuable to be used as labourers, pulling the siege train towards the town and we fanned out over the hill from the beach to foray down the slope towards the fortification. This is when we had our first sight of the enemy as a group of French horsemen, about thirty strong, came out of the town towards us. They were heavily armoured and looked determined to attack.

This was when my disciplined men started to show their worth, as the natural tendency would be to charge straight at them but Glynn and Guy, the leaders of red and green sections, looked to me for orders and their men looked to them.

"They won't stand and fight" I shouted, "there are too many of us, so don't waste your energy, just advance slowly in line ready to shoot arrows at them if they come within two hundred yards."
The French could see that it would be a losing battle for them, so they halted their mounts out of arrow range, but a couple of head strong knights galloped forward at a thunderous pace, with arrows falling all around them and I couldn't help wondering at their luck, until one their horses was injured causing them and the rest of the French horsemen to flee, to the cheers of my men.

"That's not good enough," I angrily shouted, "You have wasted all those arrows on just two men."

"Aye" said Glynn with a big smile on his face, "but we can go and pick them up again, can't we?"

I didn't want to make my lieutenants lose face with their men and quietly drew them aside asking, "And what if we are unable to pick them up again?"

I must admit, it never occurred to me until then that once we had run out of arrows we would lose the advantage of our long range weapons.

"You're right," said Guy, looking at Glynn for agreement, "we shall have to sort out some system of preserving arrows."

I then left it to them to select a few chosen men at any one time, to ward off individual challenges, and realised that this contact with the enemy had given us valuable on the job training….. Don't tell anybody, but I fired four arrows myself!

Harfleur is at the end of a valley through which two rivers, the Lezarde and the Leure join each other and flow into the river Seine, but the garrison have blocked their flow creating a lake at the northern end of the town. The distance around the perimeter of Harfleur is about three miles, which was fully enclosed by a high wall, with what looked like a couple of dozen strong towers spaced out at intervals. There are three gateways, which we eventually were able to name the Montivilliers gate on the north eastern side of the town, the Rouen gate on the southern side and the main entrance the Leure gate on the west side. Outside each of these gates, the defenders had built additional wooden Barbican fortifications.

The number of civilians in Harfleur was not known, but it was believed to be about two thousand, and from what information we had, there were no more than one hundred soldier's to defend them; but with the twenty foot high walls it would not be a simple task to capture this fortification, without a considerable loss of life.

Harfleur

A canal linked to the Seine had a chain blocking the entrance to the town's harbour and the eastern side of the town could only be reached from the west side by boat or along the river, whilst the northern side of Harfleur was protected by the lake. Therefore, there were only two possible camping sites, the west and east sides of the town. The King chose the west side, facing the Leure gate and his brother the Duke of Clarence was to make camp on the east side, between the Montivilliers gate and the road to Rouen. Due to the flooding, a circuitous route around this newly formed lake will have to be made, passing close to the fortified town of Montivilliers, two and a half miles north of Harfleur.

Therefore on the Saturday night, the Duke of Clarence, the Earl of Kent, a detachment of mounted men at arms, along with myself and two sections of my mounted archers, set off to reach the far side of Harfleur.

Montivilliers made a small attempt to harass us, sending out a detachment of what looked like fifty fully armoured men on horseback, but they soon realised that they were outnumbered and retreated back into the town after losing six men wounded, despite most of my archers holding their fire, waiting for orders. And so ended our second clash with the enemy, which I must admit was exhilarating and boosted our confidence, however some of the Duke's men at arms had galloped forward to meet the French and one man had been killed, whilst another was badly wounded from a crossbow bolt.

As we approached the north east side of Harfleur, a group of wagons was spotted heading towards the Montivilliers gate which the Duke of Clarence ordered me to capture. The wagons were loaded with provisions for the town and it was unbelievable that this transport had no protection. As there were no armed men amongst the wagoner's, we allowed them to go free, thanking them for their very kind gifts to us!

Then, just as it was starting to get light, we saw a couple of hundred mounted French soldiers riding towards the Rouen Gate. Unfortunately, my detachment was about half a mile short of their arrival and we were disappointed at not being able to loose off a few arrows at them before they had chance to enter the garrison. The supply transport must have been for them, so at least we had reduced their stocks and improved ours.

It took the best part of the day for the rest of the Duke of Clarence's three thousand men to reach the eastern side of Harfleur, meaning that the town was now fully besieged. Once again, the King sent his Heralds back into Harfleur, offering them another chance to surrender but the town leaders refused, saying that their monarch, King Charles was sending a relief army from Rouen. So it seemed likely that men were getting in and out of the town undetected. Therefore, to make sure that the French had no more spies passing through the English lines, the King ordered that the red cross of Saint George was to be painted on the front and backs of all of his men surcoats, including knights and that any spy caught, was to be hanged.

But as my men were to roam the country side, it was decided to issue us with removable surcoats with a red cross painted on, which would give us a slight advantage should we meet up with a French patrol and be mistaken for Frenchmen. More men were sent over to the east side of the town and a defence line was made across the Rouen and Montivilliers roads but no French army came anywhere near us. So we settled down to a boring siege where very little was going on…..Well, very little for the ordinary soldier or archer that is but my orders were to scout along the river Seine towards Rouen and collect whatever food supplies we could find.

Rowing boats had been brought from the fleet and put onto the lake, north of the town, which made it easy to link up both sides and I saw William, as he crossed over, with orders for the Duke. He told me that fresh supplies had come from England along with Thomas and Taff.

"What about my cart" I asked.

"I don't know about that, said William, "does it matter?"

William was not aware of my secret compartments, so I told him it was important to me that I had my own transport, because on capturing the French supply wagon's, there were two chests of French coins which I had no intention of handing over to the Duke of Clarence, or to my retinue captain the Earl of Kent, as I wanted to keep this money to distribute to my men.

William said, "Leave it with me Cris, I shall talk to Jack and find out a way to get Thomas and the cart across to you, but they will probably have to come right around the lake."

On discovering these chests, I had four of my men hide them before they were seen. I knew that it wouldn't be possible for anybody to buy anything with this booty but it was better for us to have it rather than the already rich Nobility. However, I was able to cross the lake myself to talk with Jack and we made arrangements that when he came out on patrol the next day, towards Montivilliers, I was to meet up with him at the northern end of the lake and be reunited with my horse and cart which was full of the much welcomed horse fodder.

It would have been foolish not to pay out some of these French coins to my archers straight away, so each man was given the amount of one Sou and six denier (eighteen pennies), on the understanding that if they were asked how they got this money they must say that they had changed their English money into French coins with me; as it was well known that I was a banker and that everybody would assume I had brought French coins with me from England.

Well, if the retinue captains could charge for non-existent archers, why shouldn't we gain something? Not to mention having had to pay for some of the food supplies that we were now having to find for ourselves.

What I didn't tell the men however, was that the payments had only used up one chest of coins, the other coins went into the sides of my cart, which only my trusted friends knew about. Not that I wanted to keep this money for myself, it was there to pay the local peasants for any livestock we were to take, even though King Henry had allowed us to collect provisions without payment, in fact, I paid twice as much as I thought their stock were worth.

Now that the town has been besieged on the east and west sides, with the lake blocking the north side and a salt marsh on the south, it was just a matter of waiting to see what the French would do. From what information our spies had discovered, it was expected that a large force would come from Rouen, to relieve the town. We even learnt of a French army that were waiting on the southern side of the estuary, at Honfleur, five miles directly across the mouth of the Seine; to watch for what they thought might be the expected invasion landing site (as I had done). The Duke of Clarence ordered men to keep a close eye on the eastern approaches, with strong mounted scouting parties of archers and men at arms being sent out to follow the road along the northern bank of the Seine, as far as the first bend towards a village called Tancarville. But there was no opposing enemy, only occasional scouting parties who were only too eager to vanish after short skirmishes, during which, there were no deaths on either side and very little injury. In fact it was just like 'playing at soldiers' where a good time was being had by all, with much shouting, jeering and taunting.

Most of the local peasants kept well out of our way, except the old people, who once they knew we meant them no harm and that we would not rob them, gave us food and ale. They even encouraged the remaining villagers to return to their homes, but I knew that not all of our scouting parties would be as willing to make friends as my men were and that once on the loose, they would plunder what they could. I became quite friendly with some of these people and speaking to them in French, I learnt that three hundred men, most likely the ones we had been unable to stop entering Harfleur, had come around from the other side of the river Seine, which they had been guarding against any landing by us.

The German mercenaries had a dozen large cannon lined up facing the western side of the town and were beginning to fire huge stones over and at the walls some of which weighed as much as two or three sacks of corn. As well as the cannons there were large catapults on both sides of the town, that were hurling stones over the walls as well. After two weeks of bombardment, the defences were beginning to crumble, with big gaps appearing in the walls.

William had reported to me that King Henry was deliberately launching night bombardments to keep the towns inhabitants awake hopefully forcing them to submit, and felt confident that the town would soon surrender. I was on the far side of the town, and the noise from the guns was keeping me awake, so it must have been worse on the west side and terrifying for the towns people.

The continual watching and waiting for something to happen was creating boredom throughout the army, and drunkenness was getting more and more noticeable, with men gambling and stealing to get additional supplies of ale over their daily ration. My men, were lucky as they were able to leave the camps on patrol to forage for supplies but the ordinary soldier was not allowed to roam off into the surrounding country in search of loot.

There was lots of digging going on by Welsh miners on the east side of the town, where they were trying to tunnel under the walls; which I didn't put much faith in but they were providing us with plenty of earth and sand to create protective mounds. I didn't get to see these works, which I believe were quite extensive, but as far as I could see, they had no effect on the siege whatsoever and in my opinion, it was just a waste of time and effort. The King then had the story put about that before he embarked on his rightful claim to the French throne, the French Dauphine Louis, who was acting for his father King Charles VI, had sent his ambassador to England with a present of tennis balls for him to play with, rather than waging war on France. Henry now proclaimed that he had found a suitable racquet and has changed the balls to gun stones to throw back to him, which gave our army a laugh.

I was determined to do something similar and had a word with the Duke of Kent, mentioning that Jack and I could shoot two flaming arrows joined together with something attached that would glow in the night. Sir Gilbert was in favour of the idea and Jack came over to my side of the lake where we made three pairs of joined arrows, with large linen flags tied to the wire depicting the red cross of Saint George.

That night we crept as far as we dared up to the fortification, lit the arrows and fired the first one high into the sky over the French wall. When our men saw this fiery emblem, they gave a great cheer and much to their delight, the French thought that an attack was coming. Then, two minutes later, we fired the second arrows followed straight away by the third, which received the same adulation as the first arrows. The cheering was so loud that it was heard by the men on the east side of Harfleur, who wondered what was happening, so when the joke was relayed to them by Jack on his return, they wanted a repeat performance on their side of town the next night. Only this time, other left handed and right handed archers wanted to do the shooting, resulting in dozens of arrows being fired which lost some of the effect on the French defenders.

"What else can you do?" asked King Henry when I was summoned to his presence. "The men are still laughing but I don't want my archers to waste any more of their arrows."

This was the first time I has ever spoken to the King and I felt it to be a great honour.

"Well, my liege." I said, "At our local tournament in Faversham my friend and I could shoot arrows into a wooden cart, in such a way that a man could climb up them."

"Just like Robyn Hode did to the drawbridge at Nottingham Castle," laughed the King. "And the Leure gate barbican is your target, where you can paint another red cross at the top?"

Easier said than done, for a start, we had no large iron bodkin arrow heads and no small William to climb them, but nothing was impossible once the King had sanctioned the enterprise. One of his blacksmiths was only too willing to forge the arrow heads to Jack's instruction. Whilst this was being done, Jack noticed that other blacksmiths were casting dozens of what looked like lead arrow heads.

"Why do you think they are making these?" he asked.

"Didn't your girlfriend's father in Nottingham have arrow heads like this?" I asked back.

"That's right, but they wouldn't hurt an armoured man, they are really only any good for distance." Jack replied.

But it was only when we started to come to grips with the enemy that we found out what they were to be used for.

The part of Robyn Hode was to be played by a dithering page named Harold, who was ordered to be the Painter, and a barn door was found to practice on. Harold was a nimble young boy of sixteen and he quickly mastered the climbing during daylight, but was scared stiff of having to do it at night under the noses of the French.

To make things safer for us, a number of ladders were to be carried forward, at the lake end of the town wall, just out of crossbow range, with the pretence of an attack to draw the attention of the defenders away from the Leure gate. There was just enough light coming from their burning torches for us to creep to within twenty yards of the wooden barbican to start shooting our arrows. The thud of their impact was causing us some concern, but we managed to create the steps without drawing any attention, then all three of us crept to the bottom of our readymade ladder.

Harold climbed the arrows, pulled the paint pot up on a rope and got on with painting the large Red Cross at the top of this barricade, whilst Jack and I stood guard just in case a head bobbed over the top. Once Harold had finished his task and lowered his paint pot, all he had to do was waggle out the arrows as he descended. Then with some relief, especially from Harold, we all crept back to the safety of our camp to await the reaction the following morning, and what a reaction it was.

The English army were flabbergasted at the large cross, wondering how it had been painted so high up on the barbican, without the French knowing. They kept pointing and jeering at the defenders who had no idea at first what all the laughing was about, until some brave soul leaned over the structure to have a look. None of our men took a shot at him but when efforts were made to remove the Red Cross, some of my finest archers had great sport shooting at them, and it took the best part of the morning for the defenders to poor hot tar over our handy work.

The delighted King presented our artist with two shillings and Harold became famous around the camp, basking in the glory and telling everybody how he had bravely defied the French. Me and Jack received Henry's thanks but no glory or reward came our way.

**

CHAPTER NINETEEN

The English army continued to sit and wait for something to happen, taking their turn at watching the French garrison. But soon after the siege had commenced, sickness had begun to take its toll on our army due to the lack of sanitation, and the streams close by to the camps were starting to fill up with human waste, which was not filtering out into the river. Further to this, digging into the surrounding land was uncovering previously buried dung, resulting in a vast amount of flies buzzing from the uncovered Merde onto any exposed food.

Most of my men could now see the sense in keeping clean and that by being away from the main camps on scouting duties allowed them to keep healthy, but it was still a waste of time trying to get other people to wash themselves and the stench of human waste and unwashed bodies could be smelled from miles away.

September is upon us and men are starting to die of camp sickness and these deaths were causing panic throughout the army, what is more, the illness was not just confined to the ordinary soldier as the Nobility were also falling sick. Then in the middle of the month Richard Courtney, the Bishop of Norwich died.
This caused a fearful response from the Nobles, who thought that they were immune from such maladies; but the sickness was getting worse and if any blood was seen in people's watery waste, there was a good chance that they would get sicker and die. Even the King's brother, the Duke of Clarence was taken ill, and eventually had to be invalided back to England. Then it was noticed that a lot of soldiers were starting to desert, especially the men from the English region of Aquitaine, who, being on their own soil of France could

easily slip away. Out of their original force of five hundred, there were only about fifty remaining.

The King and his council had set up their pavilion tents on a rise, up wind from the smell of the tip heap camping sites, which I was also glad to be away from, so I pity the men who had to put up with these conditions day in and day out, but I felt sure that with a little bit more cleanliness the army would have had less problems. I have even seen men using bare hands to eat their food, after having a dump and cleaning their arses! So the death rate can only get worse. Thankfully, most of my men could now see the sense in keeping clean but the camp sickness was starting to take its toll on all classes of men irrespective of rank, then when Lord John Thornbury was taken sick the gentry were beginning to panic.

The campaigning season was just about over and the weather was starting to get colder with a bitter wind coming off the sea, food and drink supplies were still trickling in from England but people's attire and boots were starting to wear thin. I was lucky, having brought extra clothing with me and three pairs of boots, but I was now down to my last pair. Normally peasant men are used to being bare-footed, except in winter, so it looked like they would have to go without anything on their feet from now on. A couple of days after Lord John's departure for home, a Faversham boat arrived bringing in fresh supplies. It had met up with the boat carrying William's sick brother home and we were given the sad news that Lord Thornbury had died the day after his boat had sailed from France and that his body was being taken back to England for burial.

William is now Lord of the Manor, making my sister a lady, but what's this, are my eyes deceiving me? Is that my father crossing the lake? Yes it is.

"What are you doing here?" I asked, as he climbed ashore from a small boat. "Surely you must know about the camp sickness that is killing everybody."

"It's only when we arrived here that we heard about the sickness." he answered, "I hitched a ride on the boat with this fellow Bob, who as you can see is not in monk's clothing, as he wants to be part of the King's cause and become an archer again."

"Bob," I asked, "shouldn't you have stayed in England to help safeguard the country against any possible trouble from the Lollard's?"

"Aye," said my archery teacher, "but Abbot Benedict let me off the hook, so here I am."

Just then, thunder crackled from the black sky and rain started bucketing down and bouncing off the hard ground.

"If you are bringing bad weather with you, you might just as well go back home." I shouted, as we all greeted each other with much soggy back slapping.

My father told me that he had wanted to get into the fight but was not allowed to, due to his bad leg, and that he would have to go straight back with the boat having only been given time to come and see his son.

Bob could stay and he has brought his great longbow with him, which worked in my favour as Thomas, my trusted aid, had suffered a mild case of the runs, and as he was not indentured to a retinue he was able to get out of the life threatening army; thus allowing Bob to become the driver of my horse and cart. This suited him down to the ground as he would not have to walk anywhere and could still take part in any battles.

My father told me that all was well at home, and as my brother has taken over the farm, life was easier for him and my mother who were now living in my house in Faversham. He also told me that the bank was still making money, as was the bakery.

Lightning was still flickering in the dark, followed a few seconds later by a clap of thunder, as I later watched my father and Thomas sail away from the French shore. I couldn't help wondering, if I would ever see them again.

With the walls of Harfleur now partially destroyed things were coming to a head, so that on Tuesday the 17th of September, the King once again sent his Heralds into the town to demand their surrender. If it was not agreed this time he would make an all-out attack, kill all of the men and allow his army to do what was normally expected when a town did not submit; as had happened only last year, to the besieged town of Soissons, where a French Armagnac army who, having given the French Burgundian defenders a chance to surrender, went back on their word and killed all the men, raped all the women and plundered the town. They had also killed about fifty English mercenary archers, which our soldiers were well aware of.

Last night, the King had ordered every cannon to fire stones into the town to keep the defenders awake, therefore as dawn broke on Wednesday morning, I was standing, with Glynn's red section and Fred's black section, behind the mounds of tunnelled earth ready to support the men at arms movement towards the enemy. As they started to advance, the Montivilliers gate was suddenly thrown open, this stopped them in their tracks and we readied ourselves for a cavalry attack. But no, the town elders had had enough and came out offering to surrender, as they were not willing to see their men put to the sword and their women defiled. However it was only the civilian population that were giving up, not the military. Only the eastern side of the town had yielded, which forced the French garrison commander to negotiate a truce, stating that, if King Charles had not relieved the town by the following Sunday, they would surrender.

Henry's threat to storm Harfleur and put it to the sword had done the trick, therefore at 1pm on Sunday the 22nd of September, once it became obvious that there would be no relieving French army, the defenders gave up.

Everybody wanted to get into the town but the King, knowing what a conquering army was like, only allowed trusted men to enter Harfleur, and I was one of them. It looked to me, like every house and dwelling had either been destroyed or badly damaged by the thousands of stones hurled at them during a siege that had lasted for thirty six days. The town's people were still unsure as to whether or not the King's promises would be kept as they also knew what had happened to the English men at Soissons, so they feared the worst. It was a good thing that the French had given up because jars of quick lime and sulphur had been placed in strategic places around the walls, ready to throw into the eyes of our soldiers. There were also vessels of fat that could be heated ready to pour on to them as well.

Henry sat enthroned in his pavilion on the mount, overlooking the Leure gate as the French military commander, Raoul 'De Gaucourt and the senior citizens, plodded up the hill to hand over the keys of the town. On the Monday morning he triumphantly entered the town bare footed, and visited the damaged church of Saint Martin's to make his thanks to God for his victory. The King set free about two hundred and fifty French soldiers who had survived the siege, on the condition that they would not bear arms again in this campaign. However, they were stripped of their weapons and armour, along with whatever clothing and boots were still useful before they were allowed to depart. As for the civilian population, the King retained some of the dignitaries for ransom, whilst the remainder, some one thousand women and children, were forced out of the town and sent along the Rouen road.

I was to provide an escort of archers for the first ten miles, to prevent any of our army molesting them. They were then passed over to a French patrol that were aware of the surrender and didn't offer us a fight. The civilian men were forced to remain, to help our stonemasons and carpenters rebuild the town's defensive walls in preparation for the awaited French attack, after which they would also be allowed to go free. The Earl of Dorset, Thomas Beaufort, along with three hundred men at arms and nine hundred archers which included Fred Hitch and his section (reduced to forty men due to sickness and death) were ordered to garrison the town.

Now that things had quietened down I had chance to talk with William, telling him how sorry I was about his brother's death.

"My lord, why do you think the French never took the trouble to send an army to relieve Harfleur?" I asked.

William replied, "You must know that there is no nationwide standing army in England, only the private armies of the King and other Nobles and that it is only in times of war with other nations that we in our country gather these forces together, as normally only a small force of men at arms are retained by Royalty, Barons and Lords to maintain order."

"Well," he continued, "it's the same in France they don't have a national army either, so they have also had to start gathering an army together but with one Duke of a region fighting another, they will no doubt be making sure there is no treachery before they give us battle. Our spies tell us that they are now massing their army at Rouen, so it won't be long before we really have a fight on our hands."

William then went on to say, "The Duke of Burgundy has made a secret pact with our King, saying that he shall not take up arms against the English, but neither would he take up arms against his own countrymen. He will just stay out of the fight altogether. However, it is well known that other French regions, loyal to their King, are suspicious about this pact and to be on the safe side they have maintained defensive garrisons in their own territories just in case he makes a sneak attack."

"By the way," he laughed, "you can still call me William."

As I approached my camping area, Jamie was grooming my horse and complaining to Bob that I wasn't looking after 'HIS' horse. Poor Bob had been forced to listen to a young boy's mumbling, so he was pleased to pass the blame on to me.

"Jamie," I said, "Red and I have been busy galloping around the country and have only just got back from escorting those poor civilians from the town, which took us long enough, and anyway Red is not your horse until we get back to England."

"Well don't let it happen again!" he ordered.

"Sorry sir," I said, as I saluted the cheeky whelp.

"So what have you been up to?" I asked.

"Well," said Jamie, "now that Lord William Thornbury is part of the King's council, I have been given his duties as a messenger and it's my job to deliver the King's orders to his captains, and what is more," he boasted, as he stroked the white blaze of his jet black stallion. "I am allowed to ride Lightning, which if you remember, is the horse that had a sore mouth, and my friend the King, wants his best steed kept fit and healthy."

"Friend of the King is it?" I proudly said. "It looks like I shall have to watch my step with you in the future."

Henry wanted a count taken of his remaining army, to find out how many men were left of the fifteen thousand that had started out on this campaign, which turned out to be about nine thousand, of which twelve hundred went to Garrison Harfleur. This left an army of seven thousand eight hundred, add or take a few, which I thought was hardly a large enough force to carry on the campaign, but this number can only get worse, as men are still dying or being sent home sick. Out of my three hundred men, Fred Hitch had lost ten from his original fifty, Jack had also lost ten men leaving him with eighty, Tom's section had been reduced from sixty to forty five but there had been no losses from my other two sections, which was a testament to cleanliness, not to mention being away from the main army. This left me with two hundred and sixty five men but now with the loss of Fred Hitch's section, I was left with two hundred and twenty five in four sections, plus my lieutenants.

The finest weapons left by the French defenders, were snapped up by those men first into town and I had picked a lighter sword which had two sharp edges. I was no good as a swordsman but every archer had to have one, so I threw my old one on the stock pile. I still had my cleaver, bought in Sittingbourne and my well used folding saw, which were kept in the secret hide out on my cart. So all I wanted now, was a long bladed dagger which was not so easy to find. There were plenty of daggers but they were all short bladed and it was only when I was rummaging through all of the safe hiding places, that the past residents of the town thought would not be discovered, that I found what I was looking for.

The obvious hideouts were under the fireplace just like my father's, or like mine under the pig sty but these well-known places had all been found. I racked my brains to work out where else things might be hidden. All the thatching had been searched, as had the wattle walls, but I found a knife along with about three hundred Sou coins when I slammed open the door of a grand looking house, which loosened a hideaway in the square wooden post that formed part of the doorway. The post looked solid enough but had been hollowed out to create a space inside, with a tight well-fitting plug acting as the opening and the join had been made to look like part of the grain. The plug was held in place with one of the door hinges, something like my cart's secret compartments.

The money was soon stashed away, and the knife was better than it first looked. It had a binding of leather around the hilt, that turned out to be covering a beautiful jewel studded handle, which I quickly rebound, the blade was twelve inches long….. Just the job. I looked for more of these hideaways but there were none to be found, so whoever had owned this house must have been rich and must have either been killed or unable to return for his treasure, anyway it was mine now.

My men were showing interest in the many crossbows left behind, as were other archers and everybody wanted to try them out. The crossbow had to be cocked using both feet on the bow, whilst the string was pulled back using both hands until it connected with its trigger catch, or you had to use a screw winding machine which took ages to do. The arrows, called bolts or quarrels, were about a foot long with only two flights, which could be fired further than our arrows and anyone with little skill can use them. This worried a lot of our men including me, as this weapon was our greatest dread.

I was instructed by my retinue captain, Sir Gilbert Umfraville, to show some of his men at arms how to fire these crossbows, not that there was much to show, but they had to practice how to aim them correctly. Therefore, the men in Glynn's red section had a crossbow each and were having to instruct a sulky man at arms how to aim at some makeshift targets. Thankfully, these crossbows proved to be too much trouble to handle, not to mention that they and their winding screws weighed a great deal heavier than a longbow…..and my men wouldn't have been seen dead with one in his hands, so they were left with the new defenders of Harfleur.

**

CHAPTER TWENTY

Now that there was no danger from Harfleur, we were able to pass through the town thus allowing the army to join up on either side, but I was happy to stay on the east side because it was cleaner and my men could still forage along the Seine. The weather is changing for the worst and it's getting colder with strong wind's coming off the sea, bringing rain showers with them. It is well over two weeks since the French capitulated and now that the defensive walls were almost rebuilt, it looks like our army will be on the move. There was a lot of grumbling coming my way from men who thought that they were due to be paid at the beginning of October. They had forgotten that the next two payments, set at Southampton, were to be paid together in December but there was nothing for them to spend it on anyway, except ale that was still coming over from England.

William told me that the King had been having heated meetings with his council and that he wanted to march his army north, to his strong fortification at Calais but was getting opposition from his military advisers who were telling him that his depleted army was not strong enough to resist what was thought to be a vast French army mustering at Rouen. William didn't know enough about conducting wars, so he didn't vote against the King's wishes but he asked me for my opinion. It seemed obvious to me that we were in no condition to continue the campaign with so many of our soldiers sick and dying, so I felt that we should run for home and live to fight another day.

Then again, most of the boats that had brought us to France had either gone home or been sent back to Zealand and Holland, where they had been hired from, and all that remained were the King's naval ships. Therefore, going home was probably out of the question.

"What do you think Cris?" he asked.
"What is the King suggesting we do?" I asked back.

"Well," he said, "and this is for your ears only. The King intends to exercise his legal rights and March north to Calais."

"What the King orders is good enough for me." I said.

"But," said William, "the Duke of Clarence argued with this decision and wants his brother to be satisfied with the capture of Harfleur." The Duke was no coward, as he had been in many battles, but because of his disagreement with Henry, he was suddenly taken sick and had to be sent home to England…..he looked well enough to me.

The main army had now moved to another camping site on the plateau above the town and west of the river Lezarde, which was flat open country, giving more space for the eastern besiegers to join them and we settled down to await our fate. Food supplies were short but we were just about managing. I was to assist in spreading a false rumour that we were going to march north to make an attack on a town called Dieppe, then march towards Rouen, which it was hoped would keep the French guessing. However, it was plain to me that anybody who knew where these towns were situated wouldn't be taken in by this ruse, as we would be going north then going south east, which more than double the travelling distance.

Having already complained to Sir Gilbert Umfraville about losing Fred Hitch and his men, I was pleased to hear that they would be returned to me and that ordinary archers were to replace them. This meant that I now had my force of two hundred and sixty five men back in five sections, which did not please some of Fred's men. They thought that they were going to have an easy life defending the town but when they found out that they would have lost the extra two pence per day, they stopped moaning. However, it was not my complaint that had them returned to me, it was the fact that they were to be replaced by archers too sick to travel. I for one, was certainly glad that I wasn't staying at Harfleur because the French will definitely try to reverse the loss of this town and would want to avenge the shameful disgrace of not making the slightest effort to lift the siege in the first place.

It is now my intention to write down events as they occur, using eye witness accounts from William and Jamie, plus any information relayed to me by my trusted lieutenants. Then on my return to Faversham, I shall write my book without padding out the campaign with a cock and bull story.

The army is about to start out for Calais, which is thought to be about one hundred miles away, so five days should cover the journey, but we were told that this march may well take up to eight days. Therefore, we had to carry sufficient food and provisions to cover this period. The large carts were to be left at Harfleur, along with all the siege engines and the massive guns but thankfully not the small carts, including mine, which was carrying the hidden money taken from the French and at least five hundred quivers of arrows, which had now been issued to me. Therefore, counting

the two quivers each of my men have with them at all times, containing twenty four arrows each, meant that we had over twenty six thousand for my men alone…..
And the rest of the King's archers will have spare arrows as well, so what would all these this add up too?

Bob was to travel at the rear of the King's army and I had given him the job of making sure that the arrows were kept dry and in good condition, which he lovingly cares for by re-sorting and turning, to keep the flights in good condition. He wasn't too happy about the square shafts though, saying that they were a sorry sight but better than nothing, he is even wearing a monk's habit again so that he can receive a food ration.

I was to be in the vanguard commanded by my captain Sir Gilbert Umfraville along with Sir John Cornewaille, who had replaced the Duke of Clarence. A book could be written about Sir John, as he was fully versed in war. He was aware of my leadership and promoted me to captain bowman at arms. On taking command, he had soon sorted out the wheat from the chaff regarding the false archers without upsetting the retinue captains, who had indentured their servants as bowmen. My men had been the job of testing the whole army of archers, which was a pleasant duty for them, and they simply weeded out the men who could not shoot ten aimed arrows in one minute.

There was over five hundred men who were unable to do this, so their lord and master would now have to pay their wages if he wanted to keep them, otherwise they were to be sent home to England, leaving us with real archers who could be relied on.

Tuesday the 8th of October 1415

Daylight broke on a chilly morning, as we collected our rations and prepared to march. We were to travel in three armies of over two thousand men each, the first army was to be led by my captain Sir Gilbert, the second would be commanded by the King, and the rear army was to be led by Edward, the Duke of York. I was to set a forward scouting party with two of my sections, along with a section of mounted men at arms, two of my sections were to flank the marching army and forage for food as we went along. Jack formed the rear-guard and later reported to me that a late ambush by the French had killed two of his men with crossbow bolts from close range, as the last of the army passed the town of Montivilliers.

"One of my men was hit in the face with a bolt flinging him backwards over his horse, with blood flowing out of his leather helmet," he said, "the bolt had gone straight between his eyes and he must have been dead before he hit the ground. The other man was skewered in the ribs and it took two hours for him to die." This reminded me of how William's father had died.

For the first five miles or so the track was pretty flat, then it was a gradual climb for another ten miles to the top of a hill, where there was a crossroad leading to a small hamlet on our right and as the local population had fled, the dwellings were used to shelter part of the army. It had taken us all day to reach this point and tomorrow it would be all downhill to a place known as Fecamp, which from our high view point, was just visible on the coast of the English Channel.

Most of the army had done nothing for the last three months, except for sitting on their butts and getting no exercise whatsoever, so it took another hour for the tail end of the army to come limping into our first camp. I couldn't see it getting any better as the march progressed, William had told me that the distance from our starting point to Fecamp was twenty nine miles, so we were about half way there.

"This is no good," moaned Jack as he reported to me. "My men are having to dawdle behind the rear of the columns, and…..as I am your best friend, can't you put us in the vanguard, so that we can see some action?"

"Alright" I agreed, "I shall swap each of my sections around now and then but there is no action to be seen anyway."

Wednesday morning was gloomy and the sky was black, which indicated that we would soon have some rain. However the going should be good today as it's all downhill. I was to ride with Tom's fifty mounted archers and the same number of lightly armoured men at arms to scout well ahead of the army, whilst Glynn's men remained at the front of the marching columns. The rain clouds had released a few sprinkles of water and fortunately it soon stopped but we were on our guard watching for any sign of the enemy. As we rode down the slope we encountered two monks, who moved to one side keeping their eyes down as we passed. After riding for three hours we reached the outskirts of the town, which nestled in a coastal valley where the river Valmont flows into the English Channel.

Our army will have to cross this river but fortunately the crossing could be reached without having to go through the town which, as we had expected, was well protected. They could see us, and we could see them, but they made no attempt to give us trouble and we were certainly going to leave them alone. There had been no opposition to our downhill journey, so after checking that the causeway was passable we split our force, with the men at arms watching the town, whilst my men crossed the river to look for a camping site. It was once again an uphill climb, which I am sure the men on foot won't be too pleased about.

"Right, this will do fine." I announced, as we reached the top of the slope overlooking Fecamp, where there was plenty of flat ground to camp the army. I sent some men to check-out a village that I could see over to our left, which proved yet again to be empty of people, so after the usual searching for plunder under fireplaces and such, it was declared fit for the King to spend the night.

The whole army passed Fecamp without incident but it had now started to rain quite heavily and men were arriving at the camp site wet and soggy. However, there was no trace of Bob or my horse and cart.

"Jack, you were at the rear, what has happened to Bob?" I enquired.

"I saw him branching off to the left, just before the river crossing." he replied.

This had me worried, so I immediately set off with twenty of my men to search for him, only to be met along the track by a drunken, dare I say, monk?

"Well, well, well," slurred Bob, "there was no need to worry about me, us monks and, and priests, are safe from any soldiers and, and, I 'ave been giving a ride down the hill to a couple of monks and, and, they were kind enough to invite me into their Abbey for some refreshment, and they have given me a dozen bottles of their liqueur.....do you want one?"

Bob went on, with more slurring, "but, even though we could not understand what each of us were saying, I was still able to let them know of our plan to invade Rouen, without of course letting them know that we are not really going to do any such thing." he finished off, trying to tap his nose, which dismally failed. It was not just for him that I was worried but also for my stock of arrows. I would have been in serious trouble if these had been lost!

Bob was put to bed and half of his liqueur was taken away from him, which I gave to his intended rescuers, to keep them from passing the story amongst the others.....I hoped. This little shock had unnerved me, and even more so when I learned that Bob had driven the cart through the town's defenders, right up to the Benedictine abbey, without being searched. Therefore, tomorrow morning, I am going to pass out another quiver to each of my men to look after and I am going to have to keep a closer eye on this troublesome monk.

Now where I had read that, or was it troublesome priest?

Even though there was to be no plundering, a lot of the dwellings lost most of their wooden interior to make fires, and what with the wet weather and the promise of more rain to come, pilfered dry straw and wood was stored in people's packs to be used in the future. The rain had been falling all night but for the time being had stopped. The men who had not been able to find shelter, were shivering as the dampness slowly steamed off them, when they were woken and bullied into a third day's march.

We still had men suffering from dysentery, who should have been sent home, but even though we could see the King's navy out in the Channel tracking our course, there was no way to reach them as there was a steep cliff stretching north as far as the eye could see. So these poor men were forced to continue plodding along, with rain washing their excrement down their legs, as the dysentery took hold of their bodies. I don't think some of them will survive much longer, if some way is not found to get them on board a ship. The army was already starting to fall apart with some men's boots dropping off their feet, forcing them to march bare footed along the coastal road towards Dieppe. However, after covering another eight miles or so, a route down to the beach was found and about forty men with the bloody flux were rowed out to the ships. Heaven knows what will happen to the men who were still ill, but not sick enough to be invalided out of the army.

I was well in advance of the main column as we approached Dieppe, when William came galloping up to me saying, "Cris, the King wants to see you right away."

"What about?" I worriedly asked. "I can't have done anything wrong?"

"Come on" he shouted, as he started to ride off, "just pretend to be a French prisoner."

What's he on about? I asked myself as we galloped along.

William told me what I was supposed to do, and half an hour later, I was being questioned in French by a Burgundian, along with a real Frenchman, to find out what we knew about the English army. If we told the truth our interrogator told us, we would be set free. I only told him my name as ordered, which is now Jack Devereux, but the other prisoner whose name was Jules, said to him,

"You can't fool us you traitor, everybody knows that the King of England is going to lay siege to Dieppe and has no intention of going backwards towards Rouen."

I looked glaringly at him as he went on, "You and your fifty thousand men will not have such an easy time as you did at Harfleur."

"That's true," our interrogator lied, "and what about you?" he asked, turning to me.

"I'm just an ordinary farmer," I cowered, "travelling home to Eu after living for five years near Paris."

"Well it's just your hard luck," our interrogator said, "you know too much, so you will have to be kept prisoners."

"You fool," I growled at my companion when we were taken away, "if you had kept your mouth shut they would have released us."

"I don't care," he growled back, "anyway, I come from Eu but I don't know you, where did you live?"

"I don't know you either," I replied, "but I lived with my grandfather Devereux, on his farm just inland from the town."

"Would that be where Catherine lives with her son?" he then asked.

I pretended not to be shocked as I said, "Catherine is the daughter of my grandfather's son, well, not my real grandfather as he was drowned and my grandmother has married his brother, but as I have been away for five years so its news to me that Catherine is married."

"So if you have been away for all that time," he said offhandedly, as he looked into my eyes, "you won't know that both of your grandparents are dead."

You couldn't keep that sort of news from showing on your face, as I was visibly shocked and with tears in my eyes, asked him when and how they had passed away.

"I don't know exactly how they died" he replied, "but it was about two years ago and they both died on the same day."

My reaction removed his suspicion of me, and he told me that he lived in the town, worked as a fisherman and that his uncle was one of the crewmen drowned when my grandfather's boat sank. I was sorry about my grandparents, who I hadn't seen since becoming a student of Brother Benedict, and I can't pretend to be pleased at hearing that Catherine was married. I had hoped to meet her again someday and perhaps make good my promises to marry her, but that's not possible anymore…..worse luck.

Jules was then taken away for further questioning, during which time I was given my final instructions.

"You don't have to become a spy for your country." said the Burgundian, "as you will probably know the penalty for spying, but we need to find out all we can about the intentions of the garrison at Eu. Therefore, I want you go there and get back as soon as you learn anything."

"Why me, when you must have lots of spies?" I asked.

"Where do I come from?" he enquired.

"Burgundy," I replied.

"How do you know that?"

"Because of your accent," I said.

"Well that's why we need you, as you have a Norman accent."

After this explanation I could hardly refuse, so when Jules returned, I said to him, "we've got to get away from here and warn the Count of Eu that Dieppe is going to be attacked very soon."

Later that evening our guard looked to be asleep, as I thumped the ground next to his head to make my escaping partner think that I had clonked him, then we stole off into the dark where would you believe, there were some unguarded horses. It would have given the game away if they had been saddled, which meant we had to ride bareback.

As we slowed down after a long night's ride, Jules asked, "so why are you going home now?"

"Probably for the same reason as you…..to fight the English." I said.

"I am" he replied. "I was part of a crew fishing in La Manche and we got trapped in Fecamp by the English ships, so I decided to walk home."

On reaching the Devereux farm we split up and arranged to meet up in the town next morning. I gingerly made my way to the farmhouse, which looked exactly as it had done the last time I was here, many years earlier and the first person I saw was a little boy playing in the yard. He looked to be about three years old and his hair was jet black…..just like Catherine's.

"Hello, who are you?" I shouted after him as he ran off.

Before I knew it, there she was, more beautiful than ever. "CRISPIN, oh CRISPIN is it really you?" She cried, as she ran forward throwing her arms around me.

"I thought that I would never see you, ever again. Are you here with the English army? Of course, you must be."

But I had a few questions of my own to ask her before I started answering hers. "I heard that you had a son, was that him?"

Catherine smiled and said "Yes, that's my wonderful boy and I have named him Crispin after his father who he has never seen…..until now."

I was flummoxed, to say the least and said, "but, but, I heard that you were married?"

"What's a girl supposed to tell everybody, when she has a baby out of wedlock, and anyway," she replied, "You did marry me on that Christmas Eve in your house, don't you remember?"

I knew I had been drunk that night and had slept on the same bed as her, but that was all I could remember, and I certainly don't remember anything else. "Crispin," she said to the little boy, who had followed her out of the house, "this is your father, who has come home at last."

"And not before time," said her father, who now appeared from the barn "but I won't believe it, until I see the marriage certificate."

"I'm sorry Crispin," Catherine butted in, "but the certificate, signed by Brother Benedict, was lost when my bag was stolen."

"Oh, that's no problem," I said, having quickly grasped her plight, "it can soon be replaced."

"Well don't think you can take advantage of my daughter until I see it," growled her father.

"I don't know how long that will take." I replied, "but if you don't believe us, why not get the Curé to perform another ceremony as soon as you like." which put a grateful smile on Catherine's face.

After this, it was just a matter of catching up on what had been happening in our lives. I learned that my grandmother had died of old age during the night and that my grandfather was so shocked when he discovered her, that he died of grief the next afternoon, which made Catherine's father the owner of the farm. I told them of my successes and that they mustn't let anybody know that I was half English.

"But which half are you loyal to?" Asked Catherine's father.

All that I could say was, "if your mother and father, whom you both love, were fighting, whose side would you take?"

After no answer was given, I said, "well, it's like that for me, I am half French and half English and all I am trying to do is let my people in France know that the King of England only wants his rightful lands back and that he would not harm his French subjects.

What sort of a liar have I turned out to be? I asked myself. It's true about not harming anybody who doesn't put up a fight that is, but I am not too sure about the rightful lands bit, as I am starting to realise that the man with the biggest army just takes what land he wants, which has already been happening in France, with the Dukes of Burgundy and Armagnac, always at each other's throats.

Catherine's father promised to keep quiet about me being half English and showed me into the barn, where I was supposed to sleep, but Catherine crept in to me during the night and took me to her bed for the few glorious hours left to us, before I was to go into Eu and do my spying bit.

CHAPTER TWENTY ONE

William….. I know what Cris is up to and I have to look after his horse and possessions, except for his longbow, which Bob is keeping whilst he is away, and he also wants me to record what the army is doing, which is not much.

We are into our fourth day's march and there is still no sign of the enemy. Last night we camped along a road close to a narrow gap in the cliff, where it was possible to send some more seriously ill men out to our ships. This however, will be the last chance for the sick to quit the campaign as we are now to march inland. Camping whilst still in column last night, made it easier to start off this morning and we are now camped six miles further on from a town called Arques, in the Leure valley, having covered less than sixty miles in four days, so that's not twenty a day is it?

We have bypassed the strong garrison of Dieppe, which the King has avoided like the plague, so their army must be uncertain of where we are, as they no doubt had been expecting us to lay siege to this town. However, it won't be long before they realise that we are making for Calais. There was a castle at Arques but the defenders did not give us any trouble, in fact they were only too willing for us to cross the nearby river Bresle, thus avoiding having their town sacked as Henry had threatened, they even supplied us with some fresh bread.

Jack….. Some friend that Cris is! I had no chance to see him last night, as he is up at the front of the column, whilst I am still at the back. It's not like him *to forget his promises, but it's getting tiring following on behind the rest of our straggling army. It was a good idea, camping in column last night, as everybody stops marching at the same time but not tonight worse luck, as we have now only just reached our camping area beyond Arques, two hours after everybody else, and we still haven't seen hide nor hair of the enemy.*

As I entered Eu, at 6am on Saturday morning, the news had come that the English had passed Dieppe and were heading our way, and as it turned out, there had been no need to go through the rigmarole of having been a prisoner of the English as the town's people had other things on their mind.

The Count of Eu, who was standing under his blue banner depicting a patterned yellow Fleur de Lis, was asking for volunteers to ride as far as Rouen and Abbeville, to let them know what was happening and to ask for assistance to fight the fifty thousand English enemy, as had been reported by Jules.

I volunteered to warn Abbeville, as did Jules and I said to him "I am going to warn my family first, so you go south of the river Somme, and I shall cross at the estuary ford and do the same on the north side."

The count heard me say this and said, as he handed each of us an official sealed message, "this crossing is now well guarded and a lovely surprise will be waiting for the English army should they be trying to reach Calais this way…..like they had done nearly seventy years ago."

This was vital information that needed to be told to King Henry, so it was important that I got away as soon as possible.

"Right," I said to Jules, "if you cross the Somme and ride along the north side of the river, I shall say goodbye to my family then ride on the south side."

There was a bad reception waiting for me when I got back to the farm, as they had already heard the news which was spreading like wildfire.

Philip was going to try and kill me as a traitor, but Catherine pleaded with him to leave me alone.

"Just go away," she said with tears in her eyes, "I don't understand all this fighting but perhaps one day you will come back to me and your son."

I had no choice, as it was important that I got word to the King, so with a reluctant heart, I parted company with Catherine.

I hoped that I wouldn't be attacked by my own men when I met up with the advance patrol at noon but as this was the only road to Eu, they had been told to watch out for me. Within less than ten minutes after my arrival, I was making my report to the King himself with a smiling William looking on.

"So, they think that we have fifty thousand men do they?' laughed Henry. "I only wish we had. I was aiming to cross the river at low tide and your information confirms to me what a French prisoner has already told us. You will no doubt be hungry, so you can eat with Lord Thornbury and then return to your archers."

"William" I said, as I tucked into some delicious beef. "I have seen Catherine and she is the mother of my son."

"That's impossible," he replied, "You haven't seen her for what must be over five years."

"Four," I said, "and young Crispin is the spitting image of his mother."

"Well, I'm amazed," he said, "but congratulations, I suppose you want Red back now do you? Well he's with Bob, so now it's back to work."

"And where do you think you've been?" asked my troublesome monk, when I met up with him.

"Only seeing my French family" I grinned "and as soon as I get my longbow and arrows back, I shall join my forward patrol."

"You had better see Jack first, as he isn't happy with you at the moment." said Bob.

I had forgotten that I was going to change my archers about, so I quickly rode to the rear of the column and made my peace with Jack, telling him what I had been doing and giving him my good news. He and his men then moved to the front of the army to swap places with Glynn's red section. It was late in the afternoon when my advanced patrol reached the farm but Catherine and her father, like all the rest of the peasants in the area, had moved into the walled town but at least I would be able to save the farm from plunderers.

Just then, Jamie came galloping up to tell me that the Duke of Kent wanted to gather my men together for some special instructions and rode off to tell my other lieutenants where we were to meet him. This was the first time that I had seen all of my men at the same time since arriving in France and was pleased to see that unlike the rest of the army, they looked strong and healthy.

Sir Gilbert gave out about fifty arrows that he had been holding and I had one in my hand as he started to speak, "can anybody see the difference between these arrows and the ones you already have?" he asked.

After everybody had looked at them, they could see that their own arrow heads were a darker colour, whilst these new arrows were almost grey. I knew what was coming when he said, "now scrape your knives against the heads of the ones I have just given you and you will see that the metal is much softer. These," he continued, "are going to be our special weapons and must only be used on a man in full armour and when you are sure of hitting him. And before you say it, no, the arrows won't go through their armour, which is what we want them to believe about all of our arrows."

With that, my men were given a dozen arrows each and threatened under pain of death, that nobody in our army was to know about these practically harmless missiles. I could see the idea … if the French knights think that their armour would protect them, it may lead them into a false sense of security and readily attack us and we can then use the deadly iron bodkin head arrows against them.

William…..We Reached Eu about 6pm as dark clouds closed in over the crenulated walls, which as Cris had reported, were twice as thick as those at Harfleur. Not that it mattered, as we had no siege equipment with us anyway. French riders came out of the town but held up, well out of arrow range and some of our horsemen went forward to meet them but the French retreated, all except for one knight, who was offering single combat. Surprisingly, one of King Henry's knights took up his challenge and donned his full armour.

The men were cheering our unknown champion and the French defenders were doing the same, as these two gallant men charged one another, but nothing was achieved because after a couple of passes they crashed headlong into each other, resulting in both their deaths. It was never revealed who our champion was but we later learned that the French Knight's name was Lancelot (just like our legendary knight of the round table).

King Henry then sent his heralds into the town, demanding that the twenty one year-old Charles d' Artois, Count of Eu, submit to his will. The Count realised that Henry could not sustain a long siege and that he was anxious to be on his way, so he did the same as the town leaders of Arques, by sending food and wine to our camp.

Bob….. Cris has told me where to find his family's farm and when I arrived, he and his men were feasting on one of the pigs his relations had thought were well hidden but Cris knew of the farm's hideouts and had taken away all of the livestock to feed the army. In payment, he has left in their place, all of the remaining

French money captured at Harfleur, which was more than enough in compensation. I was given the job of killing two pigs and two sheep and cut them up into pieces to take to Cris' men.

**

CHAPTER TWENTY TWO

I have left Catherine a note, telling her to look in the spot where she and her mother had saved my father. I had buried here a box, with a letter in it saying that hopefully I would come back and that I wanted to marry her. On top of the letter I had placed the gems, now removed from the dagger, along with the coins that I had found in the door post at Harfleur.

The morning was damp and dismal after a rainy night, as the columns moved inland, along the road that went straight to Abbeville, which Henry wanted his army well past before we made camp. It was plain to see what a sorry state our army was in, with more people suffering from dysentery, which along with exhaustion was taking its toll to such an extent that men who could not go on were having to be left behind to the mercy of the French, who we fully expect to start following in our wake.

As already mentioned, the King had intended crossing the river Somme at Blanchetaque, as his predecessor Edward III had done in 1346 but now that this route is blocked, we shall have to find another crossing. The first half of this march was all uphill across open country and the forced pace was too much for some soldiers, who were falling more and more behind the rear column. Then, after marching for five hours, we reached the summit, where we were allowed a half hours rest before the easier downhill slog to pass Abbeville.

Glynn…..*I must remember to tell Cris what is going on at the rear of the army, so he can write it down.*

I was not too happy at being put at the rear of the third army, as they are a rag tag bunch and their leaders seem to want to travel with the King and not with their men, most of whom have no boots. The sick are falling more and more behind the column and my men have to let them hang on to their horse's tails to be pulled uphill. Some men have given up and simply sat down to await their fate from the French, who are now following close behind us but not offering to give us a fight.

Why our desperate men are not allowed to ride the spare horses, is beyond me, as there must be as many horses as there are soldiers and even though these animals are carrying plunder the men should come first, I'm glad that at least I am mounted. I shall have to see if I am allowed to take the fight to the trailing French scouts tomorrow oops sorry... not me, as I have to move to the centre of the army to replace Thomas, who will go to the vanguard. It was a good job Cris sent his cart back last night with joints of meat, as our rations are almost gone so we shall have to live more off the land from now on. There was more than enough meat for my men, so after putting some of it in our packs, what remained was passed on to those soldiers who had smelt the joints roasting. But now that our wine has run out, my men shall have to get used to drinking water, which is plentiful with all the rain that we are having. So after stopping for a rest at the top of this hill and as it has started to rain again, it looks like we are in for a long wet trudge.

Jack......*This is better than kicking your heels miles behind the army. I am well ahead of the vanguard at a place that the local peasants we have captured say is called Pont-Remy, where there is a causeway across the Somme. The crossing has been broken but I can* see armoured French soldiers on the north side of the river, whereas I am on the south side, but unfortunately they are too far away to shoot dummy arrows at. I have sent twenty of my men back to the column to report this disappointment but with the good news that when they come to a small village called Miannay, there is a branch road going to the right, which will allow the army to bypass Abbeville saving at least five miles of marching. One thing I have now noticed, is that the French are well aware of our route and that we intend to cross the Somme, so they are destroying everything in our path. This rain isn't helping, but it's the same for the French, and I don't think they intend to give us a fight because they are just burning whatever crops cannot be carried away, as well as the dwellings, to deprive us of shelter and wood for our fires.

Guy…..Cris is a great leader and he does look after his men, not like some of the retinue captains who don't seem to care if their men starve, all they are concerned about is themselves, but having to tell him everything I do, is a little bit annoying, as I have to find him at the end of nearly every day. His friend Tom is travelling on the left flank of the King's army, whilst I am travelling on the right, but tomorrow I am to move to the rear of the columns and the rest of our sections will rotate around the whole army, meaning that there are always two different sections with the vanguard. One section as the rear guard and two flanking sections who are able to forage for whatever food can be found.

The flanking sections are the best because the finest pickings can be had, with the choicest of food being kept for our men, before the lords and even the King get their hands on it, which doesn't suite the gentry *because just like the ordinary soldier they are not allowed to leave the column. So they have to put up with whatever we give them but unfortunately, any good plunder we find has to go to the King. Unless of course, we can hide it or put it to our own use. Just like when my men were able to deprive some French soldiers whom we caught, of their horses and boots, which we shared among ourselves. These soldiers had mistaken us for their own countrymen as we were not wearing our surcoat's painted with the Red Cross, consequently when they noticed our longbows, it was too late to escape without losing their lives. And strange as it seems, my men are now searching for any lye soap left behind in the empty dwellings.*

William came galloping up to me shouting, "Cris, you're wanted again."

"What for this time?" I asked.

"The King knows that Abbeville is well garrisoned," he said, "and he has no intention of trying to cross the river there, but he wants to find out if the French are going to fight us, or just stay in their fortresses."

After my instructions I was on my own, as I made a dash for the town crossing. I was supposed to have stolen a horse, after being taken prisoner again but the pursuing English, who were hard on my heels, gave up the chase once I was safe amongst my French countrymen. The fact that I was being chased got me into the fortress and the Counts letter with his seal was good enough to protect me from any further mistrust, but I was questioned about the English army.

"For one thing," I reported, "there are not fifty thousand of them, more like six or seven thousand and they are scared stiff of having to fight us. They are also short of food and I think that they are trying to make a run for Calais."

I was not giving away any secrets, as this must have been reported back by their scouts but my news went down well and I was allowed to join the army in the town where I nearly missed having my name called.

"Jack, have you gone deaf?" this voice asked, as I was being tapped on the shoulder.

"Oh I'm sorry Jules, I'm just tired and hungry." I told him of my woes as he took me to where there was a plentiful supply of food and drink.

"I wondered what had happened to you," he said, "but now you can join the army here and give those English what they deserve, as men are coming from all over France to beat them in battle."

"Not before time" I gladly replied, "if they had come earlier we might have saved Harfleur."

"Yes," he agreed, "but losing Harfleur has made the country wake up and realise what they had to lose if that usurpers son was to rule France."

"So are we going out to fight them?" I hesitantly asked.

"No," he replied, "not yet anyway, we don't have enough men in Abbeville to stop their advance, so we are allowing them to proceed until we build up our army."

All I needed to know now, was what the French intended to do to challenge Henry's army.

"Should you be telling me this?" I asked "as there must be a lot of Burgundian spies just waiting to betray their country?"

"That's our problem," he replied, "because some of the Burgundian's have now rallied to King Charles but unfortunately some have not, so we don't know who to trust, therefore we don't trust any of them."

This was my chance, "so what's the plan." I asked, with my heart in my mouth.

Jules looked right then left and whispered, "we are ordered to keep pace with the English as they try to find a crossing over the Somme, which they won't find because they are all being destroyed. But this is what is being kept secret from the Burgundian's, we shall stop them at the head of the river, at Saint Quentin, in the forest of Arrouaise where thousands and thousands of our forces are starting to gather."

"I don't know where that is." I said.
"Nor me" he replied, "but I believe it's about eighty miles from here."

In no time at all, I had found out everything I wanted to know but it won't be as simple getting away from Abbeville, as it was from Eu, so I shall just have to bide my time until I get a chance.

Jack…..*I know what Cris is up to, so I hope he's safe. I just wonder how he is going to get back over the river now that the French are keeping pace with us,* *but knowing Cris he will find a way and the left section skirmishers have been warned to watch out for him.*

Last night, our army had camped in a field beyond the cottages of Pont-Remy, which straddled the Somme, but I had spent the night a couple of miles away, sheltering in a dry barn with my men. This morning as we approached the rear column, they were trampling wearily dragging their feet along the road, soaked to the skin and not caring what might happen to them. If my men had been French they wouldn't have been able to put up any defence at all, they didn't even have a flanking guard out. The rear guard, led by Guy, was having trouble getting men to keep up with the column as we joined them and Guy told me that the trailing French scouts were not offering to give his men a fight. They were just keeping an eye on what we were doing and when he sent some of his archers after them, they just simply galloped away.

William…..*We are now into our eighth day of marching and should, according to the King, be arriving at Calais. It had been another wet and windy march and the men are exhausted, but we needed to get past another well defended town called Amiens. The column has been getting longer and longer and the main army has had to camp earlier this evening, to allow the stragglers to catch up at a place called Boves, where the town's people begrudgingly supplied us with bread and wine, after we promised to spare them from destruction.*

We are on the north side of the Somme at Boves, where I can see my own army on the far bank, but Jules seems to be sticking to me like glue. When I get a chance, I am going to swim across the river but as there are so many French soldiers milling about, I shall just have wait and see what I can do later on when it gets dark.

"You don't seem yourself tonight," said Jules, "what's the matter with you, are you ill?"

This was my chance, "I must have caught the bloody flux from the English," I lied, "and I think soaking my body in the river might help, but as I can't swim will you come along and keep an eye on me?"

"Of course," he replied. "I don't want you to drown."

The current was strong at this narrow stretch, but drown I did, as I struggled and choked then sunk underwater allowing the river to take me fifty yards downstream before I surfaced and hid in some reeds alongside the bank. The search lasted for about ten minutes but nobody expected me to alive and I was able to remain 'dead' as I crossed to the other side.

"What news have you got for me this time?" asked the King.
"Sire," I choked, "all of the crossings are all being destroyed and the French army are massing at the head of the river at a place called Saint Quentin to give you battle."

The King, who had been brought out of his bed uttered, "Ah, it's as I thought, but there is not a lot I can do to prevent this battle, so we shall just have to pray for divine intervention. You wouldn't happen to know by any chance how far it is to the head of the river would you."

"Eighty miles sire." I replied.

"Thank you Crispin, you shall be well rewarded once we get to Calais."

If we live to get to Calais, I thought.

"In the meantime," he said, "I shall get my servant to find you some dry clothes."

He then had another of his servants give me a pair of the finest boots I have ever seen. They were made of tan coloured calf skin and as soft as silk, which fitted my feet perfectly.

"Thank you my liege," I stammered.

Following the river would now be a waste of time because bridges and fords are being destroyed. However, from information passed to the King by my scouts, Henry now knew that the Somme followed a curving loop, which took a wide swing north before swinging south again, meaning that his army would be able to cut across this loop, whilst the French army would still have to pass around the north side of the river. Therefore tonight, orders had been put out that we were to have an early start in the morning, whilst it was still dark, and that camp fires were to be left burning to keep the French unaware of the move.

I was ordered to double my rear-guard and set an ambush for the trailing French scouts, which turned out to be our first great victory because I decided to leave the rear-guard as it was and send the two flanking sections in a pincer movement around the rear of the camped Frenchmen. The morning light was still an hour away, as I gathered the sections together to tell them of my intended plan. Jack and his men were to move along the Somme and meet up with Glynn's men, who were to pass around the south side of what we thought to be about forty French men at arms. I was with Jack as we crept along the river, and could see the French camp fires glowing as we circled to join up with Glynn.

We were trying to move quietly but our approach was not as stealthy as I wanted it to be and we could hear their horses becoming restless. Besides myself, there were other men who were able to stalk a prey without making a noise and we discovered that the French had set three guards to watch their front, with only one to watch their rear. I took it upon myself to tackle the rear guard whilst the other guards were to be silenced by three of my stalkers. I crept to within five yards of my prey, who was sitting with his back to a tree snoozing away, and dispatched him quietly with an arrow through his neck.

This was the first man that I had ever killed and I just stood there looking at him, he hadn't moved an inch and I wondered if he was still sleeping, until I pushed his shoulder, causing his lifeless body to slowly flop over; but I didn't feel good about taking a man's life away. The three forward guards had also been silently killed and my men leisurely aroused the sleeping Frenchmen, a few of who tried to defend themselves, only to receive unnecessary wounds. However the remainder, some sixty men, surrendered without further fight. Jack's men collected our horses and the prisoners were escorted south for about ten miles, having been relieved of their mounts, equipment and boots, then we left them to their own devices.

I could see the planned route our army was taking, because they were heading for a church which was on top of a hill, visible from all directions, meaning that my men along with the captured horses, soon re-joined the army. This was a good time to hand back the King's horses loaned in England and provide my men with mounts of their own. I knew that I was doing wrong by doing this, because all captured steeds were the property of the King but what he doesn't know won't hurt him…..or me. The King's plan was a masterstroke, as in no way could the French army keep abreast of the English because the distance around the loop must be at least twice the distance across, allowing our army to steal a one day march on them.

Today is our eleventh day of marching and it has started to rain again, so it's to be another dismal muddy wet slog. Thankfully, the going is all downhill and eventually the army made camp near an un-walled town called Nesle, where the inhabitants were not as lily-livered as other towns or villages we had passed, as the King's threat to put the town to the torch was met with defiance. They even taunted our army by hanging anything that was red out of their windows, which I suppose was to signify they were ready to draw blood. Why on earth they chose to do this is a mystery, as they would have had no chance whatsoever of saving themselves from certain death and total destruction.

Whilst resting up for the evening, everybody received the news that we had to witness a hanging. Apparently, one of my men had been caught stealing a small box called a Pyx from the local Church, which was used to hold consecrated bread. The man had thought it was made of gold but it was only gilded copper. No amount of pleading from his councillors could change the King's mind and the man…..Fred Hitch, was strung up as an example to the army that the King's orders must be obeyed at all times.

I knew that Fred was a bit of rouge and was light fingered, but I ask you, hung for a box? When all of the lords and gentry had their horses loaded with plunder.

Fred's men have now been split between my lieutenants, with ten men going to each of the remaining four sections. This hanging has made the King unpopular with my men, but it certainly made everybody realise that the army must have discipline and that whatever the King commanded must be obeyed. Even if a person disagreed with it, otherwise some cowards may run away from a battle and not stand with their comrades.

As we lined up on the Saturday morning, ready to destroy the town and put it to the sword, everything changed. The King had received news that there was an unguarded river crossing at a village called Voyennes only four miles away, so the order to sack this brave town was immediately cancelled and along with Tom's archers and fifty men at arms, I galloped ahead of the army to watch for any opposition at the crossing. To our great delight there were no Frenchmen to been seen, and the King, along with the rest of the army reached the Somme about 10am.

There were two crossing points, a ford and a bridge further upstream but the central span of the bridge has been destroyed, leaving a gap of about six feet, whilst the stone footings had been removed from the ford, making it only wide enough for a couple of men to wade over at the same time. The river itself was about thirty yards wide with marshy grounds on each side, making the full crossing distance about four hundred yards. There was a rough pathway of about one hundred yards leading to the river's southern edge, leaving a distance of maximum arrow range to the far side of the northern marsh.

The strong, long distance archers, of Jack's blue section were ordered to stand guard on our side of the river, whilst I, along with Glynn's red section, stepped into the water and started to wade across, holding our longbows and arrows high above our heads. It was a long anxious ten minute struggle against the flow of freezing waist high water, whilst at the same time trying to keep my balance on the uneven footing. Everybody expected the French to appear at any moment but thankfully we reached the north side of the river with no mishap, other than a few men almost drowning and had to be helped to their feet. On climbing out of the water, my men spread out to set up a bridgehead covering the crossing.

There had not been a single Frenchman in sight and the bridgehead was getting bigger and stronger as the morning progressed, with more and more men reaching the north bank. It now became impossible for the French to stop us bringing the rest of the army across the river. I could see our soldiers using logs, planks, doors and even ladders to repair the broken bridge and by mid-afternoon wagons and horses started to cross to the north bank, which was finally completed as night was beginning to fall.

Whilst all this had been going on, one of our mounted patrols had encountered a party of twenty French riders, who were about to attempt a belated attack, but they retreated after losing a couple of men dead.

One other who was wounded, was interrogated and under the threat of death, told our King all that he wanted to know about the French movements, which William later repeated to me.

"Miracles do happen" he said, "Because as we had cut across the bend in the river and your men had removed the trailing French scouts, they had no idea where we were. A prisoner told Henry that the French army thought that we were further on up the river or had decided to march against Paris. His comrades had then rushed on upstream, leaving behind their store of food supplies, which we have found. Therefore, the King wants it known that God is on our side by providing us with food and an easy crossing."

On Sunday morning we started to march out towards the strongly fortified town of Peronne and the men at arms have now been ordered to wear full armour, as it's only a matter of time before we have to fight a full scale battle. I felt sorry for the men still suffering from the runs, as they couldn't just drop their britches and do their stuff, so you can just imagine the problems they would be having after soiling themselves.
All of our archers, not counting my men thank goodness, have been ordered to cut staves of wood six feet long and about two inches in diameter and that a sharp point was to be shaped at each end. This was to form a defensive hedge of stakes against an expected cavalry attack, as a horse will not knowingly ride against a row of spikes. One point of the staves was to be forced into the earth at an angle, so that the other point would be about four feet off the ground, just high enough to impale a horse's chest.

The great walls of the town were about half a mile away, as we by-passed Peronne the next morning. The French sent out a cavalry force to tempt some of our army to come closer, so that they could fire their cannons at us, but the King would not allow any of his men to take the bait showing that discipline was being maintained. Then after passing the town the army turned left, away from the Peronne to Calais road and marched towards the north side of the Somme. Only this time we were travelling in the same direction as the river, we then zigzagged back towards the road again.

"Why are we not moving directly along the Calais road?" I asked William, my man in the know.

"The French are attempting to bring us to battle but our zigzagging has not allowed them to and the King is trying to avoid a confrontation with them." said William. "But now they are ahead of us, so it's just a matter of time before they turn around to block our march, at a place that will give them an advantage."
The fact that they were in front of us became only too obvious to our army, as the road to Calais was found to be trodden and soiled by what must be many thousands of men, causing our morale to sink. It was also obvious that our chance of winning a battle had probably gone and from the rumours of the ever increasing strength of the French forces, our chance of living was also gone. This however hardened everybody's resolve and although the mood was dismal, it brought a brotherhood to the army…..if we are going to die, we shall die fighting.

The King was giving encouragement to his men and we felt proud when he had announced that, as his ransom would be crippling to the nation, he was in it to the death and had no intention of standing back from the fight, which made the army feel special.

We have now been on the march for two weeks. It's all slow going and even though there has been no recent rain, it was still cold and windy as we trudged to the village of Dollens, then as day followed day we arrived at another village called Frevent. The bridge that crossed the river Canche has been broken, and whilst it was under repair the French made a token attack but they were kept at bay with a few of our dummy arrows.

Then it was another slog onto the small hamlet of Blangy. We arrived late on the Thursday afternoon and there were no French to give us trouble. The completely exhausted footslogging soldiers just flopped down wherever they could get shelter, and to add to our misery it had now started to rain heavily, which combined with the strong wind was coming down at a stinging angle.

There were no local people to be seen in this hamlet that was built alongside the river Ternoise. All of the empty dwellings were soon packed out with men who thought the day's march was over. The French had no bridge to destroy at this river as the water was shallow and thankfully the crossing was unguarded, which seemed strange as we would still have to wade across up to our knees. The sheltering didn't last long, as Henry wanted his army on the other side of the river, just in case the French did arrive to stop his forces crossing. So whatever was left of the dwellings was quickly demolished to remake campfires once a new camp was chosen.

"This little paddle won't make a lot of difference to us." said Bob, as he guided Taff across the river. "We are soaking wet anyway, and it's a good job I was allowed to bring your small cart with us on this trek, as I would never have been able to walk, like the rest of our other poor souls."

My troublesome monk was worrying me, because he has been suffering from the runs…..fortunately, it had not turned into the bloody flux, yet! But I couldn't say the same for his passenger.

Jamie had been ill for several days and no amount of doctoring had had any effect on him. Thankfully, there was no blood flooding out of his bowels. His father has been allowed to march alongside this makeshift ambulance and Uncle James was constantly cleaning the poor lad down. If my cart had not been available, Jamie would have had to be left behind to take his chances with the French as so many of our sick were forced to do, but I feared for his survival.

Our spirits were being kept alive by our King, who whilst I was taking Jack's report for my book, rode by with several of his lords. When he noticed Jack's facial scar he reined in his horse and asked Jack in what battle he had acquired it?
"This man," said Jack, pointing at me "inflicted it in an accident with an arrow when we were children."

The King tut tutted at me saying, "Shame on you Crispin, but your friend's scar looks the same as this wound," which, as he indicated on his left cheek, happened when I was sixteen." Which everybody knew about anyway.

When Jack's men heard what Henry had said they cheered him on his way, so they must have forgiven him for hanging Fred Hitch….. But not me.

It was still raining on and off as we set up camp in the wet open fields and tried to start more fires, but this was soon changed. There was a flurry of excitement as riders came bounding down the slope with Tom panicking and shouting, "They're just over the hill, the French are waiting for us," as he galloped on to make his report to the King.

This was it, the enemy has been sighted blocking the road to Calais and the whole of our army stood up expecting an attack at any moment. I followed the King and his nobility as they rode up the rise and as we came over the ridge I got my first sight of the French, which caused my heart to jump into my mouth. There were thousands and thousands of them about half mile away.

When they saw our army, they shouted and jeered towards us and spread themselves out in a rough line facing our way. They looked absolutely awesome in there glistening armour and colourful regalia, with hundreds of flags and banners that were just too numerous to count. This meant another change of camp and the army moved to the top of the rise overlooking the French. Only this time our archers drove their stakes into the ground hoping they wouldn't be attacked. The French had chosen the battlefield well, as we would be hemmed in by trees that stretched along each side of ploughed fields, with a village on our left which we later learned was called Azincourt and another called Tramecourt on our right.

Both armies just stood there looking at each other with no attempt whatsoever to do battle, which suited me as it gave me more time to live. This went on until sunset and as darkness started to fall it became obvious that there would be no battle today, so we were allowed to stand down.

Sir Gilbert had been ordered to examine the battlefield and took me out into 'no man's land' along with a couple of his men at arms to test the ground and set markers at two hundred yards, not that they were needed as every archer knew this distance exactly. Walking through the ploughed furrows proved to be a bit sticky, as the rain was not soaking into the clay like soil and I knew that once men and horses started to cross these fields the ground would soon turn into a quagmire. Sir Gilbert's men were fully armoured and were sinking into the mud more than I was, so heaven only knows how boggy it would get once heavy cavalry and an army of knight's start to churn up the land.

Whilst out in these dark fields, a group of French cavalry passed by us to make a sortie against the left wing of our army. On hearing them coming we had laid in the furrows, only to be completely covered in mud. This attack was only a gesture and was soon repulsed with only a few wounded men on both sides, but nobody had heard them coming until they were nearly upon our army. Therefore, the King has given orders that no noise was to be made for the rest of the night, in case they made another attack. And if any offender was to disobey these orders they would have an ear cut off! We were also ordered to keep our camp fires small, so that their glow would not spoil our sight in the dark. As the night dragged on the noise and laughter coming from the French army sounded as if it was only yards away, and it was impossible not to hear the silent praying of Henry's fearful troops.

The King was moving through our lines giving encouragement and saying God was on our side in a righteous war, but I was in no doubt that the French would be saying the very same thing to their men. Bob and Jamie were using my tent and I was having to camp out in the open, not that this made much difference, as with death looking me in the face I wouldn't be able to sleep anyway. I was just sitting close to my small fire, brooding about Catherine and wondering if I could ever be forgiven by her father for taking his livestock.

Then a bad thought came into my head….. *I could run away which would be simple, all I had to do was slip into the forest, pretend to be French, then make my way back to Eu. None of my friends would ever know because they would all be dead. But would I be able to live with myself?*
How could I even think of deserting my comrades, I shall either live or die with them?

"How's my young messenger: Jamie?" asked Sir Gilbert Umfraville, as he rode up to my small camp fire.

"Not so good," I replied. "I only wish I could get him away to Calais, where he might have a chance of survival."

"I'm sorry to hear that." he said, "and I'm also sorry to say that the King knows what your cart driver did at Fecamp, where he passed through the French lines without being challenged."

Oh, oh, here it comes, trouble. I thought.

"But don't worry," he quickly added, "because Henry wants to try and use the same trick to get word to what he hopes might be an English army coming to our help from Calais. And a monk, hopefully, should be able get through their lines. If you look over there, behind those trees, (as he pointed to our right) there's a pathway that goes through that village. If he was to take that path and get past the French, he may be lucky enough to meet up with any relief force coming from Calais and bring them to the rear of the French. We shall then have them between both our armies."

"But my monk is also ill," I sadly uttered.

"Well we can only ask him, can't we?" replied Sir Gilbert.

Brother Arnold (alias Bob) was willing to give it a try, and a monk's habit was found for Jamie. I then decided to save Red by having him pull the cart, whilst Taff would have to take his chances with me, which I later learned turned out to be a big mistake.

The King still had spies filtering in and out of the French camp, so they must also have spies in our camp; one piece of information that was fed to our army was that the French thought we were scared into silence. It was also learned that neither the French King or his son would be present in the oncoming battle, which those in the know especially me, hoped that perhaps with no single person in command there may be confusion amongst the resplendent nobles, who may want to attain personal glory without working in a disciplined and organised attack…… Which proved to be the case.

"What do you think about this, Cris?" said William. "The King wants it to be known, that the French are going to cut off the two longbow pulling fingers from the right hand of every archer that they intend to capture tomorrow, so that they would never be able to draw a longbow again."

"What a load of rubbish," I laughed, "that's a 'Cock and Bull' story if ever I heard one! For a start, the ordinary peasant soldier will be put straight to death and it's only the King and his lords that will be allowed to live, for the ransoms they would have to pay."

William had heard the story about the two public houses in Stony Stratford and said, 'shush, I know it's a load of bull, but it will put some fighting spirit into our archers, so don't you go telling people otherwise."

"Yes sir," I replied, saluting him with a grin on my face.....

**

CHAPTER TWENTY THREE

Friday 25th October

It had rained on and off during the night and dawn was breaking over soggy ploughed fields, where a lot of soldiers were going to die. The men who had been able to get some sleep awoke, bedraggled and frightened, to another cold damp day. There were no black rainclouds in the sky, so it looked as if we were going to be able to keep our bowstrings dry, but sadly, so would the French crossbowmen.

It's Saint Crispin's day, and my birthday but shall I live to enjoy it?

The King was making a big thing of today, spreading the word that Saint Crispin was a French saint, who with his brother Saint Crispinian, was immortalised in the town of Soissons. Henry wanted an excuse to bolster his army saying that these Saints are supporting our army to avenge last year's slaughter, where the French killed and raped their own country people.

We were also reminded that a considerable number of English archers, who were aiding our Burgundian ally's, were also brutally killed.

There was no movement on our part to start the battle and the French showed no intention of doing so either. We just stood there looking at each other, as it was well understood by both the English and the French that a defending army had the better chances of winning a battle, because of the effort involved in marching forward as opposed to standing still. William told me that Henry had sent his Heralds forward offering to surrender the battle on the condition that his army could continue the march to Calais, but this was rejected out of hand as the Heralds had returned with the bad news that the French were determined to end Henry's claims to France once and for all.

"It's only too obvious that they are willing to wait for our army to attack" said William, "they have plenty of food and wine and it's plain to see that more and more men are coming from the north and swelling their army by the hour, whilst the only men we have are those who have survived the seventeen days march from Harfleur."

Our decreased army numbered less than six thousand men, of which only nine hundred were men at arms, the remainder were archers. Whilst from the hundreds of banners I could see, the French must have at least twenty thousand knights, soldiers and crossbow men. For hours and hours we stood silently waiting for the French to make the first move but they were also waiting for us to do the same.

So how's the King going to get them to attack first? I wondered. This is when the dummy arrows came into use.

About three hundred yards in front of our lines there is pathway between the two villages and I was ordered to have Jack's long range bowmen form up along this track facing the enemy, who were six hundred yards further on.

But here is the clever part of the King's plan.....

I was to take two sections of my men through the trees past Tramecourt and get as close to the French lines as possible without being seen. Then I was to hide in the undergrowth and wait until I heard Jack's loud orders to his men. We had removed our white surcoat's depicting the red cross of Saint George, in the hope that if seen, we would be taken as local peasants.

In the meantime Henry had his army up stakes and move forward one hundred yards to make it look like his army were advancing. If the French had any sense, this would have been the ideal time to charge with their heavy cavalry, because the archers would have their backs towards them whilst they were forcing their defensive spiked barriers back into the soft earth, but all they did was stand there and watch.

My men were nervous at being so isolated but we were able to get close to the left side of their army without being noticed, as the French were too busy watching Jack and his men form up in line along the pathway. I'm sure our army as well as my men, could hear the enemy's laughter at such a small attacking group.

Jack shouted as loud as he could, "Nock," which made the French more attentive….. "Draw…..Aim….. Release."

This was an order for me and my men, as Jack's men were only going through the motion of pretending to release arrows from their bowstrings.

The French could see the movement but were not close enough to notice that there were no arrows being fired at them. My men were to count, one, two, then release over one hundred dummy arrows into the air at the laughing enemy, followed straight away with another arrow fired by each man. The time lapse between Jack's order to release and my men's arrows hitting the armoured men worked perfectly and the only casualties I could see were a few Frenchmen, who, having left their visors up, were unlucky enough to receive a direct hit in the face, with the remaining arrows bouncing harmlessly off the Knight's armour and falling to the ground. Even though they had had some casualties we could hear the French merriment. Jack and his men did the same trick once more with my men firing two more dummy arrows, each in quick succession, only this time all of the French knights had lowered their visors and kept their heads down to protect their eye and face slits, resulting in more joviality.

Jack and his men then ran back into the woods alongside Azincourt and made their way back to our lines. This little sting was enough to anger the opposing army and they were straining at the leash to make an attack, thinking that our arrows were harmless. So it only took one or two itchy knights to make a move for the whole army to start an advance.

Jack…..*It worked a treat and I was congratulated by the commander of our left wing army and cheered by his three hundred men at arms and his fifteen hundred or so archers, who really thought that we had shot our arrows such a long distance because they, like the French, could only hear my orders and see the firing motions. Furthermore, I am not going to let them know any different! They don't even know about the soft arrow heads but it's no dummy arrows from now on, as I can see the French making a start.*

William…..*Although I am now Lord Thornbury, I still consider Cris to be my best friend, so I am willingly going to help him map out this battlefield but as far as writing a book is concerned, I don't think he will be able to compete with the many, many, chroniclers* that will be doing the same thing. I might even write a book myself, all of this of course depends on whether we survive today. I don't expect to be killed, as I shall probably be taken prisoner now that I can afford to pay a ransom but Cris no doubt, will be put to the sword. After moving forward, as the King had ordered, I am now looking across ploughed fields ahead of me and the French army is about half a mile away at the other end of these fields. Our men are lined up three deep with about one yard between each man, therefore, at a rough guess we have a front of roughly one mile. I am with the King's men in the centre of his three armies, with Lord Camoys on our left and Edward the Duke of York on our right. From where I am standing there is a roadway that leads on to Calais, which stretches through the centre of these fields.

There are trees growing between each village and the fields, with a pathway leading from one village to the other and the treelines along the fields funnel inwards towards this pathway, then open out again (just like an hour glass), to where their army is lined up, reducing the space across this pathway to about half a mile. This means that whoever attacks first, will have to either draw their lines closer together or their ranks would have to stretch further back. It's now 10 am, and at last the French are making a move, so their laughter won't last for long once our deadly arrows start falling amongst them. It's just like watching children 'egging on' each other to advance and now that the first moves have been made they all want to get into the fray, as they don't want to be deprived of the easy pickings and the prospect of a one sided battle with lots of prisoner's to hold for ransom.
All of our nobility knew about the King's brilliant plan regarding the dummy arrows, which has increased

their confidence in whatever Henry decides to do; and won't the French be in for a surprise once the hardened steel bodkins start tearing through their armour? Every archer and man at arms has received his orders and knows exactly what to do, and more importantly…..what not to do, such as going forward into single combat.

I can see the French slogging their way through the muddy fields, so it won't be long before they reach the pathway, which is the distance that every archer in England has been practicing for years. Then once the French reach this target, they will be showered with an initial hail of five thousand arrows. I seem to recall reading about another pathway like this, was it at the battle of Crécy or was it the battle of Poitiers?

I am not a trained soldier or even an archer, so my roll will be to relay any orders the King might wish to send to the right of his army, whilst another messenger, Sir Charles Beaurepaire, is ready to do the same on the King's left. Sir Charles is a young noble from Henry's lands in Aquitaine, who along with ten others is all that are left of the original five hundred that joined the army in England, the remainder having deserted.

Tom…..As well as some of my men, I climbed to the top of a tall tree and could see the French coming, they were all on foot in three armies, each ten rows deep. We were pretending to be peasants by waving to them, and were getting plenty of waves back. Firstly I could see what must have been at least five thousand heavily armoured knights, foot slogging through the mud and hoisting flags and banners above their heads. Then about the same number of less *armoured soldiers in the second army and from where I am looking, these are followed by men with little or no armour. But where are their thousands of crossbow men, which have caused us the greatest worry?*

We had expected them to be in the lead, or at least be formed on the French flanks, but they were nowhere to be seen. No, hang on ... there they are, at the back of their army, just sitting down twiddling their thumbs, what's going on?

If they are not going to take part in the battle we may have a chance after all, I must let Cris know about this as soon as we get back to the main army.

"Cris," shouted William, as he came up to me with fresh instructions. "You are to take three of your sections and line them out amongst the trees at Tramecourt, and orders have been given to Jack to do the same with his section amongst the trees at Azincourt, which will create a three sided box that the French will have to advance into."

I gathered my lieutenants together and started to give them the King's instructions.

"Glynn, I want you take your section past the track that joins the two villages and line them out amongst the trees but aim at the crossbow men first, then the knights as they pass you….. Guy, I want you to spread out in the woods to guard Glynn's right flank, as once the French see what we are doing they will send men into the woods to attack us from the side…..Tom, I want you to line out behind Jack's men and do the same as them, then as the French advance, move along with them picking off the crossbow men first."

Tom could only grin, saying, "there are no crossbow men Cris, they are still at the rear of their army and it doesn't look like they will be taking part in the battle."

It was beyond belief, how could the French be so stupid?

They had at least as many crossbow men as we had archers and even though their rate of fire was far slower than ours, they could do considerable damage to our army.

"What a relief," I uttered, as I changed my orders, "shoot at the knights and aim at their arm or groin joints, as the King only wants them wounded and put out of the fight. *Making plenty of prisoners for ransom of course.* I thought. And make sure that none of you waste your arrows on the same man."

Finally I ordered, "Make every arrow count!"

Uncle James.....*Too blinking clever by half that Cris, what do I know about book writing? Ah well, I must remember correctly what's happening.*

I have been unwell and been given, with twelve other sick archers and about the same number of sick men at arms, the job of guarding the baggage train behind our lines. Now that the army has moved forward a bit, we have had to follow but loading the plunder on and off the horses is no joke. Thankfully, there are at least a hundred grooms doing most of the work. I have managed to keep the runs in check as Cris, God Bless him, has found me some oats and a few chicken eggs, which seem to be binding me up, but I am completely exhausted. He has told me what Jamie and Brother

Arnold are up to, so I just hope that they have no trouble getting past the French.

The French have been struggling for at least an hour now and if it hadn't been so serious I could have burst my sides laughing. They were moving along at a snail's pace, with some knights nearly up to their knees in mud. My men are standing back about two paces into the trees and just releasing their arrows directly into their sides as they pass. A few brave knights have made an attempt to attack us but once any man came out of the battle line he made himself a prime target.

I have just sent an arrow straight into a man's groin and he has fallen forward on his hands and knees into the mud just as if he was praying. Most of my arrows were hitting a Frenchman, but some of them were ricocheting off their armour over their heads into the rest of their column, so heaven only know where these are landing or what damage they are doing. My victims were lying dead or wounded in the mire not fifty yards away and it's just like shooting fish in a barrel. I knew it was them or me, but I had tears in my eyes as I watched their pitiful struggles and listened to their cries of pain.

The best the French could do to avoid being hit was to move closer and closer together as they passed through the bottle neck of trees, in an attempt to draw away from our deadly arrows the only safe place for them would be behind other knight's as they had realised that my men were selecting targets that were directly in front of them and not shooting over their heads. As long as my men have arrows we are safe but the arrows won't last forever…..and then look out.

Slaughter is the only word that I can use to describe the punishment we were dishing out to these colourfully dressed tin soldiers. Why they don't send a detachment of men into the woods to attack us from the side is beyond me, because the trees would give them an advantage over my archers.

William…..*Not long now, the French are well passed the pathway between the two villages and our archers are starting to release their arrows high into the air. I wouldn't like to be under that hailstorm once it lands. Jack and his men are killing the enemy as they pass Azincourt and Cris is doing the same at Tramecourt, forcing their army to a frontage of less than what must now be only six or seven hundred yards, as they draw away from their deadly arrows. Oh I forgot! I must check the time….. Eleven thirty am.*

What a floundering army they are, just look at them, trying to lift their iron clad feet out of the mud and having to do it time after time as they slowly come towards us. King Henry certainly got it right when he said that God is on our side, as I can see some knights completely stuck up to their knees without the strength to lift another leg. I have just returned from relaying instructions to Edward the Duke of York. Henry wants him to maintain discipline and not to be foolish by having his men attack the French, not until he gives the order to advance in line. Only I didn't use the word foolish when delivering his message, all I said to the Duke was, the King wants you to wait until the French reach our lines before joining battle. But by the look of it, he is about ready to take the fight to them, (foolish man).

I have also been ordered to keep an eye on the baggage train and report any attempt by the French to circle around and attack it, but everything looks well to me. However, I might just pop back in a bit and see how Jamie's father is doing.

Jack....*This is too simple, my men must have put at least a thousand knights on their faces and they are being sucked into the mud as they fall, but they still keep coming. I wouldn't mind betting that Cris is doing the same over on his side of the field and as he has twice as many men as me, he must have at least doubled my score. Look at that knight crouching, just like he was having a dump, it seems a shame to put an arrow into his backside, still it's one more out of the fight once our arrows have gone. I started out with two quivers of my own blue flights and ninety six arrows supplied by the King, giving me one hundred and forty four arrows in total and my men along with the rest of Cris' men will have at least the same.*

I was disgusted when the King's arrows were given to us, as the shafts were square, but this proved to be a blessing, as we could trim the corners off them ourselves and use the dry shavings for lighting our fires. I wonder if the King had planned this as something for the men to do at night and to give us some very useful wood shavings in the bargain. Having said all this, I still haven't started to use my own two quivers of arrows and I don't intend to, until the French come to see me off, then I shall take as many of them as possible to the grave with me.

Due to the French having to draw away from our deadly arrows, there is a gap between their army and the trees on my side of the field, which has allowed their cavalry to get into the fight but their heavy horses are moving so fast that some are getting past without my men being able to hit them. However, the horses we have managed to injure have tossed their riders so hard into the ground, that they are unable to pull themselves out of the mud. After a short struggle many of them lie still, so they must have suffocated or drowned in the water soaked gooey mire, whilst their poor screeching horses have charged into the French ranks creating further problems for the closely packed tangle of men.

Up to now, none of my men are injured but how long this will last I can't say, as it will soon be hand to hand fighting when we have to join up with the men at arms.

There are dead and wounded French knights stretching right back along our side of the battlefield, whose armour is pressing them deeper and deeper into the churned up mud, whilst the rest of their army are stuck up to their knees trying to advance around and even over their fallen comrades. They are going nowhere fast and look completely exhausted but now and then after a slight rest, they pull a leg free, squelch it forward and get stuck again. There is no way for them to continue their march so they can stay where they are for the time being, whilst my men concentrate on those knights still plodding along.

Thomas Easton.....*I have seen very little of Crispin Bowyer since his uncle James and I were put in command of thirty archers each by the Duke of Kent in Faversham, but his uncle has told me about Cris' book, so I know that he shall want to hear what is happening in the Dukes retine.*

Well, due to the Bloody flux, I am down to eighteen men of my own, out of an original thirty three and I have taken command of James's archers, as he has found himself a soft job watching the baggage train….. Sick my eye!

What a ragged bunch we are, with not a pair of boots between us, but I only hope I stay alive to tell Cris what is going on in the centre of our army. I am on the left side of the King's army and have advanced with my stake plus one other, which I cut last night as did most of my men. Having to drag these poles along with us has been a bit of a pain but I'm now glad I can get some protection from our spiked wall. With nothing better to do last night, besides praying and worrying, all of our points have been whittled as sharp as our bodkin arrows, which we then careful scorched over our small fires to dry out the sap and harden the wood. There has been a lot of jeering between our armies and all of the English archers were letting the French know that they still had their fingers by sticking their hand up with only their pulling fingers showing in a two finger salute.

I have been dreading this but here we go…..I shouted nock, draw, aim, release, once I saw the signal baton tossed into the air by Sir Thomas Eppingham and hearing the army's war cry…..for God, Harry, Saint George and England.

I'm not so good at hitting a bull's eye any more but who could miss such a host of men slowly advancing all bunched up together. Our whole army of archers are firing arrow after arrow high into the air and although I can't see what damage they are causing, I can at least see that our bodkins are knocking these French knights to the ground, but where are their crossbow men? Even though they fire their bolts slower than we fire our arrows, they should now be hitting our army. Thank goodness, they are nowhere to be seen and I just hope they are out of the fight, but why can't God do the same with the French cavalry?

For here they come on their massive war horses that can simply brush us aside like chaff in a wheat field. I hope these stakes do what they are supposed to do, and as far as not letting the horses see them until the last minute…..well that can go to pot, as I want them to see my stakes at least.

Their main army is now only one hundred yards away, so I can aim straight into their close packed ranks, selecting my target with ease…..and doesn't that knight's surcoat look muddy?

Whoosh, clank, that's one more for sure as my arrow knocked him backwards but with only twelve arrows left out of five quivers, I had better make it twelve kills…..eleven now as my last arrow has hit another knight in his arm joint, as he tried to climb over his fallen comrades. A wall of enemy is building up higher and higher in front of us but still they come, scrambling over their dead and wounded. Come on then, come on….. Ten to go, now nine, if only I had more arrows, why on earth did I shoot so many in the first onslaught…..

MORE ARROWS….. MORE ARROWS!

I can see one poor beast screeching piteously, with an arrow in its neck. It has thrown it's rider into the mud, not five yards in front of me, but it would be a waste to use one of my last few arrows to kill him, putting *him out of his misery. So I had to leave him just wallowing there, as we are not to move forward or out of line.*

Thank goodness, the horses are turning away from the stakes and crashing back into their own men. Look, there's another tossed rider, he is lying floundering in the mud, surely that man at arms shouldn't be moving out of line to finish him off? Yes he is, he has killed the Frenchie with a sword thrust between his arm joint and breast plate.

Oh no, look out there's a French horseman coming at you! Clank…..he has received a hammer blow to his helmet and his head seems to be crushed in. That's the first Englishman I have seen killed. Miraculously the French knight is still galloping along our front, without a single arrow being aimed at him, as nobody wants to waste an arrow on this moving target, what's more our men are cheering him.

William*…..The road directly in front of the King is not churned up like the ploughed fields, allowing the enemy to make better progress along it. A determined group of Frenchmen, who are well ahead of the rest of their army, has reached our lines and are now battling with Henry's bodyguard but I can see my liege fighting like a man possessed, standing over a wounded knight who can only be his brother, Humphrey the Duke of Gloucester as he is wearing a surcoat that is the same as his. Henry is shouting out our battle cry, which is being picked up by the whole army.*
'For God, Saint George and England'….. 'For God, Saint George and England' over and over….. And the archers are still giving the French the two finger

salute, letting them know that they still had all their digits.

I can see Henry's flag showing the fleur de lis and the English lions, which was proudly held aloft with its bearer standing next to our King, both surrounded by exhausted fighting knights, who are clubbing, slashing jabbing, and beating the French to a standstill with nothing more than sheer determination. We seem to be winning as French noblemen are surrendering by the dozen. However, these defeated men are causing us a problem because prisoners have to be kept safe by their captors, which means that more and more of our men are out of the fight and are standing behind the army guarding their charges.

But what's all that shouting coming from the baggage train? No, it can't be….. Now we are in trouble. The enemy have got behind us and all of the servants and grooms are fleeing in terror shouting that the baggage train was being attacked.

With so many of his men guarding prisoners, Henry has realised that the French must have been able to come to the rear of his army, which could only mean that the surrendered Frenchmen may well take heart and start fighting again. So he has sent me and his other messengers out, with the order….. **KILL ALL OF THE PRISONERS!**

Uncle James…..What's this? It looks like the local peasants are gathering behind us with the intention of robbing the baggage train once our army is defeated, which won't be long now by the sound of it. The grooms are running away and the locals are getting braver!

I am supposed to stop the scavengers plundering the plunder that we have plundered in the first place, which is a hopeless task and the best we can do is save the horses close to us, but the deserting servants are shouting the wrong messages as it's not the French soldiers who are attacking…..thank goodness.

"Cris" Shouted Glynn, "my men are running out of arrows are there any more?"

"Are the French attacking your flank?" I shouted back.

"Not as far as I can see." he bellowed.

"Then see if Guy can let you have some of his." I called, "but it's the same here and if Guy is not being threatened, get him to come and line up with your men."

Guy…..*Having not seen a single Frenchman to shoot at I have willingly joined Glynn, as the second French army started to struggle past us through the mud. I was not so willing for my men to give away two of their quivers but we still have four containing twenty four arrows each, so we have joined in this killing spree.*

William…..*What's the Duke of York doing? He is moving his army forward without the King's permission. This doesn't look good as his standard is nowhere to be seen, it should be waving above his head. The King will have something to say about his lack of discipline. However Henry has now given the order for his two remaining armies to advance banners, shouting our battle cry again, 'For God, Saint George and England.' The French second army has* *halted in its tracks and is in disarray not knowing what to do, they could see that their leaders are lying dead or dying all piled up in front of them and they are fleeing back, blocking the third army's advance. It is just one big foul up, and I'm sure that they, along with the panicking horses, are trampling each other underfoot.*

I now have only one of my own red flighted quivers of arrows left, so it's now starting to look like we shall have to fight hand to hand, along with our men at arms, which will mean that I won't stand a chance against a fully trained Frenchman.....but what's this?

The French are falling back, they must be reforming their ranks or could it be that having seen what has happened to their heavily armoured leaders ,they have started to panic.....I hope so.

Yes! They are crashing into each other in an attempt to get off the battlefield. Are we winning?

There is now a lull in the battle, and orders have been passed down that we are to go out into the field and kill any knights who are still capable of fighting, whether they have surrendered or not.

"Men," I shouted, as I pulled off my boots. "Those of you who are lucky enough to have anything on your feet..... Take them off! You will be able to work your way through the churned up land easier."

It's one thing killing from a distance but going up to a defenceless man and prodding your knife into his body is something else, and even though some of my men were quite happy to commit this murder, I was not.

All I am going to do is collect the arrows that are sticking in the ground.

By now, it must be at least an hour past noon and a lot of the French are running away causing more of a lull as they fall back, but I am determined to cross this ploughed field and find my friend.

"Jack, is that you?" I called to this muddy archer as we met in the middle of the battlefield.

"Aye Cris, you mucky pup." he said, slapping me on the back. "I see that you are collecting arrows like the rest of us and from the look of things we are going to need them, as the Frenchies seem to be getting ready for another attack, so we had better get back into the woods."

"How many men have you lost?" I asked.

"None" He replied, "what about you?"

"None dead," I replied, "but some men have hurt their feet by standing on the discarded French weapon that have sunk into the mud."

After parting, with a cheery good luck to Jack, I was moving my men back into the trees when I stepped on something but it wasn't a sword or a piece of armour, it was more like a stick. On rooting it out I discovered that it was a flag pole, which had a long banner attached, which had been trodden into the mire and completely soaked in mud.
This is mine. I said to myself, as I cut the strings holding it to the pole and stuffed it into my doublet. All of the English knights were collecting flags, so now I have one.

"Stop!" I shouted, to a glazed eyed Thomas Easton, who was about to slit a man's throat, whose muddy surcoat looked blue with traces of yellow. "Let me kill this one."

"I know you," said the knight in French, "You are one of the men I sent to warn Abbeville, so just get on with it, you traitorous pig."

"Pig, maybe," I said to the Count of Eu, "but if you want to live, do you surrender to me?"

"Yes, of course you swine."

"Well shut up," I said, as I cut off of his armour, pulled him out of the mud and frog marched him to the trees.

Now that my men are back in position with a stack of arrows each, we are ready to start defending ourselves again. But hang on, I can see the heralds talking to the King, so what's happening?

The heralds had been watching the battle from the side of the pathway at Tramecourt and had been getting in the way, by blocking the aim of some of my men, but what's all that cheering?

Is it over? Have we won? **YES!**

It's too incredible to believe but the heralds have come to the King with the good news that the French were surrendering the battle.
Exhausted and drained, I sank to the ground and felt an overpowering sense of triumph, mixed with jubilation, remorse and sadness for all those dead and dying men. There were still more than twice as many Frenchmen as Englishmen but they were rapidly

disappearing in all directions, except for their leaders, who were lying in mounds skewered with arrows. I was happy to join in the rejoicing, and watched the King wave his banner in the air, to the cheers of the whole army. Henry had his horse brought forward and rode through the rank's praising them and claiming that the victory was not his but God's.

Well, God must have had something to do with it because there must be thousands of dead or dying French nobles out there in front of us, whilst others still alive but too exhausted to move, were stuck in the mud across the battlefield, like isolated trees.

The battle has been won and there is to be no more killing. Surviving French noblemen are surrendering themselves for ransom by the hundreds and servants are searching for their lost masters amongst the dead and injured. I knew that I should go searching for plunder amongst the heaps of bodies and scrap iron but I was completely spent and thoroughly ashamed of myself, so I just sat there crying with relief. It's no wonder my brother didn't want to talk about his exploits at Homildon, so I suppose that I shall keep my mouth shut as well.

**

CHAPTER TWENTY FOUR

Local scavengers, women as well as men, have joined our army in gruesomely stripping French bodies naked and thinking nothing of cutting away an arm or a leg if a piece of armour was difficult to dislodge. None of my men have been killed but our victims were either dead with arrows pointing skyward from their bodies, or they were still wallowing in the mire with a bodkin stuck in their joints. I had started out with ninety six ordinary arrows and two quivers of my finest arrows and the rest of my men had at least the same quantity, most of which were now gone. If my men had only shot one hundred arrows each, that's over seventeen thousand arrows fired from my side of the field alone, with perhaps half that amount fired by Jacks section. So when you include the rest of the King's archers, there must have been well over half a million arrows fired at the French.

A great number of these would have been shot at a range of one hundred to two hundred yards, coming down to less than eighty yards as the Frenchmen advanced. But from where my men were shooting, the distance was never over fifty yards. Therefore, if only one in ten of my men's arrows shot at Tramecourt were hitting the mark, that's seventeen hundred strikes but knowing how skilful my men are, I would say that the number of dead and injured has got to be more like three to four thousand, if not more; unbelievable though it may seem and I am ashamed to say that my tally is probably high.

The battle has lasted for less than four hours and I dreaded having to look for my red flights, as this would highlight the number of Frenchmen struck by my arrows. I knew that I must get on with the search and collect as many arrows as possible, as it was expected that another battle would soon flare up, even though this one had been won. How many of my arrows made actual hits, I don't know, as all of our archers have been collecting whatever they could find, regardless of flight colours. Thankfully, they only collected six of my red flights and I didn't ask the finders what damage they had caused.

Now that the French were in disarray, I ordered my men to pillage what food and drink they could, whilst I went to soak the mud off myself in the stream that passed Tramecourt. When I returned, the Count of Eu was sitting quietly with his back to a tree and he said, "I trusted you to take my message to Abbeville but why have you become a traitor?"

"I am not a traitor." I replied, "I'm an Englishman serving my King."

"Ah, a spy is no better than a traitor." said Charles of Artois, "but thank you anyway for saving my life."

I did feel like a traitor and saving his life helped me to ease my conscience a bit but not enough to excuse me from the deaths I have caused.

Now that the fighting has stopped, there is an eerie calm across the battlefield with some men.....English as well as French, wandering about in a daze and the only sounds I could hear were coming from the wounded men and the suffering horses. The smell of blood oozing from the many dead, was added to the existing smell of our unwashed army, which has become almost normal to my nose. People who were trying to kill each other not an hour ago, were now working together to pull living Frenchmen from under the mounds of the dead, with more and more prisoners being taken for ransom. It looked like every archer had a Frenchman in custody, which would bring them a great sum of money. I have my prisoner but I am not selling him, not yet anyway, as I want to try and become his friend so that when I return to Eu, I hoped he might help smooth things over with Catherine's father.

There are at least five thousand Frenchmen for ransom, which will boost the King's revenue, as he gets one third of all hostage ransoms with the retinue captain getting another third whilst the remaining third goes to the person who had captured the prisoner…..supposedly, but it didn't quite work out like this. The capturer was obliged to feed and protect his charge until the ransom was paid, which could take years, so what our men have been doing is selling their prisoners for thirty nobles each, to the King's representative. This was to be paid once they returned to England, along with their wages.

Fat chance, if you ask me.

William…..*It's still mid-afternoon and I have been given the job of helping to count the dead Englishmen from the Duke of York's army and just as I thought when his banner fell…..the Duke is dead, all because he wouldn't follow orders and he advanced too early. Also killed were, the Earl of Suffolk and about one hundred of his men at arms, who had taken the brunt of the French attack on their side of the battlefield.*

Our dead, totalling just over two hundred, have been put into barns which were then set on fire, which is far quicker than burying them. But the smell of burning flesh was worse than any odour I could have ever imagined. However, the bodies of the two noblemen were boiled down to the bones, ready for sending home to England for burial. Now that the killing is over, the army is getting as much plunder as they can from the dead. They have been joined by the servants of the fallen Frenchmen, who have come looking for their masters, not knowing if they were dead or alive, or even if they had been taken prisoner. They were discovering that this was a difficult task because the dead had been robbed of their clothing and armour that bore their badges of rank and due to the King's orders to kill the prisoners and the facial stabbing through their visors, quite a number of the dead were unrecognisable.

**

CHAPTER TWENTY FIVE

Saturday 26th October

The King is offering a reward of thirty nobles, to the person who finds 'The Oriflamme' and people were digging in the mud searching but not finding it….. And they won't, because whilst washing myself yesterday, I also washed my mucky find, which turned out to be the French battle flag. This is now wrapped up in my spare clothing. It's about six feet in length and twelve inches wide and has three trailing chevron strips at the bottom. It is made of bright red silk with a green border, with a golden sun emblem on the top face, casting golden sunbeams down its length. Oriflamme, in English, means 'golden flame' and I knew that the red colour was supposed to represent the blood of Saint Denis who was beheaded about the same time as my namesake, Crispin. I have no intention of selling this banner to the King, as it's worth more than ten pounds to me.

Having gorged ourselves on the vast quantity of food and wine left behind by the fleeing enemy, the order came from King Henry to march straight away towards Calais, leaving this field of carnage to whosoever wants to bury what must be at least eleven thousand dead Frenchmen, most of who were of the ruling classes.

But I just couldn't understand why none of our prisoners had tried to escape in the night, as they were not closely guarded. I would have been off like a shot but my prisoner, who I now call Charlie, was still sleeping like a baby.

"Come on," I called, tapping him with my foot, "we need to get going."

"What time is it?" he groaned, wiping the sleep out of his eyes.

"It's 7am and we need to be on our way." I replied.

Count Charles de Artois was worth about two hundred pounds to me, providing I waited until he could gather together his ransom payment and as he was one of the prisoners not sold to the King's representative…..Sir John Cornewaille, he would be riding along by my side, which will give me the chance to try and win his friendship. Even though we have won the battle, which the King has named the "Battle of Agincourt", we were still fearful of a fresh attack from the French. Therefore, my lieutenants and their men, took up their normal marching position, only this time the rear guard of Glynn's men along with fifty mounted men at arms and some of the grooms were to scour the countryside gathering back the horses and plunder that had been stolen by the local people. **Uncle James**…..*What was I supposed to do when a couple of hundred people raided the baggage train? I was lucky to get away with my life but that counted for nothing when the Duke of Kent roasted me for not dying along with a dozen others. So I have now been given the job of helping to round up the stolen horses, which is simple enough, now that the peasants are in fear of being caught with the booty, and most of the mounts along with their loads have been abandoned. We can only do our best but how am I to know what's still missing? Anyway, I don't want to lag too far behind our army and neither does the rest of the search party in case the French want their revenge,* *so after gathering at least a thousand heavily loaded horses, it was back to the rear of our army.*

The Count of Eu had calmed down a bit and although he was not too talkative, he is resigned to his fate and asked me to find out how much ransom he would be expected to pay.

"Charlie," I said, "I don't know how much it will cost you, but whatever it is I am prepared to waver my share, if you will allow me to live as Jack Devereux in Eu?"

"**NEVER**!" he shouted. "I don't want a traitorous spy in Normandie no matter how much it costs me."

So that looked like the end of my little plan for the time being. I'll just have to try and think of something else to bring him round.

There is no glory in slaughtering an enemy, even though it was a matter of their life or mine. Therefore, I was determined that once we arrived in Calais, my longbow would be broken into little pieces and burnt and that I would never shoot another arrow as long as I lived. I was ashamed and disgusted with myself for the butchery I had helped to create at Azincourt and didn't want to be a part of King Henry's killing army anymore. I had once thought, from all the stories told to me by my family of warriors, that fighting battles was glorious but none of them had ever mentioned the horror, bloodshed or carnage of battle, only the glory of winning and the collecting of loot.

On capturing Charlie, I had discovered some written parchments in his possession, which might have been instructions for the French army but on translating them into English, I found that they are notes very similar to mine; and as they will not be of any use to my King, I shall use them in my book to give my readers an insight into what the French have been up to.

CHARLES D' ARTOIS, COUNT OF EU

Notes

Sunday 13th October

I am obliged by my fealty to King Charles VI to join his army to counter the English invasion. Therefore, once the enemy had passed Eu and was well on its way to Abbeville, I gathered my fifteen men at arms, which included two knights, and have set out in pursuit. I did have three knights, but my cousin. Lancelot was killed in single combat outside the town walls. I had sent two men to follow on behind the English, to see which way they are heading, and one of them has reported back that they have bypassed Abbeville, so this is where I have joined up with our army for the chase. The fifty thousand men that they were supposed to have is incorrect, it's more like seven to ten thousand, which is bit of a relief and from the sick and dying men they have left in their wake, it looks like we shall have an easy battle once we gather all our forces together.

Sunday 20th October

It is now one week since I set out from Eu and I am in Peronne along with at least five thousand of my countrymen. For some reason, no reports had been coming back from the men following the English who, it seemed, had lost their trail for a couple of days, so it was not known what their intentions were. It was thought that they had turned towards Paris, but having picked up their trail again, we now know for sure what they are up to….. They are running for Calais, as they have crossed the river Somme and are marching north past our stronghold.

Monday 21st October

Nobody seems to be taking command of our army as the King will not be leading us, neither will his son! And from what I know about both of them this doesn't surprise me in the least. King Charles is a bit touched in the head and often thinks he is made of glass, whilst his son, the eighteen year old Dauphin Louis, is a fat layabout who only thinks of drink and debauchery, so I for one, won't miss them. They had been advised that should they be captured, their ransom would be crippling to France. Therefore we are loosely under orders to Constable Charles d' Albret and Marshal Boucicault, but both of these leaders do not seem to have full control of the many royal Dukes and Counts…..a conflict of opinion if you ask me.

Monday Afternoon

Not too daft these English…..we had hoped to draw them towards our walls by sending out a bogus charge, which if they had counter attacked would have allowed us to fire cannon stones at them, but they didn't take the bait. They continued their marched past Peronne, therefore, our so-called leaders have given orders to follow in their tracks.

Wednesday 23rd October

It's strange but for some reason we have been marching ahead of the English army, and today, a suitable battlefield has been found between two villages called Azincourt and Tramecourt, which is the only route that the enemy can take. So with plenty of food and wine to eat and drink we have turned about and shall wait here to do battle, collect a few hostages and send the rest of the rabble to their graves.

Thursday 24th October

There has been a lot of rain this morning and our scouts tell us that the English are no more than a few miles away, so we shall soon be seeing some action. I just hope I get the chance to capture a few noblemen for ransom, but this seems unlikely as I have been informed that I shall be in the rear rank of our leading army of six thousand fully armoured knights, whilst the lighter armed second and third armies shall be following up behind. Nevertheless, it should be a simple task wiping this tiny army off the face of the earth, as more of our men have started to arrive from Saint Quentin, which is where we had hoped to stop the English army crossing the Somme. From the hundreds of banners that I have counted, we must have at least twenty five thousand Frenchmen ready to do battle.

Late afternoon, Thursday

There they are, standing on a rise across the fields from us, but I don't know which one of them is King Henry even though I can see his banner. We have all lined up facing their way and our men are jeering at him, so let's get on with it…..But no, let them get on with it, because all we have to do is allow them come to us. I can see the rest of his army trickling over the rise, spreading out and facing us, but I can't see what they are doing? They seem to be sticking something in the ground and it's beginning to look like we shall not be fighting them today. So let's eat, drink and be merry, for tomorrow THEY DIE.

Friday 25th October 9.30am

No movement yet, we are looking at them and they are looking at us, still there's no rush. Thankfully, it's stopped raining. I must admit, I wasn't too happy with my position in the first army as everybody including me, wants to be in the front where the glory will be. Some of the traitorous Burgundian's, who we were fighting not long ago, having rallied to the King are placed in the front of the leading army which will allow them the greatest honour. All of this posturing is not helping one bit, and our two leaders are reluctant to give orders to royal princes who would take no notice anyway.

It has taken some time to sort the three armies out, with the high ranking heavily armoured knights in the lead, the lesser Nobles following up close behind and the ordinary armoured soldiers at the rear….. But, what's that movement along path between the two villages? It looks like their bowmen are lining up to shoot at us, well that's ridiculous for a start, as surely the distance must be too great? I don't understand English but I can hear orders being shouted and I can see their men drawing their longbows.

Good news…..word has filtered through the army that their arrows are having little effect on our armour and I can also hear laughter coming from our men, it also looks like the English are starting to move forward.

**

CHAPTER TWENTY SIX

Our army arrived in Calais on Tuesday the 29th of October without any more interference from the French. The garrison refused us entry into the town, giving us the flimsy excuse that there was insufficient food and drink for everybody, which was a bit much to say the least. Only the King and his lords were allowed inside and we have had to camp outside, however, I was in no doubt that they feared that our men would run riot.

Where are Bob and Jamie? I shall have to go looking for them as they should have been here days ago, and I wonder if they had got into the town before our army arrived. On finding William, I worriedly asked, "As you are allowed into the town, have you seen Bob and Jamie….. Are they safe?"

"Sorry Cris," he replied, "I have bad news for you, Jamie is here, but Brother Arnold is dead."

"How did he die'?" I sadly asked.
"Come on," he said, "I shall take you to see Jamie, and he can tell you himself."

"I roughly remember bouncing along in the cart dressed in the brown robes of a monk and being stopped and searched by a French road block." said Jamie. "I seem to recall Bob trying to bluff it out with them, but they were suspicious about such a fine horse as Red pulling the cart, so they insisted on a search. When they discovered his longbow the game was up."

Jaime hesitated, "I don't remember what happened next…..But the French have treated my illness, which seems to have worked as my health has improved. All due to the care of an English speaking French doctor who told me what had happened when we were caught."

"So what did he tell you?" I impatiently asked.

"He told me that the road block guards had tried to drag Bob off the driving seat but he would not surrender, resulting in fisticuffs, and that he had been making a good job of the fight, having downed three men, but with another four to put up with, he was eventually overwhelmed." said Jamie.

"Is this when Brother Arnold died?" I interrupted.

"The doctor told me that Bob was in the next tent dying of the bloody flux and that the exertion of the fight had sapped the last of his strength. He then told me that he was only able to save my life because I am young, whereas Bob is old and has less stamina, and unfortunately he was being given his last rights from a French priest."

"As I bent over Brother Arnold," Jamie continued, "he whispered….. We won, but don't ask me how? You must not fret about me my son, as I have had a good life and have made my peace with God. He then, in a very weak voice, told me to tell you that he hopes you have now come to realise the futility of fighting other people's wars….. As he did all those years ago…..and with that, he slipped into a coma and died peacefully half an hour later."

After wiping away a few tears Jaime went on, "I was reunited with Red and we made our way towards Calais but without your cart, which has been turned into firewood, and unfortunately Cris, your cleaver and folding saw have been lost.

But what do you think about this?

I have suddenly become a rich man, oh alright then, a rich boy, because once the surviving French Nobles knew that the battle was lost, ten of them surrendered to me, which means that I have a nice little sum coming to me in ransom payment. Why they have done this is beyond me as I would have just gone home, but I suppose it must have something to do with honour and chivalry." He concluded.

Thank goodness Jamie is safe but I was sad about my archery teacher, who had sent me his dying message, which has made me more determined to give up being an archer. But having said this, I am not going to turn into a monk like he did, I am going to return to Normandie and with luck, settle down and marry Catherine.

I have now returned Taff to Jamie, as well as making him the full owner of Red, and have given him written instructions for Edward, saying that he is to give him a junior position in the bank. I also asked Jamie to inform my parents that I intend to sail back to Eu and hopefully marry Catherine and that we had a son named Crispin.

I'm not too happy about Henry or his campaign at the moment, but when William found me camped outside the town walls, he said. "Come along Cris, the King wants to reward and thank you for your special efforts"

I wasn't going to let him know how I felt, nor was I going to turn down any gains that might be coming my way, so I entered the town gate to meet my liege and to my great surprise, his brother the Duke of Clarence as well, who had not gone home sick, but had sailed on to Calais after leaving Harfleur.

I was right after all…..he wasn't really sick, so *there is obviously a family feud going on here.* I thought.

"I am passing out grants to my faithful warriors." said the King. "So, what am I going to give you?" He asked.

To which I gave the usual response, "I was only doing my duty sire, which is reward enough."
"Come now," said Henry with a smile, "there must be something you would like, land … a title, what?"

"Sire," I replied, "I wish to return to Eu, where I spent some of my childhood, and settle down with a woman who is very dear to me; if perhaps you could persuade one of your prisoners, the Count of Eu, to allow me to live in his town as Jack Devereux that will be reward enough."

"Umfraville," shouts the King to Sir Gilbert, "have this Count brought to me."

"I shall not have a spy living anywhere in Normandie." said Charlie defiantly when he was ushered into the King's presence.

"Normandie is about to be part of my realm." said Henry angrily, "so you shall do as you are told, and until you have paid your ransom, which will be one thousand marks, you shall need somebody to help raise the money. Therefore, you should be grateful about my man's waiver, and if you are not careful I shall make it ten thousand marks!"

Charles of Artois had no option and was forced to accept the King's demands, thus I became the temporary ruler of Eu.

"And as for you Crispin," said my King, "you shall not go to Eu as Jack Devereux, but as Sir Crispin Bowyer and you shall be my Ambassador for the whole of Normandie."

Later, after smashing and burning my longbow, I have had the great satisfaction of burning my notes page by page…..let somebody else write the book because I could never relay the carnage and horror of war. Oh, and by the way, the Oriflamme also went up in flames, as I needed no reminding of the terrible carnage and loss of life which I helped to create.

Having convinced Charlie that I would do everything in my power to raise his ransom and look after the welfare of his people, I was able to get him to relate the end of the French ordeal on the battlefield of Azincourt.

"I can't pretend to be a good soldier." he said, "so I was put at the rear of the first army, which thank goodness probably saved my life. So when our leaderless army saw what they thought was your army advancing, it was like a red rag to a bull, and thinking that your arrows would do little harm, they couldn't wait to get going. I was not aware of the trouble we would have crossing the ploughed fields and like everybody else, was sinking deeper into the slime as we advanced."

"But why weren't any of your crossbowmen used in the battle?" I asked.

His reply was, "It was felt that if they had taken part they would not be able to pick out individual targets, such as the King or the very rich noblemen who would bring a huge ransom and that it would just be a simple matter of overwhelming your outnumbered knights."

I still wanted answers, so I asked him, "Well why didn't your army send men into the woods to combat our archers lining your advance?"

"That's easily answered" he replied, "we could see you alright….. But there was nobody giving orders."

The End.

POSTSCRIPT

Whilst this has been mainly a work of fiction, the story leading up to the battle of Agincourt is based on research into the life and times of the people of Britain in the fifteenth century, along with the conflicting evidence leading to the actual battle of Agincourt itself.

With regards to the campaign, I have taken a consensus of what I feel would be reasonable from known information. Therefore the march from Harfleur may possibly have been split into several routes to allow for foraging, but I have kept the army together in my story following what I consider to be the generally accepted route.

I found no evidence that the King's navy would track his armies march along the French coast but this could have been a possibility.

When it comes to the battle, it would only be logical to have archers in the woods at each side of the battlefield during the French advance, which has been suggested by numerous chroniclers, as just like the machine gun in the First World War this firepower would devastate the French army, and it is well documented that the French crossbow men were not used in the battle. If they had have been, the outcome would have been very different.

There were no dummy lead bodkins fired at the enemy but the French did think that their armour would protect them from the English arrows and it is also well-known that after a long morning's wait, King Henry's little move forward was sufficient enough to egg-on the leaderless French army to start their advance.

As you shall no doubt wish to read for yourself, this battle did not result in Henry V becoming the King of France, due to his untimely death, supposedly from dysentery, at the age of thirty five, some seven years after the battle.

There are various opinions as to whether the Oriflamme was displayed at the battle or not, as this banner was normally only present when the French King was leading the army, but it was reportedly lost and never seen again.

With so many French Nobles killed or taken prisoner in the battle, there was no organised resistance remaining in France, which no doubt was the reason why there were no further confrontations with Henry's army as he marched the last forty miles to Calais.

During the reign of Henry IV and his son, there was dissention with the Lollard's, who, as already mentioned wanted to establish a Church of England which simmered for over a century, until Henry VIII decided to have his reformation.

Due to, the intervention of railway travel, time zones across Great Britain were standardised in 1840 to meet timetable requirements, therefore the time for noon was set at Greenwich and is known as Greenwich Mean Time. (GMT) Therefore, if, in these times of urban lighting you are able to locate the North Star, make your own sun dial and note the difference from GMT.

There are two versions of how Wat Tyler met his end. One was that he died at Smithfield's, but I have used the second version that he was murdered at Saint Bartholomew's hospital, which fits nicely into my story.

Livre des Quatre Dames

Four French ladies were lamenting the fate of their husbands at the Battle of Azincourt and trying to decide which of them had suffered the most.

The first lady thought it was her, as her husband had been found dead.
The second lady thought it was her, because her husband was obviously dead but his body has never been found and that his estate could not be finalised.

The third lady claimed that she suffered, because her husband was a prisoner in England and that it was a hardship raising his ransom.

The fourth lady said, 'You have all suffered, but I suffer the most because my husband was a coward and shamefully ran away.'

From a poem by Alain Chatiers 1416

APPENDIX ONE

MONEY COINAGE

Money was circulated as metal coins made out of silver and gold and the weight was important to the value, except for the groat, which was first minted during the reign of King Edward I, at the same weight as 89 grains of wheat. In medieval times it was felt that individual grains of wheat all weighed the same and that they could be trusted to produce an agreed standard of measurement. This coin was made out of silver and was valued at four pennies. The weight however became progressively lighter because during the reign Edward III the weight was reduced to that of 72 grains and the groat, issued at the time of Henry IV, was again reduced to a weight of 60 grains.

Therefore consider this, if you had two old groats weighing 89 grains (and you knew how to do it) you could melt them down add a little more silver and re mint them into three coins and the same could be done with the 72 grain coins, which would produce an extra coin from every five re-minted.

There are many books on ancient coinage but I shall try to be brief in my explanation. English money was and still is, based on the pound but there was no such thing as a pound coin in 1415 as it was a unit of account, (for adding and subtracting to and from balances) neither was there a mark.

POUNDS SHILLINGS AND PENCE

Early English money was derived from the Roman coinage system *Librae ... Solidi ... Denarii* or L.s.d.

(L) An amount of pure Silver, having the weight of 11.5 ounces, was given the value of one pound.

(s) Like the pound and the mark, there was no shilling coin but for accounting reasons 20 shillings made one pound.

(d) A silver coin called the penny was minted to correspond with the Roman penny and 240 pennies were worth one pound, and 12 pennies were worth one shilling.

	VALUE	METAL
POUND	240 pennies (20 Shillings)	No coin
MARK	13 shillings, 4 pence	No coin
NOBLE	6 shillings, 8 pence	Gold
CROWN	3 shillings, 4 pence	Gold
SHILLING	Twelve pennies	No coin
GROAT	Four pennies	Silver
PENNY	One twelfth of a shilling	Silver
HALFPENNY	Half of one penny	Silver
FARTHING	One quarter of one penny	Silver

The noble and the crown were beyond the ordinary peasants' means, therefore from this list only four coins were in general circulation, the penny, the halfpenny, the farthing and the coin which nobody had any faith in....the groat.

APPENDIX TWO

WEIGHT AND MEASUREMENT OF GOODS

Unlike coins, the weight of goods was based on Greek measurements using the weight of barley grains, and roughly 27.3 grains of barley equals 1 Dram.

1 ounce = 437.5 grains of Barley   1 pound = 7000 grains of Barley

16 drams	1 ounce
16 ounces	1 pound
14 pounds	1 stone
112 pounds	1 hundredweight
20 hundredweight	1 ton

Therefore one hundredweight, weighs the same as 784,000 grains of barley; but of course iron weighs were made to match exactly the same weight as the grains and there were metal weighs made to equal: one ounce, one pound, one stone or for any weight wanted to measure any amount in between or above these mentioned.

For example: eight, one stone weights were used to measure out one hundredweight and so on. It was also accepted that the weight of three grains of barley was equal to four grains of wheat.

APPENDIX THREE

VOLUMES AND CAPACITIES

Confusingly, liquids (fluids) also use the ounce as a measurement, so for a simple explanation one ounce of a liquid is slightly heavier than one ounce of the weight of goods. (Roughly 4%)

5 Fluid ounces	1 Gill
4 Gills	1 Pint
2 Pints	1 Quart
8 Pints	1 Gallon
2 Gallons	1 Peck
4 Pecks	1 Bushel
9 Gallons	1 Firkin
4 Firkins	1 Barrel
228 Pints	1 Barrel

APPENDIX FOUR

MEDIEVAL LENGTHS

Measurements were based on the size of an average man:

One inch = the width across the widest part of the thumb.

One hand = the outside width across the hand from a pinched in thumb to the outside of the little finger.

One foot = the length of a man's foot (11 thumb inches)

One yard = the distance from the tip of the nose, when the face is strait forward, to the tips of the fingers when the arm is stretched out sideways - 30 – 33 thumb inches.

One English pace = one old yard (Modern 30 inches).

Cubit = distance from elbow to fingertips (Modern 18 inches)

One League = 1.5 Roman miles.

One Furlong = the length of a ploughed ditch. (Modern 220 yards)

Acre = the amount of ground that could be ploughed in a day (Modern 4840 square yards).
Note!! The Metric system only started to come into use during the nineteenth century.

APPENDIX FIVE

DISTANCE

Modern marching armies travel at an average rate of about 3.5 miles per hour on good dry roads carrying only their rifle and pack. They are trained to take a step of 30 inches at the rate of 120 steps per minute, therefore a modern army can march about twenty miles in six hours, not counting for stops and rest periods. However the roadways in France in 1415 would only be pitted dirt tracks, so in dry conditions with minimal or even no footwear, a rate of 3.5 miles per hour would be difficult to achieve; and in wet conditions this would obviously reduce the distance that could be travelled in an allotted time. The presence of horses and horse drawn carts would presumably have no effect on the marching pace.

Let us assume then, that in dry conditions the hourly marching rate is reduced to say 2.5 miles per hour and in wet muddy conditions to say. 2 miles per hour. Then the marching time to achieve 20 miles per day in dry conditions would be eight hours, not counting for stops and in wet conditions, at best, say ten hours. But the mile in 1415 was based on a Roman mile of 1000 paces and a Roman pace was a double step, or five feet in today's calculations. Therefore a Roman mile was 5000 feet, whereas a present mile is 5280 feet. We now know that the distance from Harfleur to Calais by the intended route marched is roughly one hundred and seventy miles, not one hundred miles as was thought at the time.

GLOSSARY

Sou coin – This was a small coin used in France which was of small denomination.

Doublet - A man's fitted and often padded buttoned jacket.

Nose Tapping – This is a gesture, which is a form of non-verbal communication. To tap the side of your nose to a person is telling them, not to be 'nosey', mind your own business or keep it a secret.

Sot (Sots) – This was an offensive term used to describe a person who was habitually drunk. Hence, drunkards were known as sots.

Melee (mêlée – French) – This generally refers to disorganised and confused scramble, between a group of people in combat. Where there is no regard for group tactics etc. each one fights as an individual.

Promontory – This is a raised mass of land where one end of it has an abrupt decline. Throughout history many forts and castles were built upon them because they were easily defensible.

Pennon – This is a type of flag that is triangular in shape, yet small in size. They did not depict coats of arms, but were often depicted with the personal ensigns of knights and had mottos and crests on them.

Rigmarole – This word only originated in the mid-18th century but has been used in this book to describe Crispin's pretend imprisonment as, a long drawn out and complicated situation, that hadn't been necessary.

Flummoxed – means bewildered or perplexed.

Dysentery – This is a bacterial infection of the intestines which causes diarrhoea, which is referred to in the book as 'the runs'. It was common during the medieval times due to the lack of sanitation and personal hygiene.

Bloody Flux – This was another name for dysentery and was used when the condition worsen and blood would be leaked from the bowels indicating the seriousness of the condition.

Feudal system – In simple terms the feudal system was a hierarchy of social position. It was based around who owned land and who was granted privileges. The order of this hierarchy would be: King, Clergy, Nobles, Knights, (Merchants, Farmers and craftsmen, who were all on the same level), and lastly peasants and serfs.

Robyn Hode – Was a mediaeval outlaw and although it cannot be proved that he actually existed, he was a well-known character who was the subject of many tales in folklore. It was in the 19th century, long after the time when this story was set, that he became known as Robin Hood.

Richard (Dick) Whittington – Was a real-life wealthy medieval merchant who became a Politian and Lord Mayor of London. It is folklore that made him the subject of many stories that inspired the folk tale of Dick Whittington and his cat. Although there is no evidence to suggest that the real person owned a cat.

And finally…….

The Two finger Salute – Today this gesture is used in an offensive and derogatory manner, with its original meaning being lost over the centuries.

Because the French were to have supposedly threatened to cut off an archer's 'drawing fingers', which were the index and middles fingers, thus rendering him unable to shoot an arrow; as a mark of defiance and to show the French

'Look, I can still shoot at you, I still have these two fingers!'

The archer's would hold up these two fingers to show that they were still able to fire their arrows at them.

Hence this became known as:

The Two Finger Salute

Visit:

www.2fingersalute.webeden.co.uk

8380115R00207

Printed in Germany
by Amazon Distribution
GmbH, Leipzig